The House of Kane

Books by Barbara Casey

Fiction
The House of Kane
The Coach's Wife
The Gospel According to Prissy
Shyla's Initiative

Young Adult Fiction
The F.I.G. Mysteries
The Cadence of Gypsies
The Wish Rider
The Clock Flower
The Nightjar's Promise
The Seraphim's Song

Nonfiction
Kathryn Kelly: The Moll behind Machine Gun Kelly
Assata Shakur: A 20th Century Escaped Slave
Velvalee Dickinson: The Doll Woman Spy

Coming Soon!
Just Like Family

The House of Kane

Barbara Casey

SPEAKING VOLUMES, LLC
NAPLES, FLORIDA
2021

The House of Kane

The poem *The Same Cannot Always Be So* was created by Barbara Casey.

ISBN 978-1-64540-602-0

To Al, for his patience and understanding
of this writer's temperament;

To my parents, George and Charlotte Woods,
for always believing in me;

To my daughters, Carla and Rene,
for keeping me supplied with inspiration;

To John and Dan, for giving so much happiness
to those I love;

And to Sophia Belle, for sharing
that magical joy that can be experienced only by a child.

With love.

For Hemingway

Prologue

If you bring forth what is inside you, what you bring forth will save you. If you do not bring forth what is inside you, what is inside you will destroy you.

St. Thomas, *Gnostic Gospels*

Timothy Richards switched off his computer not waiting for it to go through the normal shut-down procedure and rushed out of his office. He would probably have hell to pay in the morning when he tried to turn it back on. It had a tendency to lock up or lose files whenever he turned it off prematurely, but at the moment he didn't care. He paused in front of the elevator, saw from the indicator that it was stopped on the sixth floor, and took the stairs instead, racing down the two flights in the building where he worked for a computer consulting firm. He was leaving work early, especially for a Tuesday when there were time sheets to prepare, but he had plenty of comp time coming if anyone complained. Sick leave, too, if he had to use it.

His wife had said that the envelope was a cream color and that it had Kane Publishing House on the return address. That meant it wasn't the plain white envelope he always included with his submissions. The ones that were usually returned with a form letter rejecting his manuscript. No, this was the Kane Publishing House stationery which hopefully indicated its contents held more than a form rejection letter.

Outside, he literally sprinted to the last row of the parking lot where he had left his 1987 Toyota earlier that morning. It was where he normally parked since that was where he could get the best view of the intracoastal waterway each morning before going into the building and again late in the afternoon before returning home. He liked seeing the yachts lazily navigating the north-south water lane and to imagine what it would be like if he owned one. Now, however, he cursed the parking lot, he cursed the distance from the building to his car, and he cursed his own blind stupidity for even parking there in the first place.

It was June and the hot, humid south Florida temperature was brutal. Normally there was a slight breeze stirring off the intracoastal, but on this afternoon there was nothing. He could feel the sweat rolling down his sides and back, underneath his shirt. After fumbling with the keys, he finally got the ignition turned on. He rolled down the windows since the air conditioner didn't work and stomped the accelerator several times in an attempt to start the engine. The car jerked backwards in one sudden movement out of the parking space, reminding him once again that the transmission needed replacing.

It had been four weeks to the day when he sent off the rewritten copy of *The Ancients,* a historical novel based on the life of the Roman Emperor Hadrian. The first version had been rejected outright by seventeen publishers, the last one being Kane who suggested he find a professional editor to help him. After making several inquiries, he located someone by the name of Aislinn Marchánt. She was a freelance editorial consultant who had a reputation for her thoroughness and accuracy. Several manuscripts she had edited had been published by major publishing houses. She had her own publishing credits which were quite impressive as well. Someone told him that she was recently divorced from Robert Marchánt, the chief surgeon at West Palm Beach Regional Hospital, but, best of all, she lived in El Cid, the old, established residential area of West Palm Beach, conveniently not too far from his office.

Hiring her had been expensive; his wife had stayed mad at him for two weeks over that one. But he saw it as an investment rather than a frivolous waste of money which his wife claimed, and he was right.

Aislinn's edit of his manuscript had been comprehensive and critical. When he finally finished doing the rewrite and making all the changes, he was so pleased with the results that he even signed up for the two-week creative writing class she was teaching at Coastal College. Since it was held in the evenings, it was usually simple enough for him to go there directly from work. Tonight would be the final class.

It was Aislinn who had suggested that he rewrite the novel in first person rather than third, among other things, and to approach the subject of Hadrian's wall as another character. The results gave life and feeling to a story that was otherwise just another dry academic treatment of ancient Rome and one of its emperors. Aislinn worked with Timothy for three months on his rewrite. As soon as he finished, he sent it back to Kane Publishing House along with a copy of Aislinn's original written evaluation and editing suggestions. He wanted this publisher to know that he was serious about getting published, so much so that he had hired a professional editor.

Timothy turned off Olive Street and took a side street to avoid the red traffic light at the busy intersection ahead. If Kane published his book, he wouldn't have to worry about money so much. He'd be able to get some things taken care of—like his damn car. Maybe he could even quit his job and start writing full-time, which is what he wanted to do. He knew that Elizabeth, his wife, wanted things too—motherhood, for one. For some reason, though, that hadn't happened. Not yet, anyway. He couldn't help but feel that Elizabeth blamed him somehow, and that she tied it in with his desire to write. If he were to get published, maybe she wouldn't feel that way. If he were to get published, maybe she would get pregnant and she could quit that dead-end bookkeeping job with the construction outfit she worked for.

Five minutes later, he pulled into his driveway and screeched to a stop. Elizabeth was waiting at the front door, lips tightly drawn, with the envelope in her hand. The last eight years, ever since he decided he could be a writer, had been hard on her. They rarely did anything together other than eat the evening meal. Whenever they talked, it was usually complaining about work or money. Whatever spare time he had was spent on writing. If *The Ancients* got published, though, he would make it up to her. He would take some time off so the two of them could go somewhere just for fun. Then he would start his next book.

Together they went to the kitchen table, the place where all of their important matters were handled, and sat down. Hands trembling, beads of sweat covering his upper lip, Timothy slit open the envelope and pulled out the letter.

Dear Mr. Richards:
After careful consideration of your manuscript,
The Ancients, I am pleased to inform you of our decision
to offer you a contract, two copies to be sent under
separate cover. After you receive the contract, please
sign both copies and return them for countersignature.
I am looking forward to working with you.
Please contact my office if you have any questions or
concerns.

Yours sincerely,
Caldwell Kane
Publisher

Timothy grabbed his squealing, tearful wife and spun her around the room. Then he read the letter again just to be sure he hadn't mis-understood. He lightly brushed his fingers across the gold embossed

4

letters KPH in the upper left-hand corner and then, overcome with emotion, covered his face with the letter. This was what he had been hoping for. All those years of rejections; the frustrations and self-doubt; the late nights of writing until five or six in the morning, only to have to stop and get ready to go to work exhausted; the stress on his marriage. Even the other employees where he worked had started kidding him, calling him "Mr. Shakespeare" to his face and making jokes about him behind his back. He was sick of being asked, "Have you gotten published yet?" The cost had been high; with each rejection letter, a new humiliation to suffer. It was all worth it now. This is what it had been about. Now he could say he was an author; and yes, dammit, he was published. His dream had finally come true.

Part One

Chapter One

You don't write because you want to say something; you write because you've got something to say.

F. Scott Fitzgerald

"But I still don't understand why I can't write a story about a little girl's best friend who happens to be a dragon." This was the third time Aislinn had tried to explain, and the whine in the woman's voice was starting to become annoying. A large man sitting in the back of the room coughed loudly and shuffled his feet in irritation.

"It is important to write on themes that haven't been overdone. There are already several hundred titles out there in the children's market about friendly dragons. Publishers want to see something new; something that hasn't been tried before." The woman just kept shaking her head, and Aislinn knew it was useless to try to explain further. Gloria Hart was one of those writers who had blinders on where her own writing was concerned. She couldn't accept constructive criticism, no matter how valuable it was. Aislinn glanced at her watch. It was ten o'clock already. "It is getting late, so if there are no more questions, . ."

"I have just one more, Aislinn, if you don't mind. How do publishers feel about using profanity in middle grade or young adult novels? After all, it does seem to be a part of the culture now."

"That's a good question, George." George Weston was a retired US Marine Corps Captain who was writing a nonfiction photographic journal on little-known skirmishes that occurred in the South Pacific during World War II. Aislinn was quite sure it was filled with profanity, and justifiably so no doubt. "Most publishers prefer not to include it. They feel there are enough legitimate descriptive words that can be used without promoting something that is, for the most part, negative or in bad taste. This is true in adult novels as well, by the way. There are exceptions, of course, as in everything."

"Like another friendly dragon story," added Gloria.

Aislinn ignored her. "This has been a pleasant two weeks for me, class. I have seen a lot of talent, and I want to wish you all the best in your writing endeavors. Thank you all for coming these past two weeks and for making my job so enjoyable."

Everyone started getting together their papers, notepads, briefcases in some cases, and anything else they had brought to class. Several men and women came up to Aislinn to thank her. She had given them help as well as hope. Now when they returned to their normal daily lives as hair dressers, computer programmers, teachers, homemakers, and factory workers, they would have a better sense of how to achieve the goal of also becoming published.

With the classroom empty, Aislinn walked briskly down the corridor and through the side door exit into the darkness of night. She was at once aware of the scent of sweet jasmine, probably growing in the nearby arbor, and the thick, humid air enveloping her like an invisible damp sheet. It too had a scent, but more of the earth. She felt her hair, especially where it was cut short around her face, coil into ringlets, a characteristic of naturally curly hair over which she had no control.

Since this was the last session, there had been more questions during class than usual. A few had brought copies of their manuscripts to give to her to take home and edit. Then she had to gather all of her own papers together. Now everyone had already left. The other classes that were being taught in the same building as part of the Coastal College continuing education program had been dismissed long ago.

Her car was parked in an area that was illuminated, but just barely, and located at the opposite end of Sedgfield Hall from where she had just come. She considered briefly going back inside to see if there was anyone around who would walk with her to her car, but then dismissed the idea. She was just being silly. She breathed in deeply and then slowly released the air through her mouth, trying to relieve the anxiety she could feel building up inside of her.

Her writing course, "From Printed Page to Publisher," had gone extremely well, with more than twice the enrollment of the previous year. She had already received an offer of a contract renewal for next summer. Aislinn enjoyed teaching creative writing. The two weeks during the summer provided a break from her usual routine of writing and being a freelance editor, and the pay was good. It also introduced her to new writers who would hire her to evaluate their manuscripts after the course was completed.

All of her students were adults with day-time jobs but who were taking her course because they really cared about writing. Several of her students, in this class particularly, displayed an unusual amount of talent. One elderly Chinese woman, Mrs. Mon-Sun Norcroft, had written and illustrated with charcoal and water colors a picture book that beautifully and simply demonstrated the Eastern philosophy of *chi*. Aislinn felt sure it would get published by one of the major houses. She had even given her the names of some editors to contact. A retired judge was working on a nonfiction memoir of criminal court cases over which he had presided during his long tenure on the bench. Somewhat impatient with the submissions rules and guidelines required by publishers, he had typed his manuscript single-spaced, and it was filled with typographical errors and penciled-in notes. It was his contention that the publisher would "fix" it. Aislinn finally convinced him that in order for it to even get read by a publisher, his manuscript had to follow the basic rules of grammar and formatting, which meant double spaced with proper headers. Another man who worked in computer technology had written an historical novel which Aislinn had edited a few months prior to the start of her course. The spelling and grammar in it were atrocious, and the story line was disjointed and difficult to follow. But the theme and his presentation of facts were solid and unique. He had an unusually strong writing style that Aislinn felt showed promise with just a little guidance. She was surprised but delighted when he showed up to take her class, and on this final night, he had informed her that he had been offered a contract from Kane Publishing House for his novel. She couldn't have been more pleased. She remembered when she received an offer of publication for her first book. It was a middle-grade novel, there was no advance, and only five thousand copies were printed. But it didn't matter. More than anything else, she felt she was finally validated. With that contract she crossed over from being just a writer to being an author, and once she did she didn't slow down.

Aislinn felt around in her purse until she found her car keys. Tightening her grip on her briefcase, she walked in the direction of her car, reminding herself that since she had been teaching at Coastal College, there hadn't been any problem with security. In fact, in the fifteen years the small coeducational college had been operating, there had never been even the slightest hint of a problem. For some reason, though, in the two weeks she had been teaching her writing course, Aislinn's instincts seemed to be warning her of danger or some impending disaster, and her instincts were seldom wrong. Maybe it was the fact that it was a night class, and by the time each session ended it was already dark. Or maybe she just needed a break from everything. She couldn't even remember the last time she had taken time off just to relax. Certainly not since her divorce. She had even considered the possibility that she was starting her "change of life," even though she was only 37 years old, and maybe the hormonal activity was causing her to be more nervous than usual. That still didn't explain the fact that sometimes she felt she was being followed, even though she never actually saw anyone.

Several times there had been strange phone calls—annoyance calls with implied threatening or sexual undertones more than anything else—always to her answering machine at home when she wasn't there, in a voice that sounded muffled and distorted. The last call she received was two nights ago when she returned home from her writing class. Then just yesterday morning she received an instant message in her e-mail from someone called the *Predator*. *Does it feel strange to know that I know when you are working?* the message had read. At the time she received it, it was still early and she had just logged onto the Internet to do some research. Startled, she immediately deleted the message and went about her work, but it had left an uncomfortable feeling that she hadn't been able to shake off. Now she was wondering if perhaps she had deleted the message too hastily, and that she should have notified the authorities about it.

"Ms. Marchánt?"

Aislinn jumped at the touch of someone's hand on her arm.

"Sorry. I didn't mean to frighten you." It was one of the men from her class, Roy Mathews. He had been trying to write a middle-grade fantasy mystery novel that smacked heavily of the Harry Potter books. With her encouragement and a lot of suggestions, he had changed his focus from witchcraft and magic to an adventure that was contemporary and realistic. In his rewrite, the characters were more three-dimensional; the plot was stronger. He had worked hard on it. "I was just wondering if it would be all right if I send you my manuscript when I have finished making these last changes you suggested? Since tonight was the final session, I would like to have you edit the whole thing and help me find some publishers to send it to; that is, if you think it is good enough that a publisher would even want to look at it." He smiled self-consciously.

Aislinn thought about the work waiting for her at home—a box of unanswered phone messages and correspondence that she hadn't been able to look at in the past two weeks, the stack of manuscripts on her desk to be evaluated and edited plus the ones she had been given that night, and her own novel, a metaphysical fiction, she was longing to work on. "I would be happy to, Roy." She reached into her briefcase and pulled out one of the brochures she always carried with her along with her business card. "This explains my fee structure," she said handing him the folded paper. "Make sure you send me only a copy, not the original, and, of course, a stamped, self-addressed envelope."

"Will do," he said smiling more openly. His mouth became more centered on his face. "I'll talk to you later, then. Thanks, again." He walked off in the opposite direction.

Aislinn enjoyed working with writers and illustrators and guiding them through the submission process. She had found that most people who asked for her help, however, had a desire to write, but too often they didn't want to take the time or make the effort necessary to perfect what they had written before submitting it to a publisher. Aislinn blamed the computer for a lot of it. The computer made it so easy just to dash off a story and send it out to several publishers at once, not giving any thought to whether the story was suitable material for a particular publishing house or not or even if the story was any good. There was also a lack of objectivity in these writers, and an inability to judge their own work—the Gloria Harts of the world. It was the end they were interested in—a filmy dream of fame and fortune—not the journey it took to reach that end. There were some, however, who enjoyed the journey and who also revealed that certain sparkle in their writing.

They were the ones who would do whatever was necessary to get it right, no matter how long it took or how much work. They had the talent and they had the instinct. Roy Mathews was one, as was Timothy Richards. They were the ones who eventually succeeded in getting published. Aislinn had helped a few to achieve that goal. She regretted there weren't more, however.

Safely locked in her car with her seat belt on, Aislinn drove out of the parking area and headed north to the historical district of El Cid twelve miles away where she lived. Her home, part of the divorce settlement from her husband of three years, was a two-story Spanish style stucco built in the early 1900s and located a block from the intracoastal, the primary north-south water route for motorboats, yachts and sailing vessels. The house was positioned more or less in the center of two lots and completely enclosed by a six-foot stucco wall and black, wrought iron gates. She loved her home with its tall ficus hedges, climbing red bougainvillea, and detached garage. Grapefruit and orange trees that produced fruit on a regular basis filled in one far corner of the yard. Up closer to the main house, she had completely redone the flower beds, tearing out the old diseased and decayed plantings that had become much too overgrown, and replacing them with the yellow flowered alamanda, blue plumbago, and orange ixora. Those same three colors she had also carried inside her home, in fabrics, tiles, and the many decorative accessories she had collected on her occasional trips at home and abroad giving lectures and workshops.

The house itself had large, spacious rooms, and the thick plastered, ocher-colored walls helped keep it cool during the hot south Florida summers. Aislinn's office was upstairs, just off her bedroom. Because it was located in the front of the house and faced directly east, she could easily see the intracoastal and whatever nautical activity was taking place. Watching an occasional passing yacht or sailboat relaxed her and helped her to better organize her thoughts when she was working.

Aislinn's home was her sanctuary. It was where she allowed her imagination total freedom in order to create, and it was where she helped others to create. When she wasn't writing or editing, she worked in the yard, weeding, pruning her flowers and shrubs, adding a water garden here, a concrete bench there—personal touches that helped her feel in touch with her innermost self and everything around her. It was also the place where she could be completely separate and apart from the rest of the world. Aislinn Marchánt thrived on privacy, which made her anxiety over being followed, the unexplained phone calls, and the strange e-mail even more worrisome. One of her students from the previous summer was a county sheriff. He had told her if she ever needed anything to let him know. Maybe she would give him a call.

Aislinn pushed the button on the remote she kept in her car which opened the large iron gates leading onto her property and drove in. The gates closed behind her automatically. She had left several lights on outside as well as inside the house. Even with the longer summer days, it was still always dark by the time she got back. Now that she was divorced and living alone, she couldn't be too careful. Leaving the lights on also made it more cheerful for her small Seraphim Maltese who waited patiently for her to return from these four-to-five-hour sessions.

Aislinn unlocked the door and was immediately greeted by a five-pound fluff of long white hair named Hemingway. Hemingway had been a present from her husband the previous year when she received special recognition by the National Association of Writers for her collection of short stories. Since that time, he had been her constant companion.

"Well, hello, Mr. Hemingway." The small dog lovingly wove the figure eight around her legs with his small wriggling body, all the while grunting and displaying a full set of perfect, white teeth in a happy smile. Aislinn put down her briefcase and scooped him up into her arms, nuzzling his soft silky fur and smothering him in tiny kisses. "You are such a good boy. I bet you have to go outside." She reached for his leash which she kept on a hook near the back door and slipped it around his neck. On the table next to the door she noticed the blinking light on her telephone answering machine, indicating that there was one message. She leaned over and pushed the button to see who it was.

This is Caldwell Kane and I would like to speak to Ms. Aislinn Marchánt. Please call me either this evening before eleven o'clock or tomorrow morning, any time after seven.

Reaching for the pen she kept nearby for that purpose, Aislinn scribbled down the telephone number.

Caldwell Kane. She knew who he was, of course, but she had never dealt with him personally. Caldwell was the third generation to take control of the family-owned Kane Publishing House. Over the years, through mergers and acquisitions, as well as natural fruition, Kane had become one of the largest publishing houses in the country. The number of titles it published annually listed well over one thousand, and many of them consistently made it to the *New York Times* list of best-selling books in both fiction and nonfiction. The name of Kane appeared regularly in *Writer's Digest, Publishers Weekly,* and other news and trade periodicals. Most recently, Aislinn had read that Caldwell Kane, now age 60, was expanding their children's line with two new imprints in addition to opening another office in South America, Brazil she thought, in order to break into the Spanish language market. When all the other publishers seemed to be scratching for blood to just barely stay alive, Kane's tenth house, astrologically speaking, was definitely on the rise. So why was Caldwell Kane calling her? She replayed the message. For a man who made a living from words, he certainly used them sparingly.

Hemingway was licking Aislinn on her cheek in rapid-fire strokes to remind her of her duty. She glanced at the clock; it was a few minutes before eleven. Well, Caldwell would just have to wait until morning. At the moment, she had more urgent matters to attend to. "Okay, Hemingway. Let's go outside."

Chapter Two

Writing, at its best, is a lonely life. Organizations for writers palliate the writer's loneliness, but I doubt if they improve his writing. He grows in public stature as he sheds his loneliness and often his work deteriorates. For he does his work alone and if he is a good enough writer he must face eternity, or the lack of it, each day.

Ernest Hemingway

Dr. Robert Marchánt walked along the quiet, deserted corridor, head down, half-framed reading glasses perched on the end of his nose, clipboard in his hand by his side. It was five o'clock in the morning, the time he routinely checked on the hospital patients, read their medical charts from the night before, and confirmed schedules with the head nurse on duty. There were three surgeries scheduled before noon that day, two of them routine—a tonsillectomy on a six-year-old boy and a gall bladder extraction on a fifty-two-year-old man. Then there was a heart by-pass on an eighty-three-year-old woman. That one could be a little tricky; there was always the possibility of things going wrong in someone that old. But it shouldn't pose any problems—she was strong and healthy in every other respect. Her doctor performing the surgery was qualified and experienced, as were the other two surgeons scheduled that morning. Robert, being chief surgeon, wouldn't have it any other way. He glanced at his watch. The first surgery—the tonsillectomy—would be underway shortly.

Since being named chief surgeon and along with that an appointment to the board of directors at West Palm Beach Regional, everything at the hospital had changed—and for the better. A new administration had taken over, the mortality rate had dropped from six percent to less than one percent, the staff was energized, its morale high, and for the first time in fifteen years, the hospital was showing a profit. His own reputation as one of the nation's leading brain surgeons was attracting doctors from around the world wanting to be associated with him and offering their services in those critical cases needing their expertise. As a result, new sources of government as well as private funding were being received on a regular basis. A state-of-the-arts cardiac unit had been added in the past year, and a new Alzheimer's facility was two-third's complete. As with any large medical facility, of course, there continued to be problems in spite of the successes. Blood supplies were consistently low, the change-over in personnel was still too high, and Robert, himself, needed to delegate more instead of trying to personally oversee everything that took place. Nevertheless, even with these problems, in just three years West Palm Beach Regional Hospital had taken its place among the premiere health facilities in the country, and it was all because of Dr. Robert Marchánt.

"Good morning, doctor." Margaret Peters, the head nurse, was expecting Robert and had the patient files ready for him.

"Nurse Peters." He nodded and took the files, carefully scanning the information in each one. On a couple of the files he made notations to the doctor in charge; from others he copied information into a small black book which he kept with him at all times. "Let me know when Dr. Turner gets in." He handed the files back to the nurse.

"Yes, sir." The nurse watched Robert walk down the hall to his office located at the far end. "What a waste," she muttered under her breath. Everyone in the hospital knew he was divorced now even though he hadn't said anything about it. News like that just got out. And she wasn't the only nurse who had her eye on him, either. In fact, several of the women doctors had been coming around the second floor nurses' station lately, supposedly on business, but she knew better.

Different make-up, new hair styles, perfume strong enough to trigger a migraine; Dr. Marchánt would definitely be a good catch in anyone's book. He was still relatively young—forty-five, he was good looking in that strong, silent kind of way, and he obviously had money. The only thing she could see that might be on the downside was his almost obsessive dedication to his work. She had heard, in fact, that that was the reason he and his wife had divorced. Apparently his wife was some sort of writer or editor, and as anyone can tell you, a two-career marriage is difficult at best.

Margaret Peters sighed and glanced at the clock on the wall behind her. Several of the nurses under her charge were returning from their early-morning routines. It would soon be time for the cafeteria to start sending up the breakfast trays. Before that, though, she needed to check all of the medications going to the different patients. As head nurse, that was her responsibility; that, and keeping all of the other nurses on their toes.

In his office Robert sat down at his desk and pulled out a folder from the locked bottom drawer. In it was a large envelope marked "X-rays." Just as he pulled them out, there was a knock on his door. It was Josh Turner.

"Did you get those X-rays I sent you?"

"I'm looking at them now. It doesn't look too good, does it?"

"You know the answer to that better than I do. All I know is, the sooner you get it taken care of, the better off you will be. I assume you want me to do the surgery since you came to me in the first place. If that is the case, then as your doctor I want to schedule you for Friday morning."

Robert didn't say anything. It was already Wednesday. That only left Thursday, and there was just so damn much happening right now at the hospital. The last thing he needed was to get tied down to a hospital bed, even for just a couple of days. But Josh was right. He had to get it taken care of it as soon as possible. There was too much of a risk involved not to. Delaying it could result in another transient ischemic attack. It was just a matter of time before it would lead to a stroke. That was the nature of plaque in the carotid artery.

As far as Robert could tell, there had been five attacks in the past four weeks: a sudden weakness and tingling on his left side, a blurring of vision, difficulty in swallowing. Each attack had been slightly worse than the one previous. During the fifth attack, he had momentarily lost his coordination. That was when he went to see Josh Turner. He and Josh had gone through Duke Medical School together. They had specialized in the same field, neurology, and then, ironically, they both wound up in south Florida. He trusted Josh completely.

Josh immediately gave Robert a complete physical examination which included a blood profile and an endarterectomy. The results confirmed what Robert already suspected. He had a significant plaque build-up in his carotid artery. Had it been someone else, Josh might have recommended first using anticoagulants in order to improve the arterial blood supply to the brain thus avoiding stroke, but the amount of plaque was so great he didn't want to take a chance that the drugs might not work.

As in all surgeries, especially those involving the brain, there were risk factors: brain damage, paralysis, irreversible stroke. As a surgeon, Robert was aware of each and every one of them. "Go ahead and schedule it, then," said Robert. "But try to make it in the afternoon. I'll get someone to cover for me while I am incapacitated. Do you know if Mack Courie is back from his honeymoon yet?"

"I believe I heard someone mention that he was. He could certainly take care of your patients for a few days." Josh waited to see if Robert wanted to say anything else. He wouldn't go into his usual explanation of what to expect as he normally did with his patients. Robert's knowledge of this type of surgery was extensive. Robert also knew what his chances were of getting through it without any negative side effects. Hopefully, there would be none.

After Josh left, Robert closed the folder and put it back in the drawer—away from wandering eyes. Most of the staff were trustworthy and reliable, but they were also curious. For the first time in his life, he felt vulnerable. It were as though he was seeing his own mortality being taken from him. So many times he had heard his own patients say the same thing. He said he understood, but he really didn't— not until now. He stood up and walked to the window wondering if this is what it was going to come down to. After all the work and sacrifice, is this how it was going to end? Aislinn. He wanted to talk to Aislinn. Even though they were no longer married, she was the one person he could talk to. She would be able to help him get his head back on straight. She would understand because she knew him as no other person did.

Just then the red light located above the door began flashing, a warning device that Robert had insisted be installed when he first took over as chief surgeon at West Palm Beach Regional. It tied in directly to the surgery room upstairs. Briefly he thought of the scheduled surgeries for that morning. The heart by-pass wasn't supposed to take place until ten o'clock. Robert rushed out into the hall and to the main nurses' station. Something was wrong. Margaret quickly handed Robert the phone. The nurse on the other end of the line relayed the message. It was the six-year-old boy. There was hemorrhaging. Apparently his blood wouldn't clot. He needed a blood transfusion, but his was a rare blood type, AB-Rh negative.

Robert threw the phone down and quickly explained what was happening to Margaret. "Get hold of his parents and any other relatives who are here at the hospital with them and get them tested. We need blood now. Let me know what you find out. I'll be in surgery." He disappeared into the private express elevator leading up to the third floor where all of the operations were performed. This wasn't supposed to happen. A tonsillectomy was as routine as you could get. And yet they were going to lose a six-year-old child because the hospital didn't have reserves of AB negative blood. Exiting the elevator, he immediately went to the gallery where he could see everything taking place. Dr. Miller was working frantically trying to stop the flow of blood. The heart monitor and respirator were fluctuating, an indication of problems.

The phone in the gallery buzzed. It was Nurse Peters. There was an aunt with the same type. They would send up the first amount in a matter of minutes. More would soon follow. Robert pressed the intercom button on the wall next to the window where he was standing. "Dr. Miller, blood is on the way. Hang in there."

Miller glanced up at the gallery and nodded. A nurse wiped the perspiration off his forehead. He secured a clamp just above the one he had already attached to the artery. Another monitor sounded and then showed a straight green line. Miller ordered the electrical cardioversion to be administered. The green line fluttered, and then went straight again. Robert gripped the handrail in front of him. "Don't lose him, dammit, don't lose him."

Moments later a nurse ran in with the life-saving blood, the blood from the child's aunt, and handed it to one of the nurses on the surgical team. She quickly and efficiently hooked it up to the intravenous tube already inserted in the boy's arm in order to start the transfusion. Once again Miller ordered the electrical cardioversion. Nothing happened.

Later that morning, a follow-up examination determined that the boy had suffered a heart attack, and that was the cause of death rather than the loss of blood. Knowing that didn't help when Robert went with Miller to try to explain to the parents why their son, Julio, was dead.

* * *

Aislinn's latest novel she had been working on was a contemporary fiction which delved into the lives of two families united through marriage but separated by different cultures. Part of the story line involved a Hispanic woman who practiced the ancient religion of Santeria. Aislinn had spent a great deal of time researching the Santerian beliefs and practices for her novel. She had visited a Santeria place of worship and observed *ébo*, the ritual of animal sacrifice. She had even gone to a botanica, the place where those of the faith purchased special healing herbs, statues, beads and other sacred things pertaining to their religion. These were the things that filled her mind early the next morning, and having been away from her novel for two weeks, she was eager to write about them.

After walking Hemingway, she took a quick shower and dressed in shorts and a T-shirt. Rather than taking time to style her hair with the blow dryer and curling iron, she brushed it up off her neck and tied it with a ribbon. It was easier that way and a lot cooler. She could be casual since she planned to stay home and work all day. With Hemingway settled with his toys, and her favorite yellow-flowered mug filled with fresh hot coffee on her desk, she turned on her computer and began writing where she had left off two weeks earlier. She was so absorbed in her work, she didn't even notice how late it was getting until Hemingway scratched at her desk chair indicating that he needed to go outside. By then it was almost noon. On her way out the back door she noticed the telephone number she had written down the night before. She slipped the leash around Hemingway's neck, promising herself she would return Caldwell Kane's call as soon as she came back in.

The efficient-sounding woman who answered the phone at the publishing house put Aislinn through without any wait once she identified herself.

"Thank you for returning my call, Ms. Marchánt. I have something I would like to discuss with you, and I think you will find it interesting." Caldwell Kane's deep voice was more soft-spoken than Aislinn had expected. She also sensed a certain amount of tension in it. Regardless, he had certainly gotten her full attention.

"I must tell you, Mr. Kane, you have me extremely curious."

"Please call me Caldwell, and may I call you Aislinn?"

Aislinn didn't know whether to be flattered or frightened. "Certainly."

"It means 'inspiration' but I am sure you already know that."

Aislinn felt she had been tossed into another dimension. Had she missed part of the conversation?

He quickly picked up on her silence. "Your name. Aislinn. It is from the Greek word meaning 'inspiration.' It is very pretty and very appropriate."

"Oh, I see. Yes, I did know that. My great grandmother was Greek, and I was named after her." Caldwell certainly didn't waste time on any preliminaries.

"Aislinn, the reason I called is that recently a manuscript came across my desk that you had edited. Earlier I had seen the original draft of this same manuscript, and I have to say in all honesty that it wasn't the worst I have ever read, but it was close. What you were able to do with it is something just short of a miracle."

He had to be talking about *The Ancients*. "Are you referring to Timothy Richard's manuscript?"

"Yes. That was good work, Aislinn. In all of my years in publishing, that was the most thorough and imaginative job of editing I have ever had the pleasure of reading. In fact, I have offered Mr. Richards a contract."

"Well, thank you, Mr. Kane, for your kind words. That is so nice of you."

"Caldwell."

"Yes . . . Caldwell."

"Which brings me to my purpose for calling you. I'm not sure how familiar you are with Kane Publishing House."

"I know it is one of the largest and most respected houses on either side of the Atlantic. And that it was started by your grandfather."

Caldwell chuckled. "Back then there was just my grandfather and one assistant working in the back room of a dry goods store. The first year they managed to publish two slim volumes. One was a reference book on herbal home remedies, and the other was a collection of poetry that my grandmother had written. That was probably the reason my grandfather went into the business in the first place—so my grandmother would have someone to publish her poetry. Family stories have her as a fairly head-strong woman. In just a few years, however, those two volumes grew to over twenty-five. That was when my father, Carl, took over the business, eventually passing it down to me. At the present time in the home office here in New York, we have eight associate editors, including my two sons, Jason and Tyler, sixteen assistant editors, and at last count twenty or so staff assistants.

"Just to tell you a little about our operations here, when we receive a submission, it is first "read" by one of the staff assistants to see if the manuscript follows the general rules of format and also to determine whether it is fiction, nonfiction, or children's. There is also a miscellaneous pile for things that don't fall into any category as well as the different genres such as romance, mystery, science fiction, and, of course, poetry. If the manuscript is not formatted correctly, it is returned, providing there is a stamped, self-addressed envelope enclosed. If there is no envelope, the manuscript is recycled. Amazingly, about fifty percent of the submissions we received fall into this category. The other fifty percent—fiction, nonfiction, and children's—are then passed on to the various assistant editors specializing in those categories. The miscellaneous manuscripts are also distributed among the assistant editors. They read the manuscripts for such things as content, theme development, characterization, overall presentation of material, that sort of thing. Out of these, roughly eight out of every ten are rejected. The two that are remaining are then sent to the appropriate associate editor for another read. It is up to the associate editor to determine, in addition to whether it is a good read or not, such things as the practicality of publishing the manuscript, the cost involved, the market, and predicted forecasts for the manuscript's success once it is published. If the associate editor accepts it, then the manuscript is passed out to the other seven associates and to me to read. The final decision is then made at our editorial staff meeting the first Monday of every month."

So far, the things Caldwell was telling Aislinn were typical of most of the larger publishing houses. She still didn't understand why he had called.

"This brings me to you. I need someone with your talent and ability—no, it's more than that. I need someone with your instinct to ferret out those submissions we receive that have the potential to be good books. In the past several months, we have lost a number of titles to other publishing houses, primarily Sheldon-Talbert Publishing House the best that I can tell, that have gone on to be best sellers. I don't need to tell you what that has done to our profit margin. These were submissions that had been sent to us first, but for whatever reasons, they were rejected. Most didn't even make it to that final step with the associate editor. Aislinn, I want you to evaluate the manuscripts that come in before they are sent to the associate editors. If there is a manuscript in this group that is rejected by one of the associate editors, but you feel it is good material, then I want to know about it."

Aislinn was caught completely off guard. She simply didn't know what to say.

Caldwell continued, "This isn't a casual offer, Aislinn. I don't want you to be offended, but I did some checking into your background. I know that you have your own editorial consulting business and that your reputation is sterling. Your own credentials as a writer are unusual in that you are published in fiction, nonfiction, children's and poetry; therefore, you know the markets and your knowledge of publishing is comprehensive. You have received numerous awards for your published works, you occasionally give workshops around the country, and for the past two summers you have taught a two-week creative writing course to adults at a liberal arts college there in West Palm Beach. I also know that you have been divorced for just a little over a year, and I believe that you were married for slightly less than three years. Is that correct?"

Aislinn ignored his last question. After all, that was private between Robert and herself, and Caldwell Kane seemed to already know enough about her as it was. "Then you must realize that my plate is pretty full already," said Aislinn, "and I don't think at this point I want to change anything." She definitely felt at a disadvantage. He seemed to know so much about her, and she knew absolutely nothing about him.

"I'm not asking you to. What I have in mind should fit easily into what you have already built up for yourself. It would just be a matter of logistics. Basically, I would be hiring you to be a consultant for Kane Publishing; more specifically, for me personally. Each month you would be sent copies of the manuscripts that the associate editors receive. I don't expect you to edit them. All I want from you is your evaluation: Is it something that would benefit the House of Kane if it were to be published? I would also like for you to attend the editorial staff meetings once a month. That way the others will be able to hear your input. You will, of course, receive a monthly salary and all of your expenses will be paid."

Aislinn did some quick calculations. Even if less than two percent of the submissions made it to an associate editor, it would mean having to read a minimum of twenty or twenty-five manuscripts a month. With all the work she had now, she wasn't sure she could do it.

"Aislinn, there is something else, but I don't care to discuss it over the phone. All I can say is, I really need your help. Don't make up your mind right now. What I would like to suggest is that you come to our next editorial staff meeting. That way you can meet everyone and find out what Kane Publishing House is all about. The meeting is scheduled for nine o'clock Friday morning. You can fly up here to-morrow, spend the night, and then return home following the meeting on Friday."

All of the numbers in Aislinn's head disappeared. She found her-self even more curious about Caldwell Kane and what that "something else" was that he couldn't discuss on the phone. She knew he didn't want to hire her just so he wouldn't lose a few titles to other publishing houses. It had to be something more serious. Besides, she loved New York. She and Robert had gone there several times while they were married to see plays, shop, try new restaurants, and to just spend some time together away from their usual routines. It would be nice to go back, even if Robert wasn't with her. "That sounds like a good idea, Caldwell."

"Wonderful. Mrs. McLaughlin, my secretary, will make all of the arrangements and be back in touch with you later today." For a moment Aislinn thought he was going to say something else. After a pause she asked, "What was the title of your grandmother's book of poetry?"

Again she heard him laugh. "*A Dusting of Petals.* Apparently it was a pretty good seller in spite of the fact that back then it was considered improper for a woman to write anything other than correspondence and recipes."

After hanging up the phone, Aislinn couldn't get focused enough to work. She kept thinking about her conversation with Caldwell and, strangely enough, his grandmother. She wondered what her name was. Finally, after sitting in front of the computer screen for an hour and having nothing to show for it, she gave up. Besides, with Thursday less than twenty-four hours away, she had a lot of things to take care of before flying off to the Big Apple. She glanced down at Hemingway who was sitting at her feet with a braided rope, his favorite toy, in his mouth. "Come here, you," she said lifting him up into her arms along with his soggy "stringy." Once she knew what time she would be leaving, she would ask her neighbor, Miss Howard, if she could take care of Hemingway while she was gone.

Chapter Three

Writing is an adventure. To begin with, it is a toy and an amusement. Then it becomes a mistress, then it becomes a master, then it becomes a tyrant. The last phase is that just as you are about to be reconciled to your servitude, you kill the monster and fling him to the public.

Winston Churchill

Moving slightly beyond the shade of the seventh column, the old man carefully positioned the shopping cart so that its four wheels were perfectly aligned with the expansion cracks in the sidewalk. Then, one by one, he lined up all seven plastic bags in the cart so that they, too, were parallel to the cracks. The bags were important for they contained the sum of everything he owned. Next, he felt the inside pocket of his old jacket for his Bible. He knew all of the Old Testament by heart and most of the New Testament, but he needed to feel its physical presence. It was there.

The hot sun was now overhead and the shadows had disappeared. It was time to move to the other side of the building, to the recess of another column. This was also the seventh column if you starting counting from where he had just come. In numerology, his birth date added up to seven, as did his name. The number seven was important in his life path. It was the number that controlled his destiny, along with the parallel lines and his Bible. Without these things in his life, the voice would become too loud and the universe would dissolve. Without these things in his life, he wouldn't survive. *Clouds and thick darkness surround him; righteousness and justice are the foundation of his throne* (PSA 97:2), the voice reminded him.

With the cart and the bags in place, he was ready to leave the recessed area in the granite façade of the multi-storied building, the area that was hidden from the street by the large Doric columns. The name on his birth certificate was Clarence Tirell Wood, born 7/11/34. The name on his Army discharge papers was Clarence Tirell Woods, discharged for medical reasons 5/05/69. On the street he was known as "the Professor" because of his love for books. It was also because of his love for books that he chose this particular place to call home. It was the Sheldon-Talbert Publishing House, and he had been living there in its shadowed recesses for two years.

The bags were his friends. He had named them after the twelve disciples in the New Testament—Matthew, Judas, Thomas, James—he had a bag for each one. Occasionally, he became confused, thinking that the pilgrims in Chaucer's *Canterbury Tales* were disciples of Christ, and that he was one of the Canterbury pilgrims, "The Knight," who, like God, dispensed justice along with mercy. The green leather-bound edition of *Canterbury Tales*, something he had found in the dumpster behind the building, was in one of the bags—the one named "Simon."

Except for the Bible which he had carried with him into the military service, the dumpster was where he found all of the books and discarded, unpublished manuscripts he read, along with most of the food he ate. He had read this particular volume of *Canterbury Tales* many times because, like Chaucer, he considered himself to be a student of physiognomy. Each day he watched the editors entering and leaving the building. He observed how they walked, gestured, and interacted with each other. He also noted other things: a weak chin, slumped shoulders, broad forehead, narrow eyes. From these observations he felt he knew these people, not by name, but by their physical characteristics. He recognized their weaknesses and strengths.

From one of the bags, the one he called "Philip," he pulled out a calendar and a short, blunt yellow pencil, both salvaged from the dumpster. He placed a big "X" through the date: June 27. It was that time of month when an unexplained activity occurred at the publishing house. Each of the other days were all pretty much the same. The editors arrived in the morning with large envelopes containing manuscripts they had taken home with them the evening before to read. Other large brown envelopes containing rejected manuscripts that were being returned would get picked up at lunch time by the US Postal Service. But for the past several months, on the last Wednesday of every month, one of the editors brought a large brown envelope back from lunch. She was the only editor to do this, which was why the old man had noticed it. He had also noticed that she had narrow eyes, an indication of untrustworthiness. According to his calendar, this was the day when she would once again go out to lunch alone and return with a large brown envelope.

He could feel his heart beat a little faster. Identifying the puzzles in life and trying to solve them was what kept him alive. Just like discovering the importance of the number seven in his life and the importance of existing within parallel lines, it had become important that he discover the meaning behind the single brown envelope. It was no longer just a casual interest in what was taking place; there was now a sense of urgency about it.

The sun was directly overhead. Within minutes, just as he had figured, she came out of the building and started walking in the direction of downtown. She was wearing a smart dark gray suit and a bright mustard-colored blouse. Her stockings and high heels matched the suit. He slipped back into the recess of his hiding place just as she glanced around. She didn't see him. She never did. He watched her until she got to the end of the block where she caught a taxi. Now he would wait for her to return. His heart started pounding harder. Maybe he would be wrong this time and she would come back empty-handed. He didn't like being wrong. That would upset him. He had gotten upset when that stupid military clerk made a mistake with his name. It threw his life force off balance with the "s" added onto his last name like that. That was when he learned just how important the number seven was in his life. Up until that time, everything had been all right. Everything had been in balance. It was afterwards that he began hearing the voice. *Vengeance is mine, sayeth the Lord* (PS94:1), and Clarence Tirell Wood was His instrument.

He placed the calendar and pencil back into the bag, making sure the bag was positioned correctly. The idea of being wrong troubled him. He began quoting a mixture of Bible scripture and quotations from Chaucer. His hands trembled and his eyes began blinking uncontrollably making them feel like they were too large for their sockets. He tried to focus on the parallel lines; he rechecked the wheels on his cart to make sure they were aligned properly. He felt his breast pocket. Rocking back and forth and muttering things that only he could understand, the feeling of panic gradually subsided. Soon the trembling stopped. His eyes stopped blinking. *Watch out for those dogs, those men who do evil, those mutilators of the flesh* (PHI 3:2), he muttered. Quietly he squatted in the recess of the building behind the seventh column and watched for the editor to return.

* * *

"Mrs. McLaughlin, I want you to make plane reservations for Ms. Aislinn Marchánt from West Palm Beach International to La Guardia for tomorrow early afternoon arrival. Book her a room—make that a suite—at the Waldorf Astoria."

Lorraine McLaughlin scribbled away in her notepad as Caldwell barked his instructions. Immediately after hanging up from talking to Aislinn, he had commandeered his secretary on her way out to lunch, insisting that he had something that needed to be taken care of immediately.

"See that there are fresh flowers delivered to her suite before her arrival. Roses. Red."

"Do you want a card?"

Caldwell fumbled with a button on his shirt and thought for a moment. He never knew what to write on a card. He could write a five-hundred-page book that sold over 250,000 copies, and had done so many times over the years, but a little card stumped him. "How about, 'In celebration of a mutually beneficial arrangement.'"

Mrs. McLaughlin dropped one corner of her red lipsticked mouth, something she had perfected in the nineteen years she had worked as Caldwell Kane's personal secretary. She had found him to have a good head for business, be knowledgeable on practically every subject, and fairly entertaining to be around. But when it came to women, he just seemed to miss the mark somehow. She was convinced it was because he did nothing but read all of the time; that, and the fact that he had been widowed since his two boys were just babies.

"What's wrong with that?"

"It sounds like you are hiring her to be your prostitute."

Caldwell's eyebrows shot up. "Well, what would you say?"

"Why don't you just say, 'I hope you enjoy your visit to New York.'"

"Isn't that what I said?"

Mrs. McLaughlin shook her head and scribbled some more notes. "Anything else?"

"Call Ms. Marchánt with the information once you have everything nailed down. And once you have done that, make dinner reservations for two on Thursday night at Apollo's. Make it early, say around six-thirty."

"That Greek restaurant?"

"That's right. Anything wrong with that?"

Mrs. McLaughlin shook her head and smiled. She just loved giving him a hard time. She had worked for his father until his retirement and was ready to retire then as well, thinking that the younger Kane would want to hire his own secretary. But Caldwell wouldn't let her. He convinced her that the success of the company was in her hands. If she left, it would be the end of the House of Kane. She stayed on, working as Caldwell's personal secretary and treating him as if he were her own family. "Anything else?" she asked.

"Could we have something—maybe pastries and coffee—set up in the conference room for the editorial staff meeting? And maybe some fresh flowers on the table."

Mrs. McLaughlin scribbled some more notes and then returned to her office to start making phone calls. Lunch could wait. Ms. Marchánt was obviously someone important to Caldwell.

Meanwhile, now having talked to Aislinn, Caldwell felt sure he could convince her to work for him. She would understand once he explained everything. Whistling a series of off-key notes, he walked down the hall to his son's office. "Want to go out for lunch?" he asked sticking his head in the door.

Jason glanced up from the stack of papers he was reading, looked at his watch, then leaned back and stretched. "You buying?" he asked.

"Don't I always?"

Jason grinned and grabbed his jacket hanging on the back of his chair.

"Is Tyler around?"

"Nope." Jason matched his father's long stride as they headed toward the main foyer of the office building. "He stopped by earlier and said he had some errands to take care of."

Caldwell pushed through the massive glass doors into the bright sunlight outdoors. Hiring Aislinn was something he had decided to do on his own. He hadn't told either of his sons about her. They would find out at the meeting the next day along with everyone else. "Pizza or Chinese?"

"Chinese."

The two men turned left and started walking down the street toward the location of several small restaurants.

* * *

"So, did you have a nice lunch?" Scott Darnell smiled at the young, attractive woman sitting at her desk. Stacks of manuscripts surrounded her. Scott had been working as an assistant editor with Sheldon-Talbert Publishing for five years with little to show for it. He seemed to try hard and he was enthusiastic, but he just didn't have a feel for what would make a best seller. His editing was sloppy at best, but it didn't seem to bother him or those he worked for. He was friendly, helpful, and a good listener, especially to the women who were employed there. And he was good to have around just to move large, heavy stacks of manuscripts from one place to another, if nothing else.

Tracy Cord glanced up from the manuscript she was reading, another romance novel. It wasn't the kind of thing she enjoyed reading, but because she was the only female associate editor, she usually got stuck with them. "Of course." She smiled showing off her perfect white teeth, the result of some expensive dental surgery during her childhood no doubt. She leaned back in her padded chair and stuck out a bare stockinged foot. Two perfectly shaped breasts pulled against the buttons on her silk blouse, also the result of some expensive surgery no doubt, although Scott didn't know that for sure.

"Do you need help with anything?"

"Would you mind taking these to the mailroom?" She motioned to a stack of rejected manuscripts on the credenza behind her desk that were leaning precariously toward the left. If I need anything else, I'll let you know," she answered still smiling. "Thanks for offering."

Scott nodded, picked up the manuscripts, and continued down the hallway, looking in each office that he passed. It wasn't that he was nosy, he just liked keeping up with what everyone else was doing. After dropping off the manuscripts in the mail room, he returned to his office at the end of the hall next to a make-shift lounge area. His office was smaller than the other offices, with one window overlooking the docking area and the rear lot where the dumpsters were located. But he was lucky to even get that much. All of the other assistants were assigned desks in one large work space divided into cubicles.

Not wanting to settle down to work, he walked over to the window and looked out. The old man was rummaging through the dumpster again. Scott watched him pull out some rejected manuscripts and a couple of books that had been discarded. Editors were always getting books from other publishers, old returns and remaindered books, and books that had been self-published, the majority of which got thrown out. A couple of times Scott had been tempted to give the old guy money, but then had second thoughts about it. He had to be unstable as hell at the very least to live that way. And who knows what might trigger him off.

As if he sensed he was being watched, the old man suddenly jerked his head up and looked directly at Scott. Startled, Scott shrank away from the window and sat down at his cluttered desk. When he glanced up again, the old man was gone.

* * *

Tracy waited until she was sure Scott was gone. Then she reached into her briefcase under her desk and dug out the big brown envelope she had brought back with her from lunch. He had said this one would insure her own imprint, something she had wanted ever since getting into the publishing business. She pulled out the manuscript and read the title, *Then There Was Light.* It had been written by someone in North Carolina and it had 85,000 words. She stuffed the manuscript with the envelope back into her briefcase. She would work on it that night.

Since her promotion to associate editor she had come up with absolutely nothing to show for it. Everything she had recommended for publication had been turned down. The last manuscript she managed to push through had been over six months ago, and although the forecasts for its success were good, it wouldn't be released for at least another eight months. In the meantime, she needed to come up with some better material, something that would make her look good so that when she asked for her own imprint, Sheldon-Talbert would let her have it.

Tracy's real name was Trista Cordillio. She was born in Buenos Aires where her family settled after leaving Italy during the war. When she was a teenager, she moved to Miami and completed high school, later worked her way through Indiana University where she graduated with a double major in English and journalism, and then went on to attend the University of California at Berkeley School of Journalism on a full scholarship. She graduated in the top five percent of her class. Attractive, aggressive, and determined, she immediately set her career sites on Washington, DC. She worked as an intern, or gopher, depending on one's perspective, at *The Post* for one year before getting her first legitimate assignment: reporting on the crime rates in the city. It was a filler piece that required little effort. From that assignment came others, most of them insignificant, until one day, just on a fluke, she stumbled across a story that involved "latch-key kids" in the inner city. She wrote it up and presented it to her editor who gave it first-page status. She followed up with three additional stories, these focusing on the hardships of the families with latch-key kids, all single parents trying to survive. At the end of the year she was nominated for the prestigious Pulitzer Award in journalism. The only problem was, she had made up everything. Nothing about any of the stories was true. She took a gamble and got caught, ending her career in journalism. It was just a minor setback, however, as far as she was concerned. After all, in Buenos Aires where she was from originally, that kind of "editorializing" was done all the time. No one really cared. And she certainly didn't see any harm in it.

After leaving *The Post*, she moved to New York, changed her name, invented a new resumé, and began working as a reader with Sheldon-Talbert. She was good. Having received her formal education in the United States, she had a superior command of the English language and a critical eye for detail. Most important of all, she had a feel for what would sell. After two years, she was promoted to assistant editor. Her first assignment as assistant was to attend the Bologna Book Fair in Bologna, Italy, as representative of Sheldon-Talbert Publishing House. This was an annual event that all of the major publishers and most of the smaller ones from around the world attended. Booths for the various publishers were set up in a central location, and, as luck would have it, Sheldon-Talbert was wedged next to Kane Publishing House being represented by Tyler Kane, younger son of Caldwell.

For Tracy, experiencing Bologna for the first time was like returning to her roots. The city itself was one of the most beautiful in Italy, medieval in plan, a jumble of red brick, tiled roofs and balconies, fountains and monuments, and ochre-colored porticoes. Tracy was filled with a sense of truly belonging, and for the first time since leaving Washington, she felt she could stop looking over her shoulder.

Quite naturally, Tracy and Tyler became inseparable; she a beautiful, flamboyant and intelligent Latina with energy and ambition to burn, and he the wealthy son in a publishing empire, old enough to feel competitive toward his father and older brother, but still young enough to need the flattering attentions of an attractive woman. During the day they worked at their booths. At night they strolled the streets, attended the theater, shopped in the markets, and sat at outdoor cafes sipping the local wines. They even found time to look up some of Tracy's distant relatives who still lived just outside the city. By the end of the six days, Tracy and Tyler had become lovers. By the end of six months, Tyler was doing everything he could to help Tracy professionally.

In a year and a half, thanks to Tyler, Tracy had managed to push through a half-dozen manuscripts, four of which made it to the *New York Times* best-seller list. With that much success, it was no wonder she was promoted to associate editor. But that was six months ago, and lately she had been getting primarily junk to read. She was tired of being just another editor. She wanted her own imprint where she could decide what would or would not get published. She would be able to set the focus and eventually, who knows, she might even start her own publishing company. But right now she needed another best seller. Hopefully, *Then There Was Light* would be it.

Chapter Four

Really, in the end, the only thing that can make you a writer is the per-
son that you are, the intensity of your feeling, the honesty of your vision,
the unsentimental acknowledgment of the endless interest of the life
around and within you. Virtually nobody can help you deliberately—
many people will help you unintentionally.

Santha Raema Rau

"Now hold still for just a moment so I can put this rubber band in your hair." Hemingway squirmed harder as Aislinn tried to manipulate a hair brush, a handful of Hemingway's hair, and an elastic spongee she used to keep the hair out of his eyes. She had already washed his face and "belly" which involved a more delicate maneuver. Being groomed wasn't one of his favorite things to do, but Aislinn performed the task religiously each day, thinking that at least he could see better if she did and the daily brushing definitely kept so many knots from forming in his long, thick hair.

Lorraine McLaughlin, Caldwell Kane's secretary, had called earlier to give her the flight itinerary and the name of the hotel where she would be staying. Aislinn could pick up the plane ticket at the airport in West Palm on Thursday when she got there. Mrs. McLaughlin also told her that Caldwell had made dinner reservations for the two of them on Thursday evening.

Now that Aislinn knew what her schedule would be, she wanted to walk over to see Miss Howard next door and find out if she would be able to keep Hemingway while she was away. Since Hemingway had come into her life, she had found it easy to just take him with her most of the time. But occasionally, like now, it was better if he stayed at home. And the idea of leaving him at a kennel just made her physically ill. Fortunately, Miss Howard didn't seem to mind keeping him on those rare occasions. And the cuter Hemingway looked, Aislinn reasoned, the more receptive Miss Howard would be to the idea.

With nimble fingers, Aislinn managed to secure the red spongee with one quick twist and fluff Hemingway's top knot at the same time. Then she kissed him. "Good boy. You are so handsome."

Hemingway shook his entire body starting with his head and working down to his tail in an effort to resettle the hair on his body that had gotten so messed. Aislinn lifted him off the vanity in her bathroom, his usual place to be groomed, and took him downstairs. With the leash fastened around his neck, Hemingway and Aislinn walked out the front door and down the sidewalk.

Miss Howard had lived in the same house her entire life. She was born in it, grew up there, and inherited it when first her mother, then her father died. Her father had been a successful land developer back in the early 1900s with the Model Land Company when Henry Flagler, already in his 50s, was completing the Florida East Coast Railway from Jacksonville, Florida, to Key West. The two men shared the same vision, and by linking the entire east coast of Florida, in just a short period of time agriculture and tourism were established as Florida's leading industries. As a result, the Howards became part of a "Gilded Age" that included money, beautiful stately homes, and vacations at resort hotels in St. Augustine, Daytona, Palm Beach and Miami.

The Howards lived in El Cid, an exclusive area of West Palm Beach that visually demonstrated their status in society. They had only the one daughter, Lottie, who remained at home and cared after her parents in their old age. Over the years, the neighborhood lost some of its original luster as the *nouveau riche* began relocating to the northern end of Palm Beach Island. It was here that the Palm Beach domestics had once lived, but with land at a premium on the island, the small homes were bought, torn down, and replaced by large, opulent mansions. El Cid, just across the intracoastal from Palm Beach, became like a distant relative, somewhat ignored and forgotten.

Lately, however, that had started to change. There had been a surge of renewed interest in restoring the old mansions that bordered the west side of the intracoastal and bringing them back to their original state of splendor. Real estate prices for anything of an historical nature were sky rocketing, especially in El Cid. Aislinn had been fortunate to see the trend before the real estate markets got beyond her reach. It wasn't just the home's value, though, that had made her decide to live there. She really felt as though she belonged in that environment.

As far as Aislinn knew, Lottie Howard had never been married; in fact, Aislinn doubted if she ever even had a boyfriend. It was a shame, really. But she was a good neighbor. She took care of her home, she was quiet, and during those times when Aislinn needed her, she seemed more than willing to help.

Aislinn knew, of course, that her given name was Lottie, but when they first met she had introduced herself as "Miss Howard," a practice that emphasized her formal, Southern upbringing. This was something that Aislinn, also being from the South, understood and respected. Calling her anything else would have felt uncomfortable.

Aislinn picked up Hemingway and walked up the steps to Miss Howard's front porch. The porch, anchored in gingerbread, spanned the entire front of the house. Groupings of wicker furniture, large green ferns, pots of white impatiens, and a couple of small palms were strategically placed around the area. Ceiling paddle fans quietly circulated the air above. Each side of the massive double front door revealed a beveled glass window in which tall grasses and cranes or some similar south Florida bird had been etched. It was quite beautiful and Aislinn often thought of doing something similar to her front door, if and when she had the time to look into it. Everything had a freshly scrubbed look about it, the result of many hours of labor by the people who worked for Miss Howard.

Aislinn pushed the door chime and waited. From somewhere inside she heard a door close and the sound of someone walking. Aislinn shifted Hemingway slightly in her arm and refluffed his top knot of white hair.

"Aislinn, how nice to see you. You, too, Hemingway." Miss Howard smiled and scratched Hemingway's chin. "Please come in." She stepped back, inviting Aislinn into her home. Miss Howard was a large woman—big boned, wide shoulders, and heavy. She kept her hair short, red, and fingerwaved close to her head, a style that most probably was popular when she was a young girl. Normally, she wore long, loose-fitting cotton dresses in an old-fashioned print, which was what she was wearing this day. They were cool and comfortable, Aislinn guessed, and much easier to manage for someone of Miss Howard's stature.

"Isn't this heat simply wilting?" She waved her arm in the general direction of outdoors while she led Aislinn and her furry friend to a sitting room that was located at a right angle to the formal living room. Even though Aislinn had taken Miss Howard all through her own house when she first moved in, this was the only room in Miss Howard's house that Aislinn had been invited. The room was cool; the sunlight filtered through white lace sheers covering the tall, narrow windows. It was heavily furnished with antiques—darkly stained mahogany woods, silk brocades, thick carpets, and rich velvets. Every surface was covered with *objets d'art*, mostly porcelain, that had been passed down from generation to generation in her family. Wedgewood, Lalique, Dresden, Meissen—Aislinn recognized the work of so many of the beautiful objects, and each time she saw them she felt as though she were taking a step back in time. She wondered if the entire house was furnished in antiques. It probably was, she thought.

Somewhat breathless, Miss Howard sat down heavily on the deep red velvet Victorian sofa and motioned Aislinn to a chair just opposite her. "I don't know if it is my age or what, but I honestly think it gets hotter every year." From somewhere in the folds of her dress she produced a small ivory fan which she flipped open in front of her face and immediately started fanning. "All that global warming and such. And, of course, now that we are in the season. . ."

For most people, the season was that time of year when the "snow birds" arrived from the north to spend their winters in warmer climates. It normally ran from Thanksgiving through Easter. The season Miss Howard referred to, however, was the hurricane season which ran from June through November. Fortunately, in the short time Aislinn had been living in her home, she had been spared from any serious storm damage, but she knew that Miss Howard had been through some terrible experiences, and the subject of "the season" was usually foremost in her mind whenever she and Aislinn visited together.

Eliane, a middle-aged Columbian woman, was one of the several people who seemed to always be around Miss Howard's home, working in some capacity, Aislinn supposed. She came into the room carrying a silver tray with two crystal glasses of iced tea. A green sprig of mint decorated each glass. Aislinn wondered how Eliane knew she was there.

"You can just put that on the table, Eliane. Thank you."

Eliane did as she was told and left, glancing briefly at Aislinn and Hemingway.

"The meteorologists do seem to be better at tracking storms now," offered Aislinn in an attempt to throw the conversation into a more positive tone.

Miss Howard narrowed her eyes and sighed, beating her fan toward her face more forcefully. For the next several minutes they sipped their tea and chatted about the increase in crime around the city, the devastation of the citrus beetle on the fruit tree growers, and the large number of Hispanics who were migrating from South America and the Caribbean into the county. Finally Aislinn got around to why she was there in the first place. As if on cue, Hemingway jumped down from Aislinn's lap and trotted over to the sofa where Miss Howard was sitting. She leaned down and effortlessly picked him up, all the while fanning her face vigorously.

"I will be happy to look after Hemingway," she said gently stroking his soft furry neck. "We'll have a good time, won't we?" Hemingway answered with a rapid round of tongue licks aimed toward Miss Howard's plump cheek, but landing mostly in mid-air.

"I certainly appreciate it, Miss Howard. I'll bring him over just before I go to the airport tomorrow." Aislinn placed her empty glass back on the silver tray and stood up to leave. Hemingway immediately wiggled out of Miss Howard's arm and jumped down to where his mistress was.

On the way out, Aislinn noticed a door, partially hidden by a large, four-panel Oriental screen, that opened into another room off the sitting room. Apparently Eliane had not closed it all the way and Aislinn was surprised to see that the room appeared to be a modern, well-furnished office. There was a massive mahogany desk, some file cabinets that were also mahogany, a large copy machine, as well as a couple of smaller machines that looked like a fax and printer. She only caught a glimpse, but she thought she saw a computer as well. She had never thought of Miss Howard as being computer literate, and she wondered what she used the office for. Miss Howard wasn't the type of person Aislinn felt she could ask a direct question of, so she didn't. It wasn't any of her business anyway.

When she got back to her house, the phone was ringing. It was Robert, which wasn't unusual since they usually talked at least once a week. But hearing the dejection in his voice was unusual.

"What's going on?" asked Aislinn.

"It's just been a bad day."

Aislinn waited while dread filled first her heart, then her head. She knew all about his bad days. It usually meant he had lost a patient. Unlike most doctors who with time and experience were able to eventually build up a protective callous around their feelings and emotions when dealing with their patients, Robert was extremely sensitive. He had no defenses. And unable or unwilling to share his burden, he carried each patient's problem deep inside him as though he were entirely responsible. Worrying about him had almost destroyed Aislinn. His inability to distance himself from his work and his patients was eating him away, just like it did their marriage. Eventually it would kill him.

She stretched the phone cord to the refrigerator where she could look inside. There wasn't much there, but she did have the makings for a nice tossed salad, and she knew there were some baking potatoes in the pantry. "I have an idea. If you pick up a couple of steaks, I'll fix us a salad and baked potato to go with them. How does that sound?"

She heard him sigh. "I'd like that. I'll bring the wine, too. About six?"

Aislinn glanced at the clock. It was already five-thirty. "That will be fine. See you in a few minutes."

Aislinn pulled out the fresh vegetables and began preparing dinner. She would have to fortify herself mentally to be able to help him. She had thought it would be easier if they weren't married. Now she wasn't so sure. She still felt his pain, and she still got angry because he couldn't or wouldn't deal with it by turning it loose.

Salads made and potatoes in the oven, she went upstairs to change out of her shorts into a long crinkled cotton dress. She would tell him about going to New York. Maybe that would help take his mind off whatever had happened that day.

As she slipped on some sandals, Hemingway began yapping in his happy high-pitched screeching voice which was reserved for only one person: Robert. Taking one last quick look in the mirror, she went downstairs to let him in.

"Don't you look nice." He smiled and pulled his tall muscular body away from the door jam where he had been leaning. "I have always liked the color blue on you."

Aislinn smirked and kissed him lightly on the cheek. "I know. It blends in so well with my blue scales." She took the plastic bag dangling from his hand and peeked inside. "Rib eyes. That will certainly work for me." She let him carry the wine as she led him into the kitchen.

Meanwhile, Hemingway had resurrected his favorite toy, stringy, from behind a cushion on a chair and was practically doing cartwheels to get attention from the one man he adored. Robert put the wine down on the kitchen counter and picked up the little dog, wet stringy and all. "You really need to show a little more restraint, my friend." Hemingway licked eagerly toward Robert's face. "That's all right, I know exactly how you feel."

Aislinn laughed. There had been serious problems in their marriage, but enjoying each other physically hadn't been one of them.

Robert continued holding Hemingway and planted himself on a stool where he could watch Aislinn prepare the steaks for the oven broiler. She reached into a drawer and pulled out a cork screw and handed it along with the bottle of wine to Robert. Then she got out two glasses from the cupboard. She wouldn't ask Robert any questions. She knew from past experience that it would only make him close himself off that much more. She would wait. And when he was ready to tell her what was bothering him, he would.

Robert deftly pulled the cork from the bottle while Hemingway methodically sniffed first the cork screw, then the cork, then the bottle, and finally the cork again. Robert filled the two glasses and handed one to Aislinn. "Here is to only good days," he said.

Aislinn smiled and sipped her wine. Then, without warning, Robert burst into tears.

Aislinn took Hemingway and put him down on the floor with his stringy and a treat. Then she wrapped her arms around Robert. Her stomach was clenched in a knot; her heart thudded in her ears. She tried to take a deep breath, but it hurt too much. She took shallow breaths instead. "There, there," she soothed. "It's all right now."

"We lost a six-year-old kid," Robert said trying to dry his eyes with his shirt sleeves. Aislinn ripped off a paper towel and handed it to him. Losing a child was the worst. With an older person, you felt like they at least enjoyed life for a while. But a child. . .

"What happened?"

Robert looked at her, then at Hemingway. "We didn't have the right kind of blood available. It was just a routine tonsillectomy, but he was a bleeder."

Aislinn continued holding him. She could fill in the pieces. For three years she had heard these stories. For three years she had been awakened in the middle of the night by his screams. It had completely drained her physically and emotionally, as well as her desire to write. While being married to Robert, she simply had no creative urge in her.

Instead, something negative replaced it, a fear and bitterness that almost destroyed her identity, making her into someone she didn't recognize or even like. As much as she wanted to and tried, she couldn't cope with the constant tension and pressure of Robert's work and still function with her own needs being ignored. That was when she decided that they could no longer stay together.

Robert blew his nose soundly into the paper towel. Then he took a deep breath. It had passed. He would be all right now. But Aislinn would feel it for the rest of her life. It was the way she was. It was why she was a writer. She not only empathized with people, she could literally feel their pain, especially when it was someone she loved. And more than anything, she loved Robert.

* * *

Tracy left work early. She lived within walking distance from her office in a recently renovated upscale apartment building. She rented a downstairs garden apartment in the first of three buildings that would eventually fill a space once occupied by warehouses. It was expensive but convenient to her work as well as downtown.

By leaving early, she would allow herself plenty of time to read *Then There Was Light*. The author's biographical sketch that had been enclosed with the manuscript said that the woman was self-taught. Her name was Snow Henderson, and she lived somewhere in the Blue Ridge Mountains about thirty miles west of Asheville, North Carolina.

What kind of name was that? After checking the atlas, from what Tracy could tell, thirty miles west of Asheville was nothing but mountains. There wasn't even a small black dot on the map. So far, the information wasn't exactly building confidence in Tracy that she was in possession of a good manuscript—let alone something that would get her her own imprint. She changed out of her suit and pulled on some comfortable jeans and a cotton knit shirt. Curling up on one end of her leather couch, she began reading the story of a woman who had been struck by lightning six times and lived to write about it. Two hours later, she was still reading. It wasn't just that the story was extraordinary, but that it was told in such a bold, lyrical way. Her use of mountain dialect and back-woods philosophy was hypnotic and produced a fountain of images in the mind of the reader. The language was poetic, yet simple. It was absolutely incredible.

It was after midnight when Tracy finally put the manuscript away. She had read over it two additional times, each time getting more insight into the hidden layers of this author's meaning and understanding. The author had written it as nonfiction. Without much effort, Tracy could rewrite it as a work of fiction, and no one would ever know the difference. Certainly not some hick from the sticks of North Carolina. She had thought she wanted her own imprint, but now, if she were to get this published in her name and it did as well as she thought it could, she would rank right up there with the big boys. A multi-million-dollar contract; movie, screen, and television rights, foreign rights and translations—she could have it all. Then, if she still wanted her own imprint, it would be easy to attract big-name authors who already had a proven track record.

Exhausted, Tracy lay down on her bed, her mind still working. The woman had talked a lot about the "gifts" she was left with each time she had been struck by lightning. Many of these gifts had been negative, such as temporary loss of sight, hearing, and her ability to reason—especially where numbers were concerned. But other gifts—things like enhanced sensory perception, extraordinary energy levels, and intuitive flashes—had become an intricate and constant part of her identify. Tracy lay in the darkness unable to close her eyes, thinking and planning. This could be the big opportunity she had been hoping for. She would title her book *The Enlightened.*

Chapter Five

It is necessary to write, if the days are not to slip emptily by. How else, indeed, to clap the net over the butterfly of the moment? For the moment passes, it is forgotten; the mood is gone; life itself is gone. That is where the writer scores over his fellows: he catches the changes of his mind on the hop. Growth is exciting; growth is dynamic and alarming. Growth of the soul, growth of the mind.

Vita Sackville-West

The old man had seen the editor return from lunch carrying a brown envelope. He had also seen her leave work early carrying a briefcase. He thought the brown envelope must be inside the briefcase. That was why he had followed her, just as he had many times before. He had to make sure.

Standing outside the apartment building, hidden by piles of construction debris, he watched the lights on the first floor apartment until they went dark. The voice was distinct: *For God's love, endure in patience our prison, for there's no choice; fortune has given us this adversity* (CT, Lines 226-228).

Immediately following his discharge from the military service, he had worked for a while in real estate management. That was when he was still taking the drugs: ativan, stavudine, and valium for anxiety; compazine for schizophrenia; serax for depression; zoloft for panic and his obsessive-compulsive disorder. Some he didn't even know why he was taking them. But it hadn't lasted. The regiment of prescription medications he was required to take destroyed his energy and made him physically ill. Besides that, they were expensive. He felt better by not taking them at all.

Not taking them, however, created other problems. He learned that the people he once trusted could no longer be trusted. Somehow everyone was involved in a conspiracy against him. He could fight them one at a time—like that stupid military file clerk who put the "s" on the end of his name. He just couldn't fight all of them at once, and he wouldn't try. He was smarter than that. So he left his job, his drugs, and the conspirators behind. All he had left from that experience was a ring of keys capable of opening any door in New York. He kept them in his sack, "Bartholomew," unless he needed them—like now.

He quietly moved through the shadows to the back of the apartment. He knew the layout; he had been there before. He even remembered which key opened the door off the patio. Once inside he stood silently, listening, sniffing the air, and allowing his eyes to adjust to the darkness. *Be self-controlled and alert. Your enemy the devil prowls around like a roaring lion looking for someone to devour* (IPE5:8), he heard the voice warn.

A streetlight outside filtered through a drawn window shade casting a soft reddish glow. On a table next to the sofa he saw the envelope. Carefully he picked it up and removed the contents. Holding the papers up to the reddish glow he read, *Let There Be Light*, written by Snow Henderson. This was a sign. He replaced the manuscript inside the envelope and put it back on the table. Then, as quietly as he came, he left.

Back outside he walked past the chain-link fenced area of new construction. A guard dog suddenly jumped out at him, snarling, barking and biting at the air. Slowly the old man approached the dog and held out his hand palm down. The dog lunged forward, digging his feet into the dirt and thrusting his entire body against the metal fence that restrained him. The old man stood there without moving, looking into the dog's eyes. Gradually the dog stopped lunging and growling. He became still. He sniffed the outstretched hand, then the shoes and trousers and coat. Then he looked into the eyes of the old man. The old man moved toward him, not saying anything, only looking at the dog. When the dog sat down, the old man reached through the fence links and patted him on his head. Then he walked away. This, too, was a sign.

Now satisfied, Clarence Tirell Wood walked slowly back to his sacks, to his parallel lines, to the number seven. The old man slept behind a lattice-fenced area next to the trash containers on a narrow spit of land that for whatever reason the developers had ignored when building on that location. Overgrown with weeds and wild saplings, it was completely hidden from everyone and everything, even the big truck that came twice a week to empty the large containers. On this night, however, he didn't sleep. The excitement inside of him was too great; the voice too loud. He was The Knight who personified the idea of just and reasonable leadership. He was the instrument of God. There was an injustice taking place, and it was his responsibility—his duty—to understand what it was and set it right. *He who does what is sinful is of the devil. . .* (1JO8).

* * *

Unable to sleep, Aislinn got up and went downstairs to get an apple to eat. The evening had been pleasant, considering. After Robert's emotional outburst, they had settled down to a nice, relaxing dinner. Robert didn't mention the young boy again, but he did talk about the new construction going on at the hospital. Aislinn told him about Caldwell Kane's telephone call and that she was flying to New York the next morning. "You'll be there on Friday, then?" Robert had asked rather pointedly. Aislinn explained again about the editorial staff meeting scheduled at 9 Friday morning, but that she would return Friday evening. They moved onto other things to talk about, and later they took Hemingway for a leisurely walk along the intracoastal. It was only after Robert had left and Aislinn was in bed that she remembered the strange look on his face when she told him she would be in New York on Friday.

Back upstairs, she went into her office. If she couldn't sleep, at least she could get some work done. She picked up the manuscript on top of the stack of brown envelopes that had been sent to her in the mail. In the past by working on manuscripts in the order they were received, she had been able to edit them, write her evaluation report, and return them usually within a three-week period. Now, however, with so much of a backlog, she would need longer.

This manuscript was a collection of illustrated bedtime poems for children titled *Sleepy Is the Sandman*. There were sixteen poems and sixteen illustrations. The illustrations had been done in acrylics and, considering they all had been done by the same artist, displayed an amazing range of subjects: children performing different activities as well as animals, vegetation, and inanimate objects. They were quite good.

Aislinn worked through each poem first, adding a coma here to help with the flow or structure, and changing a word or sentence there where the rhyme or meter seemed forced. With each illustration she made suggestions as to what could be done to give it more interest, or what colors needed to be changed to better accommodate the process of color separation in the eventual printing of the work if it were to get published. By the time she finished, she had written a three-page evaluation report to send back to the author. It was well past one o'clock in the morning.

Just before shutting down her computer, she decided to check her e-mail. No sooner had she logged on when an "instant message" appeared. *So, you're going to New York,* it read. *You're working a little late, aren't you? The Predator.*

Aislinn felt as though someone had thrown a bucket of ice water in her face. She stared at the ugly font the message was printed in and the bold pinks and yellows and greens used to highlight the wording. She was too tired to deal with it then. It would have to wait until she got back from New York. She shut down her computer, this time saving the message, and went back to bed. With Hemingway curled into a ball at her feet, she once again thought of Robert. She would call him as soon as she returned home.

* * *

The noise of a vacuum cleaner brought Caldwell out of his deep concentration. He glanced at the clock above his desk. It was an antique Seth Thomas in its original mahogany case and gilt banding, a Father's Day gift several years back from his two sons. The black scrolled hands told him it was ten minutes past midnight.

"Working late again, are we?" The short stout woman entered his office dragging the offending noise-maker behind her. She wore a yellow scarf tied securely around her head and a loose-fitting smock that showed off various colors and geometrical designs. Her name was Ruby, and she had been cleaning the offices at Kane Publishing House for as long as Caldwell could remember.

"I guess it is about that time to call it quits." Caldwell gathered up the pages of the manuscript he had been reading and put them back into a folder. It was a book on the Vietnam War that his younger son, Tyler, was going to recommend for publication at their next editorial staff meeting. To say that Caldwell was disappointed was putting it mildly. There were already too many war books, especially on Vietnam, written by soldiers wanting to share their particular horror story. It just wasn't the kind of thing that would show much profit. This one wasn't even written well. Frankly, Caldwell was surprised at his son for even suggesting it.

For months now Tyler seemed to have lost his drive—ever since returning from Bologna. Caldwell had grown to depend on his sons and trust their judgment where business matters were concerned. He had invested a great deal of time and energy into grooming them for eventually taking over Kane Publishing House, just as he had done, and his father before that. Lately, however, he wasn't as convinced as he once was that Tyler could handle it. He was four years younger than Jason. Maybe Caldwell was expecting too much of him.

Jason had mentioned that he thought Tyler had met someone while in Bologna, another editor who also worked with a publishing house in New York. If that was the case, then maybe it was time for Caldwell to meet her and find out for himself if it was a serious relationship. If it wasn't serious, then he needed to find that out as well. One thing was for certain, if it had been anyone else besides his son turning out the poor quality of work and showing the lack of professionalism that Tyler had these past several months, he would have already been fired.

Caldwell didn't linger to make small talk with Ruby; she had her work to do and was eager to get it done. The security guard unlocked the front door to let Caldwell out and then relocked it once he was outside. Still brooding, he walked to the street and flagged down a taxi. The Kane family home was a large estate situated on eight acres of land on the west end of Long Island. It was where Caldwell spent the weekends and those difficult periods of time when he needed to get away from the constant demands of publishing. For the rest of the time he kept a penthouse apartment with ten rooms, a nice view of the city, and a garden terrace. It was also convenient to his office. One of the rooms was occupied by Frederick, a sort of gentleman's gentleman, cook, and housekeeper combined. He kept things at the penthouse organized, clean, and operating as they should, leaving Caldwell free to concentrate on other things. Whenever Caldwell stayed at the family home on Long Island, Frederick stayed there as well in a room that had been chosen specifically for him many years earlier. Other than Lorraine McLaughlin, Frederick knew Caldwell Kane better than any person alive.

Caldwell gave the cab driver the penthouse address and sat back in the seat suddenly feeling fatigued. Aislinn would arrive the next afternoon. He would be open and honest with her about everything. Hopefully, she would be able to help put Kane back on the right track; or, at the very least, help him sort through whatever was going on. He could tell a lot from the sound of a person's voice and what they said and how they said it. Judging from his brief conversation with Aislinn, he knew that she was smart, dependable, trustworthy, and sensitive. She was also a very private person, which he understood and respected. The other thing he had sensed from their conversation was that she still loved her ex-husband.

Caldwell looked out the window at the passing lights and sighed. Maybe he was just being a foolish and stubborn old man in thinking that this young woman could do anything for him or the House of Kane, but now having spoken to her he didn't think so. There was something about her voice.

Chapter Six

You get your readers emotionally involved in your characters by being emotionally involved yourself. Your characters must come alive for you. When you are writing about them, you have to feel all the emotions they are going through—hunger, pain, joy, despair. If you suffer along with them and care what happens to them, so will the reader.

Sidney Sheldon

Robert had two surgeries scheduled for Thursday—one that morning and one in the afternoon. Both required the removal of a small tumor. The first was a primary tumor that had developed directly on the brain, probably due to some congenital abnormality in the patient although he couldn't be sure. The other, which Robert had already determined to be malignant, was a metastatic tumor that had originated in the lung. Of the two surgeries, this one would be the more difficult. He had cancelled his appointments for Friday, rescheduling them for later. He would use Friday morning to take care of his patients before putting himself in the hands of Josh Turner that afternoon.

He had intended to tell Aislinn about his own surgery, but when she started talking about going to New York, he just couldn't bring himself to tell her. He was afraid she would cancel her trip in order to be with him, and he didn't want that. Besides, she was a worrier and she had enough things going on in her life without having to worry about him. He would get through Thursday and then Friday. By the time she returned Friday evening, it would be over—hopefully.

"Let me see the folders on Harris and Rodriguez."

Margaret slid the two files already on the counter toward Robert and smiled sweetly. She had known he would want to see them and had pulled them out of the filing cabinet earlier, but he didn't seem to notice her efficiency. As he glanced over the paperwork, she studied his face. He looked tired. Maybe he had been on a hot date the night before, but she doubted it. She would have heard about it if he was seeing anyone.

Robert put the folders down and walked away. He made it a point to always talk to each of his patients before any type of surgery. He found that it helped ease the tension. Harris was scheduled first. Both the CT and the MRI had indicated that the tumor was attached to the pituitary and had already caused the patient's heart to be enlarged and his blood pressure erratic. There was also significant damage to his eyesight. Even if Robert successfully removed the tumor, there was no guarantee that the patient's vision would return to normal, or his blood pressure for that matter. To not remove the tumor, though, would leave the patient only months to live.

"Robert, can I talk to you for a moment?" Josh Turner came down the hall toward Robert.

"Sure. What's up?"

Josh glanced around to make sure they couldn't be overheard and lowered his voice. "I see you are operating today. Do you think that is wise?"

Robert shifted his clipboard to his other hand. "What in the hell do you mean?"

"Look, I'm not questioning your ability as a surgeon." Josh glanced around again. "I'm only concerned about you as my patient and the episodes you've been having. I don't think it's a good idea to risk having another one—especially if it occurs while you are operating. I don't have to tell you that these episodes are pejorative—they can only get worse."

Robert stared at him blankly. He hadn't even considered that his medical problem would interfere with his performance as a doctor. That was bad enough, but being reminded of it now from another doctor made it even worse. He looked at the notes on his clipboard he had written down earlier. The Rodriguez surgery was a simple procedure. He expected no problems. But the Harris surgery was complicated and there was no room for error on his part. One tiny mistake and the man could die. Josh was waiting for him to say something. "I'll find out who else is available to operate," Robert said.

* * *

Lottie Howard watched Aislinn hurrying up the walk carrying Hemingway, his basket that he slept in, and a shoulder bag that she used to carry his food and toys. By the time Aislinn got to her front door, she was already there with Eliane in tow.

"I just can't thank you enough for this, Miss Howard." She handed her a slip of paper with the name and telephone number of the hotel where she would be staying as well as the telephone number of Lorraine McLaughlin's office.

"Don't even give it a thought. Go and have a good time and don't work too hard. Hemingway will be just fine." She reached out with her massive arms and enfolded Hemingway into her ample bosom while Eliane took the basket and bag.

As soon as Aislinn left, Miss Howard carried Hemingway to the sun porch where she instructed Eliane to set up his bed and pull out his toys. He had stayed there on previous occasions and seemed to like being able to watch the birds and squirrels in the trees. Once he was settled in, Miss Howard went back to her office and sat down in front of her desk. A computer was angled off to one side. She scrolled down several lines, reading, and then began keying in more text.

She had been more than just a little upset when she had first received the evaluation. She was, after all, an educated woman; she had graduated from Sweet Briar College. She knew about punctuation and a thing or two about sentence structure. But the evaluation said that it wasn't enough to just have a nice, tender story about her father. She needed more action and tension to make it interesting. She needed more problems and solutions to keep the reader involved. Her manuscript, although sentimental, lacked a certain passion. The entire thing had made her quite snippy which led to her feeling ill for several days. Thank goodness Aislinn never knew that it was she who had written *My Father's Keeper*. She had given herself a pseudonym as well as a post office box where any correspondence could be sent.

As if that wasn't bad enough, she had encouraged her hired help, Eliane, to write a children's story based on a South American folktale where she was from. Not only did she write one, she also illustrated it. Aislinn's evaluation of that came back glowing, along with a list of publishers for her to send it to.

At first Lottie Howard refused to make any changes to her manuscript, thinking that it was perfect the way it was. It was about the loving relationship she had had with her father, and to change that seemed almost irreverent. After she thought about it, though, Aislinn's suggestions made sense. And the parts that she had rewritten based on those suggestions really did sound better. She remembered so many history-making events that occurred during that time when Henry Flagler was as much a part of their household as she was. She knew the difficulties he and her father struggled with, as well as the accomplishments. To write only of the feelings that had transpired between father and daughter wouldn't be doing justice to his memory or what he achieved. She could see that now—thanks to Aislinn.

Aislinn had said in her letter that she would be happy to look at the manuscript again if she decided to rewrite it. Well, she would do just that, only this time she wouldn't fool around with a pseudonym or post office box. It had all seemed so clandestine anyhow. No, when she finished it, she would take it personally to Aislinn. After all, what good was it to have a well-known author and editor living right next door to you if you couldn't take advantage of it.

* * *

The plane was scheduled for take-off at 11:30 Thursday morning, putting Aislinn in New York at 4:15, after a short stop in Atlanta. She had packed the day before, but even so, found herself rushing to leave Hemingway with Miss Howard and then get to the airport in time to catch her flight. She also called the "help line" of her Internet server and reported the instant messages she had received. She was instructed to forward all such messages to a special number they gave her, but other than that there was nothing else she could do. It didn't sound particularly encouraging.

By spending only the one night in New York, Aislinn had packed light, using a small case which she carried with her on board the plane. She also had her shoulder bag, something she always took with her when she traveled. In it was her lap-top computer and a couple of manuscripts to work on that night in the hotel room.

Lorraine McLaughlin had said there would be someone at La Guardia to meet her, so there was nothing for her to worry about. She had also reserved a seat in the first-class section for her. Settled comfortably in her seat, and her suitcase securely stowed overhead, she pulled out a notebook in which she made notes for her own novel she was writing. She was about halfway through the first draft.

The story involved a young woman, recently married, who was finding her husband's Hispanic culture and beliefs somewhat overwhelming, especially when she learned that his relatives practice Santeria. Going into the research of her novel, Aislinn's own beliefs regarding Santeria, or "the way of the saints," had been negative. She felt the sacrificial rituals were primitive and crude, especially since she abhorred animal torture or cruelty of any kind.

As part of her research, she had attended a religious ceremony involving *ébo*, in this case the slaughter of a goat. It was conducted in a hot and foul-smelling Miami apartment, and the goat was an offering to four *orishas* or gods—*Chango, Agallu, Elegua*, and *Ochun*. The Santeria priest cut the carotid arteries in the neck of the goat, letting its blood drip from the hog-tied animal into a bowl stuffed with stones, feathers, animal teeth and the dried blood of previous sacrifices. "These animals do not suffer," the priest had told Aislinn, but the goat was still alive after its neck was cut and a sharper knife had to be fetched as the mutilated animal bobbed its head. Aislinn was sickened by the entire proceeding and left before it was over.

The next day she visited a botanica, the place that sells spiritual aids not found in typical religious stores. It was especially hot that day, and the only source of air in the shop was a small oscillating fan that had been placed on an old marred table near the back exit.

When Aislinn entered the shop, all of her senses were immediately bombarded. The mixture of scents, the disorderly placement of so many objects, and the bright contrasting colors were confusing to one of the uninitiated. The shop keeper, a man dressed completely in white except for a strand of mixed-colored beads called *elekes*, studied her that day as she slowly moved from aisle to aisle, shelf to shelf, trying to get an understanding of what the religion was about. When she got to the rear of the shop, she saw a large black enamel bowl containing what appeared to be entrails from a rather large animal soaking in blood. It was more than she could take. "Come again for the *Ifá* and the *Merindilogún*," the shop keeper told her as she rushed toward the exit. "Soon you will feel the need." He had then given her a strand of the beads—blue and white. "These will protect you," he had said. "Wear them."

Aislinn felt totally foolish by the time she got home, blaming the heat on her quick retreat. Oddly enough, she also felt what she could only describe as empathy for the followers of this strange religion that had its roots embedded in ancient Africa. It wasn't necessarily evil or something to fear, as she had first believed.

As Aislinn learned more about this religion, she discovered that the color of the beads was important, for it was the color that signified which god was being summoned for help. The shop keeper had given her blue and white beads which appealed to the *orisha*, *Yemayá*, protector of women. Aislinn wore the beads on occasion, even to the college where she taught her writing course. She also packed them in her shoulder bag to bring with her to New York. The *Ifá* and the *Merindilogún* the man at the botanica had spoken of referred to consultations using cowrie shells to look into a person's past, present and future. The man had said she would feel the need to return. She wondered if he could be referring to the strange e-mail messages she was receiving, or the fact that, even now, she sensed she was being followed.

Aislinn continued to write down her thoughts, detailing everything she could remember from the two experiences. This would be an important theme in her novel, and she wanted to be clear on what she as the author projected in her writing.

Four and a half hours later, she landed in New York. She watched from her window as the plane turned, first left, then right, to prepare for its approach to the runway. The view of the city was breathtaking, and Aislinn felt a sharp jab of regret that Robert wasn't there with her to see it.

Because of her seat assignment, she was allowed to be one of the first to exit the plane. Pulling her suitcase with one hand and her shoulder bag in the other, she was soon inside the waiting area of the terminal and wondering how she would know which person of the many waiting there would be the one sent to meet her. She didn't have to wonder long. Near the front of everyone anxiously watching was an older gentleman, tall and thin, his hair graying at the temples, wearing a dark blue blazer, tan slacks, light blue Oxford button-down shirt, and a maroon tie. In his hand he had a copy of her latest novel. She recognized him from his pictures she had seen in the different trade magazines. It was Caldwell Kane.

As soon as he saw her, he smiled and rushed up to her. "Aislinn?" he said offering his hand.

"Hello, Caldwell. It is so nice to meet you."

"Believe me, the pleasure is all mine." He removed the bag hanging from her shoulder and took the handle of the suitcase she was pulling as well. Then he steered her through the crowd out of the waiting area and to the nearest exit. Parked just outside was a limousine. When the driver saw them he nodded and quickly opened the door.

"Aislinn, this is Dan. He will be your driver while you are visiting with us."

Dan nodded once again and took charge of the luggage.

Aislinn slipped into the backseat, enjoying the soft feel and rich smell of leather. Caldwell Kane was definitely a take charge kind of guy. He climbed in next to her, still holding the book, and still smiling.

Uncertain what to do with his long legs, he tried bending them, but that made his knees higher than his waist. After several adjustments, he finally just stuck them out in front of him.

"Have you read any good books lately?" she teased looking down at her novel that had been published the previous year.

Caldwell laughed. "Very few, actually, but this one I am happy to say, was one of the better ones." He removed a pen from the inside pocket of his jacket and handed it to Aislinn along with her book. "I collect autographs from my favorite authors. Would you?" he asked.

"I'm glad you liked it." Aislinn opened the book to the title page and wrote, "To my new friend, Caldwell," and then signed her name. She was completely charmed by this unassuming man sitting next to her who coincidentally was also one of the wealthiest men in publishing.

"I have read everything you have written, including your children's books," said Caldwell as he took back the pen and book, "and I can honestly say that I enjoyed each and every one of them. You are quite a talented lady."

"Thank you." Again, Aislinn felt embarrassed by his compliments. She glanced out the window to see where they were. They were on 50th Street, not too far from Fifth Avenue.

"I thought we would go to your hotel first and get you checked in. I hope you don't mind, but I made dinner reservations for 6:30. That way, you will have a little time to get settled before dinner, and we can make an early evening of it. I don't want to tire you out before the meeting tomorrow."

"That sounds fine, but I hope you don't think that I expected you. . ."

"Not at all," he interrupted. "I did this for purely selfish motives. I want to get to know you, first of all, but also, I didn't know when we would have the chance to talk in private if it wasn't tonight."

Aislinn nodded. *There is something else, but I don't care to discuss it over the phone,* he told her when she had returned his call. She would find out at dinner what that something else was.

Dan parked the limo in front of a hotel. It was the Waldorf Astoria. Aislinn could feel her heart quicken with excitement. Of all the hotels in New York, this was probably her favorite. It had character, style, elegance, and history as an Art Deco landmark in mid-town Manhattan. As far as Aislinn was concerned, the Waldorf was the grande dame of them all.

Caldwell escorted her into the lobby and told the clerk at the desk that they were holding a reservation for Ms. Aislinn Marchánt. A sudden flurry of activity produced a key and a bellhop to handle her luggage. "It's 5:30 now," Caldwell told Aislinn, looking at his watch, "and I have some phone calls to make. Why don't we plan to meet here in half an hour. Will that give you enough time?"

"That will be fine. I'll see you in half an hour." Aislinn smiled and then followed the bellhop to the elevator that was being held open for her. Thirty minutes would be plenty of time to freshen up and change into the long, red-print silk dress with the short bolero jacket she had brought to wear, just in case she needed it. The elevator stopped on the sixteenth floor. She followed the bellhop to the end of the hall where he unlocked the beautifully carved double doors. It was only after she entered the room that she realized she was staying in a suite. She immediately walked over to the bank of windows that overlooked downtown Manhattan. The view was magnificent and would be even more so once the sun went down.

"Would you like this here, Ms. Marchánt, or in the bedroom?" The bellhop was holding out her shoulder bag.

"Just put it in the bedroom with my other bag," she answered. She followed him to the bedroom and unzipped a side pocket on the shoulder bag in order to retrieve her purse. She wanted to give the bellhop a tip.

"Mr. Kane has already taken care of that, Ms. Marchánt," he said when she offered him the money. "Enjoy your stay in New York."

After he left, Aislinn walked through the large rooms. The mixture of floral gold tones and soft green and beige pastels on the walls and in the fabrics that covered the upholstered furniture was simply beautiful. Back in the living room, for the first time she noticed a desk, and on the desk was a large crystal vase filled with long-stemmed red roses. Aislinn read the card that had been tucked into the foliage. They were from Caldwell.

When Aislinn went downstairs, Caldwell was already there waiting. "My, don't you look pretty," he said pausing momentarily before ushering her out the revolving door to the limousine.

At the last minute Aislinn had snipped one of the roses from its long stem and fastened it to her bolero with the brooch she had brought to wear with her dress. Caldwell smiled when he noticed it. "They are just so beautiful, I thought you might enjoy seeing one of them," Aislinn explained.

The Apollo Restaurant was a short drive from the hotel, and Aislinn couldn't have been more pleased. "It has been months—maybe even years—since I have had any good Greek food," she said when she realized where they were going.

"This is supposed to be one of the best Greek restaurants around," he said, looking rather pleased with himself. "I just thought anyone with a grandmother named Aislinn ought to eat Greek food."

After their order was taken, Caldwell began talking about Kane. There was no question about how much the company meant to him, and how concerned he was over recent unexplained events. It wasn't the loss of monthly revenues that had him most concerned, however. It was the fear that someone in the company was recycling submissions that had been sent to Kane Publishing House to another publisher before they had even been considered at Kane.

"What makes you think that these incidents are something more than just simultaneous or multiple submissions? I have a feeling that most writers today send out their work to several publishers at a time." Aislinn sipped her glass of *retsina* and was making a gallant effort at trying each of the dishes Caldwell had insisted on ordering. She had made it through the *choriatiki selata*, the *keftedes*, and the *spanakopita*. Still to come was the *mousaka* and a *mastelo* made with lamb.

"I considered that, thinking that maybe it was just a case of where we were slow in reading the submissions and, in the meantime, another publisher read them, liked them, and accepted them for publication. But then late one evening after everyone had already left I picked up a couple of manuscripts that had come in that day to take home with me to read. One obviously didn't fit any of our lists. But the other, an exclusive submission according to the cover letter with it, was a surprisingly good adult novel. Under normal circumstances, it should have been handed off to one of the assistant editors to read after I returned it the next day, and then on to an associate editor. I had no doubt that it would be brought up for discussion at the next staff meeting. The next thing I knew, it was being published by Sheldon-Talbert, and no one at Kane remembered even seeing it."

Aislinn put down her fork and looked at Caldwell. This type of thing simply wasn't done in the publishing industry. There were enough manuscripts being sent to each of the publishing houses without one publisher stealing submissions from another publisher.

Caldwell seemed to read Aislinn's mind. "I know. It just doesn't even make sense. And it could have just been a coincidence. After all, strange things do happen. But, unfortunately, the same thing happened a few weeks later. Again, I was leaving the office late. No one saw me take the manuscripts to read or return them. This time one of the manuscripts was a collection of poems written by a man who suffers with a degenerative spine disorder. The poems reflected the pain he endures, but they also reflected a universal hope of overcoming adversity. Even though we don't publish many poetry collections, this one was worth consideration. I kept waiting for someone to bring it up at one of the staff meetings, but it never was. Then, a short time later when the new fall releases were announced, there it was under Sheldon-Talbert's list."

The waiter brought to their table a covered clay pot. In it was the *mastelo*. After ceremoniously removing the lid, he proceeded to dish up the baked lamb and vegetables onto Aislinn's and Caldwell's plates.

"What bothers me the most is suspecting someone in the company. Most of the people who work at Kane Publishing have been with me for a while. They are all pretty much like my own family. I can't begin to tell you how much it hurts me to think that someone is being disloyal."

"Have you discussed any of this with anyone—perhaps your sons?"

"No. I felt it best not to until I know what is going on. Other than Mrs. McLaughlin, no one even knows you are here."

Aislinn glanced around the colorful dining room. Candles illuminated every table. Greek music played in the background. Marble statues, an assortment of plants, and the sound of bubbling water from a fountain nearby created the feeling of being in a private garden. She remembered another time, another Greek meal, and the words of her grandmother: *People give strange things in the name of love, when in fact all they have to do is give of themselves.* Aislinn wasn't sure why she thought of those particular words now.

"I still don't understand why you have asked me to help you. I know there are people you could hire who do nothing but investigate things like corporate fraud. I would think that this situation would fall within their expertise."

"That's true. But I just don't feel comfortable bringing in someone like that, especially if there is a possibility that I have completely misconstrued everything. When Timothy Richards resubmitted his work, *The Ancients,* he also included your evaluation report to him, his first draft which included your editorial changes, and all of your correspondence relating to his writing. No one had ever done that before, and I was curious. After reading everything, there was no doubt in my mind that you had a true gift for seeing value in the written word where most professionals wouldn't, but you also had a way of dealing with people that I felt was sensitive and extraordinary. It wasn't just your suggestions on how Timothy could improve his novel; it was the way you suggested those changes. You obviously have a deep understanding of the needs and feelings of others, and I thought that maybe, once you had a chance to meet everyone at Kane, you would be able to shed some light on something that I obviously can't.

"Aislinn, I honestly don't know if you can help with this. Or if you even want to. I just felt that somehow if you knew about it, it wouldn't be so bad. I don't mind telling you, I haven't slept very well since learning that Sheldon-Talbert published that first manuscript. I think I'm too close to the situation to be able to figure it out."

"Well, I'm no detective, but I can certainly evaluate your submissions when they come in. Who knows, maybe we can learn something from that."

They continued talking through the meal, about their work, the manuscript Aislinn was currently writing, Hemingway, and Caldwell's sons. Aislinn didn't talk about Robert, and Caldwell didn't mention his late wife. By the time they had finished eating, it was already past nine o'clock. Dan was waiting for them when they left the restaurant. When they got back to the Waldorff, Caldwell insisted on going in with Aislinn and walking her as far as the elevator. "What was your grand-mother's name, Caldwell?" Aislinn asked as she pushed the elevator button to stop at the sixteenth floor.

Caldwell's look of surprise quickly changed to amusement. "Aislinn," he answered. "My grandmother's name was Aislinn."

Chapter Seven

Writers seldom choose as friends those self-contained characters who are never in trouble, never unhappy or ill, never make mistakes, and always count their change when it is handed to them.

Catherine Drinker Bowen

Tracy didn't go in to work Thursday, deciding to stay at home and start on the novel. When Friday morning came, she called in sick. She wanted to work on an outline using the information in *Then There Was Light*. Then she could decide on her characters. She would have to avoid even mentioning anyone resembling Snow Henderson, just in case someone was familiar with the story. But that would be easy enough. She would simply make the protagonist a man, and instead of living in the mountains of North Carolina, he could live in Florida. After all, that was supposed to be the lightning capital of the world. Tracy smiled as she tapped away on her computer. This was going to be so easy.

When the phone rang for the third time in less than an hour, she frowned but kept working. A little later it rang again. This time she answered.

"Hi. They told me at your office that you called in sick this morning. Is everything all right?"

It was Tyler. "Oh sure, just a little stomach virus or something." The last person she wanted to know about what she was doing was Tyler Kane.

"I guess that means you won't feel like going out for dinner tonight?"

Tracy slumped down in her chair. She had forgotten all about it being Friday. Ever since Bologna they had been going out for dinner on Friday nights. "Tyler, I really don't feel like it. Do you mind if we just make it next week?"

"Of course not. Can I bring you anything? Chicken soup? Grilled cheese sandwich? An empanada? A slice of pecan pie?"

He really was trying to be helpful in his silly way, but Tracy wanted to work and he was interrupting. "No, nothing, but thanks just the same." She wanted him just to hang up.

"Did you get a chance to read the manuscript?"

"Which manuscript?" Tracy glanced at her computer screen at the notes she had been writing. She would have to be really careful about what she said.

"*Then There Was Light,* the one I just gave to you."

"Oh, yes, I did. It started out pretty good, but it lost its focus after about the first fifty or so pages. Not only that, I have a feeling the person who wrote it is some sort of nut."

"Oh? I honestly thought it was pretty good. Oh, well. I'll see what else I can come up with."

"Tyler, I was just getting ready to go back to bed, so. . ."

"Oh, sure. Well, be sure to call me if you need anything."

"Thanks. You are so sweet."

Tracy had no sooner started working when the telephone rang again. "Honestly! What does he want now?" She impatiently jerked up the receiver. It was her mother calling from Miami. Tracy hadn't spoken to her since Christmas; she hadn't seen her in over six years.

"What do you want, Mama?"

"Is that any way to speak to your mother, Trista?" came the answer.

Tracy felt herself cringe. Her family had lived in this country for almost ten years, and they couldn't speak English any better now than they could before they left Buenos Aires. Tracy thought back to the last time her mother had called. It was because her Uncle Loui needed some money to start up his own meat business. Before that, some cousin wanted to go to beauty school, but didn't have the money to pay for the tuition. And before that, someone else, Tracy couldn't even remember who, had some legal fees.

Ever since Tracy left home, her family had treated her like it was her responsibility to support all of them. All they had to do was ask, they thought. Tracy would do all the rest. After all, she was a successful editor with a publishing firm in New York making lots of money. It didn't matter that she had made tremendous sacrifices and worked hard to get where she was and had received no help, least of all from her family, in getting there. At first it was just her mother and father and two sisters needing financial help. But then her two sisters got married, increasing the size of the family and the number of demands on Tracy. Soon other family members came to visit from Buenos Aires and wound up staying in Miami, all of them poor, all of them wanting money. Over time, the resentment became so great that Tracy started to distance herself not only from the relatives she didn't even know, but from her own parents as well. She convinced herself she no longer had a family. Hearing her mother's loud, whining voice now didn't change her mind.

"What do you want?" Tracy repeated.

"Your papa needs an operation."

"How much?"

"Fifty thousand dollars."

Tracy stood up, knocking over her chair. "Fifty thousand dollars? What kind of operation? Didn't you get that health insurance I told you to get?"

"He has the cancer, Trista. He needs a lot of treatment."

Tracy was furious. Just when she thought she might stand a chance to really make it big, to get ahead, this had to happen. Well, she wasn't going to let them drag her down—not now, not ever. "I'm sorry, Mama, I don't have it. You'll just have to get it from someone else. Now, I must go."

Tracy slammed down the phone trembling with rage. She had been used all she was going to be used—never again. Tears fell from her eyes and splashed on the computer. She reached out and grabbed the phone cord, and in one hard jerk, yanked it from the wall jack.

* * *

Tyler pulled another manuscript from the stack he was supposed to read and stared at the pages. He knew it had been pretty early when he called Tracy, but usually she didn't mind. In fact, usually she was already at her office working. She had sounded a little strange, like she thought he was being a nuisance or something. She hadn't sounded like that before. In fact, quite the opposite. She couldn't wait to see him, especially if he was going to give her a manuscript. He rubbed his stomach and felt it churn, an indication that a run to the bathroom would soon be necessary. From the bottom drawer in his desk he brought out a large bottle of stomach acid pills. Dumping three of them into his hand, he tossed them into his mouth and began to chew. The pills didn't seem to be helping much lately. Maybe this last bottle was old. He checked the expiration date printed on the twist cap. It wasn't.

He had really liked *Then There Was Light*. He had read it through twice before deciding to give Tracy a shot at it. He wished now that he hadn't given it to her. He would have talked about it in the staff meeting instead of that Vietnam War book. The author of *Then There Was Light* had sent an extra copy of the manuscript which he still had. He could always slip it back in with the other new submissions, and that way he would probably get it before next month's meeting.

He glanced at his watch. He still had fifteen minutes. Mrs. McLaughlin had set up a table with coffee and pastries in the conference room. He wondered what that was all about. No one had mentioned anything special going on.

Still rubbing his stomach he gathered up all the manuscripts that were supposed to be discussed at the meeting. His was the weakest one, and he knew that no one would support him in wanting to see it get published. In fact, he hadn't been able to get anything through for several months now. His father hadn't said anything to him, but Jason sure had, and it was just a matter of time before his father did, too. Maybe he should just back off a bit and let Tracy find her own manuscripts—at least for a while. Long enough for him to come up with a couple of best sellers for Kane Publishing. In fact, he would bet that *Then There Was Light* would be one of them. The problem was, he wasn't sure how long Tracy would stay interested in him if he didn't try to help her.

Just as he gathered up everything he was taking with him into the meeting, his stomach churned once more, this time leaving no doubt. He dropped the manuscripts, scattering them across his desk and made a dash down the hall toward the men's room.

* * *

Open books and loose-leaf manuscripts lay in the weeds, lined up parallel to the latticed fence that concealed the trash dumpster. The old man sat facing the organized litter, reading from the Bible, muttering to himself, and rocking back and forth. Occasionally he picked up one of the other books on the ground before him and read from it. It was the green leather book. He had been given a task, but he was finding it difficult to completely understand. He recognized the signs. He recognized the evil. The voice had told him, *He who does what is sinful is of the devil* (1JO8). Now he had to figure out exactly what that evil was, how to punish that evil and make it right.

He hadn't seen the woman since the night he went into her apartment. She was still there, plotting and scheming, and it all had to do with what was in the brown envelope. On the page inside the envelope was written, *Then There Was Light.* Whatever he was trying to decipher had to do with light. *Everyone who does evil hates the light, and will not come into the light for fear that his deeds will be exposed. But whoever lives by the truth comes into the light, so that it may be seen plainly that what he has done has been done through God* (John 3/20-21).

Dark clouds started forming overhead casting a gray dullness over everything, and the dull pain in his right temple worsened. He put his head down in his folded arms and rocked harder. His mutterings became louder. Soon the pain would be excruciating. Was he being punished for not knowing the answer? He cried out, *Stern discipline awaits him who leaves the path; he who hates correction will die* (PRO10). A drop of rain fell onto his hand. Then another. Quickly he gathered up his books and sheets of paper and began placing them methodically back into the sacks. The rain fell harder. He pushed his cart to the opposite side of the lattice fence next to the large dumpster. There he opened the heavy metal, double-hinged lid, letting it flop over onto a board he used to prop it with. This protected his cart and everything in it from the rain. Lightning flashed around him, while the thunder drowned out his loud cries. The pain in his head was unbearable. He curled up into a ball next to his cart, careful to keep within the perimeter of the front and back wheels. Lying there on the concrete, his eyes squeezed tightly shut, he once more heard the voice. And it said: *The king will mourn, the prince will be clothed with despair, and the hands of the people of the land will tremble. I will deal with them according to their conduct, and by their own standards I will judge them. Then they will know that I am the LORD* (EZE 27).

* * *

"What in the world are you peeking at?" Darlene, one of the secretaries at Sheldon-Talbert, had stopped by Scott Darnell's office with some more manuscripts and saw him trying to look through his blinds that were half closed.

Scott jumped at the sound of her voice and then tried to look busy. He moved to his desk and shuffled some papers around. "That crazy old man out there. Have you seen him?"

"You mean the Professor?" She walked over to the window and snapped the blinds to their full, open position.

"Is that what people call him?"

"As far as I know. He came with the building. Everyone knows the Professor. He's harmless."

"How do you know he's harmless?" Scott angled back over to the window and closed the blinds a fraction. "I mean, he's out there under a dumpster lid, for pity's sake, screaming like a banshee."

"It's the storm. Any change in barometric pressure causes him to have migraines."

Scott looked at the young woman in astonishment. "How do you know these things? Have you talked to him?"

"Of course. You don't think I want to be a secretary the rest of my life, do you? I want to be a writer. And the way I see it, in order to be a good writer I need to be observant of everything, especially the frailties of mankind." She dumped the manuscripts on his desk. "He's really not a bad guy once you get to know him. It's just that he doesn't take his medication any more, and that causes him to hear voices and hallucinate once in a while. When that happens he develops a conspiracy complex."

"What do you mean by that?"

She looked at Scott like she was trying to explain potty training to a two-year-old. "It's just that he creates imaginary problems that he feels he must solve in order to keep his life on track. Remember Susan in marketing? She used to bring the same shoulder bag to work every day until one day a strap broke on it so she got a new bag. When she stopped carrying the old bag, though, the Professor thought there was something evil going on. He followed her around for a month until finally she had to show him the old bag with the broken strap."

"Jeesus, no wonder she quit working here."

Darlene walked over next to Scott and looked out. "Poor soul. He's working on a conspiracy now. Eventually he'll figure it out, though, and then he'll be back to normal. He used to be an editor, you know," she said as she continued down the hall with her other deliveries.

Scott ran to the door and yelled, "Did he really?"

Darlene glanced back at Scott laughing. "No."

* * *

"Be careful, now, you hear? I don't want anything broken up there." Lottie Howard held Hemingway safely in her arms and stood at the bottom of the pull-down stairs leading up into the attic. She had been unable to climb the stairs for years, so on those rare occasions when she wanted something that had been safely stored there, she usually sent Eliane. On this particular early-morning occasion, however, what she wanted proved to be too heavy for Eliane, so Miguel had to be fetched and told to ascend the stairs as well.

Lottie strained, trying to see what all the bumping noises were. "It's an old trunk," she repeated. "And it has a dome-shaped lid with brass hinges." She moved to the other side of the stairs. "What are you doing up there?"

Just then Eliane appeared at the opening, slightly smudged but smiling. They had located the trunk. Carefully Miguel moved down the steps while Eliane steadied the trunk on his shoulder from above. "Eliane, wipe if off with something, and then I would like for Miguel to put it in my office next to the big chair." The big chair was just that—large, overstuffed, and comfortable for someone of Lottie's stature. The small white pillow placed in the chair had been hand crocheted by her mother and was just the right size to fit that tender arthritic spot in the small of Lottie Howard's back. During the time she spent in her office if she wasn't actually sitting at her desk, she was in the big chair.

One of the things that Aislinn had suggested in her report regarding Lottie's manuscript was that in order to reconnect with feelings and experiences from the past, it was sometimes helpful to look through old photographs. And photographs she had plenty of, for her mother had taken up photography as a sort of hobby while her husband was away so much of the time on business.

Settled with a cup of sweetened coffee, the large trunk next to her, and Hemingway scrunched next to her in the chair, Lottie began the tedious job of sorting through the numerous old albums and loose photographs and trying to recognize who in the world had been photographed and where they were taken. She recognized herself, of course. Her baby pictures—on a deep shag rug, in a footed porcelain tub, in her wooden cradle, taking her first steps. The childhood pictures—on a pony, eating an ice cream cone, on her father's shoulders, on a swing with her mother, starting school, her first cotillion. Even as a child she had a statuesque build and bright red hair, although much longer, which she wore coiled on top of her head like a coronet. Her parents she also recognized, standing in front of the various new cars they acquired each year, the bushes that were flowering according to whatever season, walking on the beach, or entertaining friends and business associates at their home. And, of course, the holidays. Aislinn had been right. The photographs brought back a lot of memories. Most of the people Miss Howard recognized were gone now.

She continued sorting and examining the contents of the trunk until she reached the very bottom where she discovered a small box tied shut with a lavender ribbon. At first she only looked at it, reluctant to even touch the box or the ribbon that held it closed. There was something vaguely familiar about it, as though she was remembering it from a deep dream of long ago. She sipped her coffee thoughtfully and returned the cup to the silver tray on the table next to her. Carefully she lifted the box from the trunk, put it in her lap, and untied the ribbon.

* * *

Aislinn awoke early to a sound she couldn't immediately identify. Slowly she began reconstructing the events of the day before—dropping off Hemingway at Miss Howard's, the flight from West Palm Beach to New York, meeting Caldwell, and the Greek restaurant—right up to the present. The sound she heard was that of rain splattering against the many windows in the suite where she was staying.

Dan had been instructed to meet Aislinn at 8:30 in the lobby of the Waldorf and drive her to Kane Publishing House. Caldwell was waiting for her at the door when she arrived. With Dan holding a large umbrella over her, Caldwell watched Aislinn stop and admire two concrete planter boxes at the entrance filled with newly-planted pink geraniums. She was wearing a soft blue, two-piece knit dress with taupe stockings and matching medium-heeled shoes. From what he could see, her only jewelry was a single long strand of blue and white beads. Another red rose was pinned on her shoulder.

When Aislinn noticed Caldwell standing by the door, she smiled. Apparently he had already been working because his reading glasses were pushed up on his forehead and he was holding a handful of papers.

"How did you sleep? Sometimes being in a strange bed and all. . ."

"I slept fine," she answered. "I even got up early this morning and finished editing a manuscript I started last night."

Caldwell led Aislinn past the receptionist's desk and Lorraine McLaughlin's office, after introducing her, and down a long, carpeted hall to his office.

"Oh, my," said Aislinn looking around. "This is really very nice."

"Thank you." He closed the door. "I spend so much time here, it's almost like another home to me."

Aislinn smiled. His office was set up much like a living room—warm, inviting, and comfortable. There was a large sofa covered with large plump pillows, chairs of various sizes and styles, and several tables, all serving some purpose and function. And, of course, there was his desk, a huge piece of solid pine furniture obviously picked out for its usefulness and practicality. Everything on the surface of the desk had to do with work: pads of paper, stacks of manuscripts, an assortment of writing instruments, a telephone covered in stick'em notes. On one end of the desk, however, there were two framed photographs, particularly noticeable because they alone seemed to be unrelated to work or anything else on the desk. The one photograph was of Caldwell taken when he was much younger sprawled on a grassy lawn with two young boys, probably his sons, Aislinn guessed. The other photo, framed in silver, was of a woman sitting outdoors on a log and wistfully looking out over a blue body of water. It had been taken in the fall of the year, judging from the brightly colored trees on the surrounding hills, and she wore a baggy orange sweater and jeans. She's beautiful, Aislinn thought, and wondered if it was his late wife.

"I feel I ought to give you one last chance to say no before going into the meeting this morning." Caldwell was leaning awkwardly against his desk, and for a moment it was hard for Aislinn to believe that this endearingly self-conscious man was responsible for such a huge publishing empire.

"What? And miss out helping you solve what might turn out to be the mystery of the century? I wouldn't think of it."

Caldwell took command of his body once again then and smiled broadly. "Right."

Everyone who was supposed to attend the meeting was already in the conference room when Aislinn and Caldwell arrived. Several of the editors were milling around the table with the coffee and pastries. Others were seated at the large table. An arrangement of fresh flowers had been placed in the center of the table, and stacks of manuscripts, pads of paper, and writing pens were everywhere. Lorraine McLaughlin was busy passing out pieces of paper, presumably some sort of agenda, while another younger woman, an assistant, seemed to be taking notes.

"People, I'd like your attention, please." Caldwell took his place at the head of the table, pulling Aislinn next to him. Within minutes everyone was seated and quiet. "I would like to introduce you to Aislinn Marchánt. She has agreed to work as a consultant to Kane Publishing, and I would like to ask each of you to make her feel welcome and to give her any assistance she might need."

Lorraine McLaughlin pushed up a chair next to where Caldwell was standing for Aislinn. She sat down next to him on the other side. The assistant sat toward the back of the room still taking notes. Aislinn couldn't help but notice the surprised looks around the table. Surprised, but not antagonistic. One attractive sandy-haired young man quickly got up and came over to shake Aislinn's hand. "Welcome aboard, Aislinn. I am Tyler Kane. If I can help you, just let me know." Tyler was as charming as his smile. "And if it means getting some more of these pastry things, I hope you'll come to all the editorial staff meetings from now on, too." Everyone laughed.

Others murmured their words of welcome, one voice a little louder than the others. "I'm sure all of us here want you to feel at home," he said. He was a serious-looking man with the dark brooding eyes she had noticed in the photograph on Caldwell's desk. He obviously felt comfortable in a leadership role.

"That is my older son, Jason," Caldwell said.

The difference between the two sons in appearance as well as manner was quite dramatic.

"Thank you. I'm looking forward to getting to know all of you." Aislinn smiled and stopped at that point. Caldwell obviously had a lot of material to go over, and she didn't want to waste his time. Besides, she didn't want to leave herself open to too many questions. The fact that she was working as a consultant was all anyone needed to know.

* * *

"So, how are we doing this beautiful day?" Josh smiled sarcastically.

Robert glanced up from reading his own medical chart. "Couldn't be better. You ready to get this dog and pony act on the road?" With

Harris and Rodriguez now taken care of, Josh had convinced Robert that there was no need putting off his own surgery for later that afternoon and had rescheduled it for the morning instead.

"Sure am." Josh took the chart from Robert. "Do you mind if I see for myself?" After reading it he returned it to the holder located on the foot of the bed. "Any last-minute requests? Favorite songs you'd like to hear, maybe? Or, I can do a pretty mean Jimmy Durante impersonation, if you like."

"I'll pass. Thanks anyway."

Josh nodded and began taking Robert's pulse. "Did you tell Aislinn?"

"No. She had to fly up to New York yesterday, but she'll be back this evening. I'll tell her when I see her."

"See you upstairs then."

A few moments later Robert was being wheeled through the corridor to the large elevator that would take him up to surgery. He had been given a sedative earlier. Now he was being given the strong stuff intravenously and he was starting to feel its effects. Once on the third floor, he was pushed through the wide double doors of the operating room. Several nurses were already there making the necessary preparations. Their voices sounded slightly muffled and the light they had parked him under was too bright. He tried to raise up to see if Josh was there yet, but his body refused to move. He thought he heard Josh then. "I'm here, doctor. You have nothing to worry about." The last thing Robert remembered was thinking about Aislinn and wondering where she had eaten dinner the night before.

* * *

The meeting went pretty much as Aislinn thought it would, stopping only briefly while sandwiches were brought in around noon. Some of the manuscripts being considered were good, a couple of them exceptional. It was the exceptional ones that would be given the full marketing treatment—author's book signings, radio and television interviews, full-page advertisements in national newspapers. One was already being considered for a possible movie deal. The remaining manuscripts to get published would receive moderate advance publicity and intense exposure at the time of release. Of those manuscripts that were left, more than likely they would be rejected. Aislinn found it interesting that the manuscript Tyler had brought to the table to discuss had gotten very little discussion. Even he hadn't pushed very hard for its publication.

It was late afternoon by the time the meeting ended, and Caldwell still wanted to take Aislinn around to the various departments. Mrs. McLaughlin caught up with them a short time later downstairs in marketing. Apparently there was a problem that needed Caldwell's immediate attention. "I'll try to make this fast," he told Aislinn. "Mrs. McLaughlin, would you mind showing Aislinn around the rest of the place?"

"I'll be happy to," she said, leading Aislinn in an entirely different direction toward the ladies' room. "Men never think of these things," she said.

Aislinn liked Lorraine. She had a feeling that if anyone knew what was going on at Kane, she did. It wasn't the right time to ask any questions, though. Lorraine would have to feel she could trust Aislinn first. When Caldwell hadn't returned in thirty minutes, Aislinn became concerned. She didn't want to miss her plane. Fortunately, she had already given Dan her luggage that morning, so she wouldn't need to return to the hotel. Caldwell finally came rushing into Lorraine's office where the two women were chatting. "I was hoping I could ride with you to the airport, Aislinn, but it looks like I am needed here. Will you be all right?"

"Of course. Thank you for everything." She smiled and offered her hand. "We'll talk later when you have more time."

He continued looking at her for a moment and then amazingly bent down and kissed her cheek. "Right," he said.

Lorraine found something terribly interesting to do in her top file drawer until Caldwell dashed out of her office. When he was gone, she pulled out a brown envelope along with a small paper sack. "Aislinn, Caldwell has instructed me to start sending you copies of all the manuscripts as they get distributed to our editors for consideration, so I'll be getting some out to you by overnight delivery the first of the week."

"Thank you, Lorraine. I appreciate that. I know it's asking a lot, but would it be possible to send me a copy of every manuscript that comes in, even the ones that are recycled—say, for the first couple of months?"

"It's not asking too much at all. I'll get a couple of the young men with strong backs who work in the mail room to box them up for me."

Lorraine pushed up the sleeves on her sweater and closed the door to her office. "Look, I'm not trying to stick my nose in where it doesn't belong, but I think you might want to read this one first." She handed Aislinn the brown envelope. "It is a manuscript that was logged in a week ago as a new submission. Then it disappeared. Now, sometime this morning, it showed back up. It might mean something."

Aislinn took the envelope from her and put it safely away in her shoulder bag. "Lorraine, is there any kind of tracking information kept on where the manuscripts are assigned once they are logged in?"

"Yes. I keep up with all of that, although I don't think anyone even knows that I do. I'll send you copies of that information along with the manuscripts."

Just then Dan knocked on the office door and stuck his head in. "If you are ready, we'd better be leaving. With it being Friday and all the late-afternoon cross-town traffic, I want to allow plenty of time to get to the airport."

Lorraine handed the paper sack to Aislinn. "Now, these are in case you get hungry and you don't want to eat whatever they feed you on the plane." The sack was filled with pastries.

Aislinn hugged her and smiled. "Thank you, Lorraine. I'll be talking to you soon."

"You do that."

Lorraine watched Aislinn climb into the limousine and disappear down the street. For the first time in weeks she felt hopeful. Something sure had been chewing at Caldwell for the past several months, and she didn't like it one bit. He was just like his father used to be—locked everything inside. Well, maybe Aislinn could get to the bottom of it.

* * *

Of course, she knew there would be more photographs in it, and right on top, in a small leather pouch, was a gold chain with a small heart hanging from it. Her heart quickened and her face felt flushed. She located the fan that was in her dress pocket and began briskly fanning herself. Then, after fastening the necklace around her neck, she carefully removed the photographs from the box, examining each image, one by one, of the tall thin young man with skin the color of brown sugar and the statuesque young lady who wore her hair on her head like a crown. It were as though in that one moment, her entire young life was there in front of her, spread out on her ample lap in faded capsules of time. The memory of heartache, bitterness, and *waste* came pouring back. So many dreams—lost. "C.T.," she whispered. With Hemingway licking her damp cheeks, she leaned back on the small white pillow and wept uncontrollably.

She had just turned sixteen—"Sweet Sixteen and never been kissed," everyone had teased. Her parents had planned her party for months. All of her friends were invited, dressed in their finest and excited about attending the first big event of the summer. The invitations, hand decorated with dried, pressed flowers and lavender ribbons, had called it a "garden party." Tables covered in white linen cloths were scattered about the lawn, small glass-globed gypsy lanterns added to the frivolity of the occasion, and a harpist had been hired to play music. Everything cooperated until something malfunctioned in the kitchen— Lottie couldn't even remember what. Her father immediately called Charles, his handyman, to fix whatever it was, which was what he had always done in the past. As he frequently did, Charles brought his son with him to help.

Of course, Lottie knew both Charles and his son. She always had. Over the years they had become practically a part of the family. C.T. and Lottie had even played together as young children. Lottie didn't have many friends. She was painfully shy and awkward, feelings brought on by the fact that she was so much larger than the other children her age. As they grew older, it was C.T. rather than her parents that Lottie turned to during those moments when life simply proved too difficult. He was a couple of years older than Lottie and in many ways the older brother she didn't have, with the knowledge and experienced that up to that point in her young life Lottie had only imagined.

For some reason, C.T. wanted Lottie to leave her party and walk down to the intracoastal. He had something important to tell her.

Lottie's mother found them there a short while later, holding hands and kissing. Lottie never saw him again.

There hadn't been an ugly scene—that simply wasn't permitted in her mother's understanding of etiquette and proper behavior. In fact, Lottie didn't even realize the seriousness of the situation until a few days later when she tried to contact C.T. It was then that his father told her that he had gone up north to live. She never found out where he was, or even what it was that he wanted to tell her that day. That fall, she was shipped off to Virginia to complete her secondary schooling and then begin college.

At first she hated her father, and her mother for not standing up to him. But that hate softened with time and then with the long, debilitating illness of her mother, it eventually disappeared. She was, after all, a dutiful daughter, and to prove it she returned home after graduating with high honors from Sweet Briar, a highly acclaimed college for young women, to look after her mother's many needs. When her father became ill several years later, Lottie lost all hope of ever having any life of her own. She forgot about C.T. and concentrated instead on her responsibilities as a devoted daughter. Any time she had for herself she reserved for her writing—poetry and short stories mainly—something she had started as a child and continued while attending Sweet Briar. She was so afraid that this, too, would be taken from her that she hid everything she wrote somewhere in her room. It was only after her father died that she collected everything that she had ever written together in one large drawer of her bureau, and it was from many of these things that she was able to piece together the biography of her father, *My Father's Keeper.* Now, seeing the old faded photographs of her and C.T., an entirely different story was taking shape. This was the passion Aislinn had said was so vital to any written work. This was

Lottie's passion and this was her story. The accomplishments of her father were only footnotes. She could see that now.

* * *

Because of the large amount of calcification in Robert's arteries, Josh had elected to perform a laser assisted angioplasty procedure rather than the carotid artery bypass operation. There was less risk involved, and the recovery time was much faster.

By using a laser catheter, a high intensity light beam would then vaporize the affected area without damaging the surrounding tissues. After this was accomplished, a stent made of Nitinol material could be delivered to the obstructed site on a balloon catheter passed over a wire. Once the balloon was inflated, the stent would expand; and the balloon catheter could then be removed leaving the stent in place to keep the artery open. This particular procedure Josh used only as a treatment in those patients with the high degree of calcification that Robert had. By pulverizing the obstructing fibrous plaque into minute micro particles, it would be washed away into the bloodstream with no trauma to any of the surrounding tissues.

Josh felt confident in this procedure's outcome. However, one thing did concern him. In past experiences he had found that many arterial blockages as severe as Robert's also contained blood clots at the site of obstruction. To further reduce any risk factor, Josh instilled a clot buster immediately before initiating the interventional procedure. He didn't want to take any chances.

Within the hour, Josh had completed the procedure and Robert was taken to the recovery room where a nurse continued to monitor his vital signs. The important thing was that there be no signs of bleeding or swelling, and all the pulses registered normally. So far, everything was going as it should.

By the time Josh went to see him, Robert was awake and arguing with the nurse. He wanted to get up.

"On your back, doctor," ordered Josh. "Otherwise you will mess up my perfectly executed procedure."

Robert frowned.

"Nurse, I don't want him to move for the next three hours. If he tries, shoot him."

"Yes, sir."

"Robert, I mean it. After three hours, if I feel everything is all right, I will let you go. But not before then. I don't need to remind you how important it is that there be no swelling or bleeding."

Robert didn't argue. He knew Josh was right. "Could you at least find out about Harris and Rodriguez?" he asked.

"Already have," said Josh. "They are both on their way to a full recovery."

"Good," Robert tried to say, but his eyelids got in the way and somehow the word didn't come out like it should. He was asleep.

* * *

Aislinn leaned forward on the cool leather seat. "Dan, do you know where Sheldon-Talbert Publishing is located?"

She saw Dan's eyebrows raise slightly as he glanced at her in the rearview mirror.

"Sure do. You want to go by there on the way to the airport?"

"Please. If it isn't too much trouble."

In a few minutes they were driving down a street flanked by tall oak trees and several multi-storied office buildings. Dan drove slowly past an older red brick structure with a deep, gray-marbled portico. The big bold brass lettering on the front of the building read "Sheldon-Talbert."

"This is it," he said. He stopped at the curb for Aislinn to get a good look and then drove on past in order to turn into the alleyway located right next to the building. Rather than back into traffic, he pulled all the way in and came out on the other side at the rear of the building where there was a parking area, loading docks, and large metal trash containers. The rain was only a light drizzle now, and the sun sparkled through the leafy branches of the large trees growing on the perimeter of the property. Aislinn looked around at the surrounding area, not really knowing what it was she expected to see. Somehow, though, Sheldon-Talbert was connected to the problems Caldwell was having.

"Stop, Dan." Aislinn peered through the droplets of water running down on the outside of the windowpane next to where she was sitting. There was an old man pushing a shopping basket filled with sacks of different sizes toward an area behind the dumpsters.

"It's just some homeless guy," Dan said. "He probably hangs out around here."

* * *

Once the rain stopped, the pain in the old man's head eased. He had survived the demons from Hell. He would be all right now. After checking each of his bags to make sure none of them had gotten wet from the rain, he began pushing his cart back to the other side of the trellis fence where he couldn't be seen.

The sound of an engine caught his attention. It wasn't the same sound as what the big trucks made that came around all the time. He paused and looked toward the alley. There he saw a gleaming silver chariot slowly coming toward him. God was answering his pleas to give him guidance. *This is how it will be at the end of the age. The angels will come and separate the wicked from the righteous* (MAT49).

As the chariot came closer, the old man began to pray for understanding, for knowledge, and for guidance. *Praise the LORD, you his angels, you mighty ones who do his bidding, who obey his word. Praise the LORD, all his heavenly hosts, you his servants who do his will* (PSA103:20,21). The chariot stopped and then started turning around. "Then There Was Light," the old man said. But the chariot began moving away. "Then There Was Light," the old man screamed at the chariot and he ran toward it. Near the rear of the chariot, a panel of sparkling diamonds slid into the chariot's sterling casing, and he saw the face of an angel. *He makes winds his messengers, flames of fire his servants* (PSA104:4). *Praise him, all his angels, praise him, all his heavenly hosts* (PSA148:2). "Then There Was Light," he repeated breathlessly. It was a sign from God Almighty. The angel heard and understood. Now he would soon receive the answer. He would know what to do. *An angel from heaven appeared to him and strengthened him* (LUK22:43), the voice said.

Chapter Eight

In any really good subject, one has only to probe deep enough to come to tears.

Edith Wharton

"I thought you were on duty this morning. What are you doing back here now?" One of the night-duty nurses poked her head into Margaret's office where she was working on the computer.

"I was, but a couple of the nurses on night duty called in sick, so I'm working." She smirked and shrugged her shoulders as if to say, "What else can I do?"

"Gee, that's too bad. I'm on my way up to the fourth floor. Do you need anything?"

"No, but thanks." Margaret watched the young nurse disappear down the hall. Actually, no one had called in sick. She had rescheduled herself when she learned that Dr. Turner had refused to release Dr. Marchánt earlier that afternoon. Apparently Dr. Marchánt was experiencing some swelling, and Turner wanted to keep him overnight for observation.

Margaret had gone home on her break in order to shower and change into a fresh uniform—the one with a fitted waist and buttons down the front. She had also splashed on an extra dose of scent—a little heady, but not too much. From past experience she knew that a man was most vulnerable when he was flat on his back, and she sure the hell wasn't going to miss this opportunity to make herself as indispensable as possible to the good doctor, Robert Marchánt. At the very least, maybe she could get him to start calling her Margaret like all the other doctors did instead of "Nurse Peters."

She tapped a few more keys on the keyboard of the computer and then shut it down. It was almost time for the nurse who was with him now to go off duty. She walked over to the door and pushed it partly closed, looking at herself in the mirror attached there. Not bad for a forty-nine-year-old woman, divorced with two sons and a daughter, all grown, if you could consider them grown. The two sons still lived with her which made it tough trying to attract eligible men. It didn't matter how much money they had, most men didn't want to support another man's kids, especially when they were old enough to be out on their own. She didn't even know where her daughter was. She would just suddenly turn up whenever she needed money, usually around Christmas. Quite frankly, she was getting a little tired of trying to support all of them. Getting married again would help things a lot, especially if she married someone like Robert Marchánt.

She fluffed her straight, brown hair and smoothed her lips. She had paid way too much for a new shade of lipstick—a dark maroon. It was what all the beautiful, stylish, and famous women were wearing, according to the sales clerk. The color was pretty on the model in the slick-papered, full-color brochure she had seen. Looking at it now on her own lips, though, in the glaring fluorescent light of her office, she wondered if it made her face look tired and washed out. Oh well, it would have to do. She didn't have any other lipstick with her. One more glance and she unfastened another button on her dress, exposing as much cleavage as possible without having one of her breasts pop out. Satisfied, she grabbed a notepad and walked briskly down the hall toward the room that was occupied by Dr. Robert Marchánt.

* * *

Aislinn's return flight to West Palm was direct and nonstop from New York, but it was delayed in LaGuardia for over two hours. The weather front that had produced all the rain in the northeast earlier was now moving south and creating another disturbance. The pilot wanted to wait it out rather than try to fly around it.

Aislinn found a quiet, comfortable lounge that wasn't full of disgruntled passengers and ordered a glass of *Chenin blanc*. Situated in a corner booth she pulled out the brown envelope that Lorraine McLaughlin had given to her and opened it. The words on the title page literally jumped out at her. *THEN THERE WAS LIGHT.* They were the very words that the homeless man at Sheldon-Talbert had been yelling when Dan drove her there.

At first she was just going to scan over the manuscript, but once she started to read it, she couldn't put it down. Without question, *Then There Was Light* would be a best seller. An announcement was made that the passengers on her flight could now load. She quickly gathered up her things and walked to the loading gate wondering who else had already read the story of the young mountain woman who had been struck by lightning so many times.

It was after eight o'clock when Aislinn arrived back at West Palm Beach. She had left her car in over-night parking at the airport. That was easier to do that than trying to make arrangements for someone to pick her up, especially when she wasn't certain when she would be getting back. Once back home, she didn't bother taking her luggage into the house. Instead, she went immediately over to Miss Howard's to collect Hemingway. She had a feeling Miss Howard usually went to bed early, and she didn't want to keep her up any longer than necessary.

Hemingway recognized the sound of her footsteps on the front porch and her scent and immediately began "talking" to her in excited squeals and happy piggy grunts that only a five-pound Maltese can make. Within seconds Miss Howard opened the door and let him out to greet his mistress. He jumped into Aislinn's arms and began licking her all over.

"Thank you so much, Miss Howard, for taking care of Hemingway."

"Any time, Aislinn. Any time at all. He is absolutely no trouble. In fact, I'll miss the little guy."

While waiting for her plane to leave, Aislinn had gone into one of the small specialty shops at the airport and bought a ceramic ink well for Miss Howard. The sales clerk was even kind enough to wrap it for her. "I hope you can use this somewhere," she said handing Miss Howard the box wrapped in pretty floral paper.

"Oh my goodness. You shouldn't have done this." Miss Howard carefully removed the ribbon and wrapping and opened the box. "Oh my goodness," she repeated. "This is beautiful, Aislinn. How thoughtful of you. I collect them, you know."

Aislinn didn't know, but she was glad she had been able to find something that Miss Howard would enjoy. With Hemingway still in her arms, she gathered up his bag of toys and his wicker bed and returned home to change clothes and begin the tedious job of unpacking, checking phone messages, and correcting whatever had broken while she was away. It always amazed her how things happened in her absence—water pipes burst, paintings fell from the wall, the air conditioner refused to cool. It came with owning an older home, she guessed.

It didn't take her long to unpack since she hadn't taken that much to begin with. Her answering machine indicated there were eight messages. One of them was from Josh Turner, a friend of Robert's who also worked at the hospital. He and his wife, in fact, lived just down the street. She dialed the number that he had left.

"I just felt you should know," he said after explaining the reason for his call. "Robert didn't want to concern you, but as you are aware, this is a serious operation. As far as I know, he will be fine, but it all depends on him. He needs to stay quiet for a few days."

"What are the chances that the problem will recur?" Aislinn eased herself down on a stool at the kitchen counter. The last thing she expected to hear was that Robert had needed surgery of any kind. He always took such good care of himself.

Aislinn heard Josh take a deep breath and slowly release it. "That's hard to say. He might never be bothered again. On the other hand, he might have plaque redevelop in a couple of months. We'll just have to keep it monitored."

Aislinn thanked Josh for telling her and hung up the phone. Then she grabbed Hemingway's travel bag from out of the small closet beneath the stairs and put him in it. She had planned to call Robert as soon as she got home, but now, knowing he had just gotten out of surgery, a phone call wouldn't do it. "You want to go see Robert?" she asked the small dog. He grinned his doggy grin. "Of course you do."

Minutes later she arrived at the hospital. It was after nine o'clock and past visiting hours, so the parking lot was practically empty. She drove to the side entrance closest to where the elevators were located and parked. There would be fewer people there to notice Hemingway. Hospital regulations didn't allow for pets on the premises. Aislinn was furious with Robert for not telling her. And she was going to let him know just what she thought about the whole thing—but only after kissing him and making sure he was all right.

Josh had given Aislinn Robert's room number. She rode the elevator up to the fourth floor and turned left. There was a dim light shining from his room, and when she got there a nurse was bent over him in the

102

bed. When the nurse saw her she straightened up. "Mrs. Marchánt, we weren't expecting you."

"Obviously." Aislinn marched into the room and plopped Hemingway on the foot of Robert's bed.

"I'm afraid it is after visiting hours." Margaret fumbled with a button on her dress and glanced at the bag Aislinn had put on the bed. Hemingway peered through the meshed screen and displayed his beautiful set of white teeth. "And that is strictly against hospital rules. Absolutely no pets are allowed." She was obviously flustered.

"Nurse Peters, I would like for you to go check on Harris and Rodriguez for me now," said Robert. "I'll explain the hospital rules to Aislinn."

Margaret grabbed her notepad from the top of the air conditioning unit where she had put it earlier and quickly left the room. "It's totally against the rules," she mumbled.

Aislinn bent down and kissed Robert. "I am so angry with you for not telling me."

Robert smiled. "You have a funny way of showing it."

"Why didn't you let me know?" Aislinn unzipped the bag and let Hemingway out. He licked Robert happily and then curled up in a little ball next to him.

"And what could you do? You were going to New York. You're back now, so now you know. How did you find out?"

"Just never mind." His color wasn't very good, although it might have been because of the dim light. She looked at his neck where the incisions had been made. There was still a little swelling, but not a lot.

"That isn't anything to worry about," Robert said watching her expression. "I got up too soon following surgery and it caused a slight swelling. It will be gone by morning."

"Why did you get up in the first place?"

"I wanted to check on two of my patients who were in recovery. I was supposed to operate on them, but Josh told me I couldn't. Peter Hays stepped in for me. I just wanted to make sure they were all right."

Aislinn sighed and took Robert's hand, putting it up to her face. Of course, it was his patients. They would always come first, no matter what. She told Robert briefly about her trip and the meeting at Kane Publishing House. She didn't tell him about the problem Caldwell was faced with. She would wait until Robert was feeling better.

"I'll come by in the morning just to check on you." She leaned down and kissed him again, this time long and tender. "I don't want any big-buxomed nurse taking advantage of you when you are flat on your back."

"I think I like it better when you aren't mad at me," Robert said grinning.

Aislinn scooped up Hemingway and stuck him back in his bag. "We'd better leave before that nurse gets the canine cops after me. I'll see you in the morning."

No sooner had she left the hospital grounds when she once again sensed danger. Hemingway growled lightly and then began to nervously dig at the bottom of his travel bag. Aislinn locked the doors of her car and watched the mirrors to see if anyone was following her. She didn't see anything out of the ordinary, but still. . .

When she got home she double-checked all the doors and windows, making sure all the locks were in place. She was probably just tired, she thought. It had, after all, been a long day. She took a hot shower to help relax her and went to bed. It was too late to check her e-mails. She would start early the next morning editing as many of the manuscripts piled up in her office as she could. Hopefully, she would get the pile whittled down before Lorraine sent the manuscripts from Kane.

With Hemingway snuggled next to her, Aislinn slowly drifted off to sleep. The last thing she remembered thinking about was the old man at Sheldon-Talbert and hearing the words, *Then There Was Light.*

* * *

After leaving Robert's room, Margaret had stomped down the hall to see first Harris and then Rodriguez as he had requested. Of course, both men were asleep, as she knew they would be. So she stomped back to her office. She didn't like the way she had been "dismissed." She didn't like the fact that Aislinn had barged in the way she did. And she certainly didn't like a damn dog in a patient's room. If it weren't for the fact that it was Robert Marchánt's room, she would have reported it.

She glanced at herself in the mirror behind the door. She looked terrible. Her hair was messed up, a black smudge was on the sleeve of her dress—where had that come from? Probably from that damn dog. And there was a run in her stocking wide enough to accommodate an eighteen wheeler. She had gotten absolutely nowhere with the good doctor, even though, Lord only knows, she tried. Thinking back on it now, she must have made a complete fool of herself.

Women like Aislinn had always made her feel inferior. Petite, perky, and pretty. How she could look the way she did after just flying in from New York was a mystery to her. Dressed in blue jeans, white tennis shoes, and a crisp white blouse, Aislinn had looked more like a teenager than a grown woman. Seeing Aislinn like that had only made her feel even more overweight than she was, not to mention dowdy. She didn't like it one bit. Still, she'd better watch out. After behaving the way she did in Robert Marchánt's room, she could lose her job if she wasn't careful.

She tossed the notepad she was still carrying on her desk and headed for the ladies' room to wash off whatever was on her dress. She was scheduled for the afternoon shift the next day. If Dr. Marchánt was still in his room, she would just act like nothing had happened. There was a good chance he didn't even know what she was trying to do anyway. Aislinn knew, though. It was all over her face when she first walked into the room.

* * *

Behind the lattice fence, he lay on the ground with his back parallel to the cart that contained all his worldly possessions. He faced east, as he always did when he slept, in order to wake to the first hint of dawn. Clarence Tirell Wood slept like a baby—undisturbed and untroubled. For the first time in weeks he felt a calmness. The Lord Almighty had sent His angel as a sign. Now the problem would be solved. Somewhere deep in his sleep the old man saw the license number on the silver chariot that had brought the angel to Earth. The numbers were 5, 8, 1, 7, 4, which added up to 7 according to the practice of numerology. Once again the number seven appeared in his life, an indication that he was on the right path. His eyes shut, his breathing deep and steady, a faint smile appeared briefly on the lips of the old man. Soon everything would be all right.

* * *

Lorraine McLaughlin reached behind her and rubbed the area just below her ribs in the small of her back. She had been troubled with muscle spasms in her lower back on and off for years. They usually occurred after a particularly long day at work, and this had been a long day. The editorial staff meeting had gone on later than usual, and then Caldwell had needed her to follow up on a problem they were having in the distribution center.

In spite of the long hours, it had been an interesting day, especially with Aislinn being there. She had brought something into the House of Kane that Lorraine hadn't seen in quite a while. It was like a positive energy. Maybe it was no more than just a pretty face with a Southern accent, but whatever it was, Caldwell had noticed it, too.

She pulled out her purse from a bottom desk drawer and turned off the light. Down the hall she could see the light still on in Caldwell's office and his door ajar. He was working late again. Everyone else, other than Tyler, had left hours ago.

"I really like Aislinn," she said walking into his office and sitting down in a straight-back arm chair. Caldwell was sitting with his back to the door and his feet resting on the credenza behind his desk. He turned around and glanced up from what he was reading.

"You do?"

"Yes, I do. She's bright, she's honest, she's friendly—not stuck up like a lot of the women around here, and she's sincere."

Caldwell nodded. "I think so, too. Not to mention attractive."

Lorraine continued to look at Caldwell. "I know you have a business arrangement with her, but it wouldn't hurt to get to know her on a personal level, don't you think?" She got up and walked toward the door. "You could sure do a lot worse."

Caldwell took off his glasses and laid them on his desk. "I'm old enough to be her father."

"So what?" Lorraine slung her pocketbook over her shoulder and left. Some things Caldwell would simply have to figure out for himself. The chance of two people meeting, falling in love, and being truly compatible was next to nil. But if it did occur, then the chronological age difference didn't matter a fat fig. She didn't know if Aislinn and Caldwell were right for each other or not. She only knew what she had observed seeing the two of them together. There was definitely a chemistry, and her observations were telling her that Aislinn could be the best thing that ever happened to Caldwell. If there was anything at all she could do to encourage matters between them, she would.

* * *

Now that Lottie Howard had defined the true direction of her novel, she couldn't stop thinking about it. It were as though she was obsessed. She would keep the same title, *My Father's Keeper,* but refocus the story line. She started working on the rewrite before Aislinn returned home. Then, after Aislinn picked up Hemingway, she went back to work on it. It had been so long since she had felt this much interest or excitement about anything, other than worrying over the citrus canker that attacked her fruit trees that one year.

This was hard work, it was also painful, having to go back and relive so many things that she had long ago either hidden or forgotten. In doing it, she found she no longer thought of her father as the idol she once had. There had been a lot of things to take place in his business that, even as a child, she knew were unethical at the very least and most probably illegal. There were also many things that he did as a father that by today's standards would be considered unforgivable.

Grain by grain, she removed the sugar coating from her original story to reveal an uneven and raw truth. It didn't matter now. This was her story, and by telling it, she felt a freedom she never knew existed.

* * *

Tyler had tried calling Tracy several times during the day, but only got a busy signal. Then right before the editorial staff meeting broke up, he tried once again. This time a taped message told him there was trouble on the telephone line. As soon as the meeting was over, he drove over to Tracy's apartment. After all, if something had happened to her and something was wrong with her phone, she might not be able to call for help.

Tracy came to the door dressed in jeans and a baggy shirt. She had obviously been working on something because she hadn't bothered taking off her reading glasses and she was holding what appeared to be the outline of a manuscript.

"Tyler! What are you doing here?"

"I thought you might need something." He tried not to notice her obvious lack of enthusiasm in seeing him. "Your phone is dead."

She glanced toward her desk where she had been working. The phone cord still lay on the floor where she had pulled it from the wall. "I was trying to get some work done. You know how these marketing solicitors are—they just don't leave you alone." She continued to stand in the doorway.

"You're feeling better then?" Tyler didn't want to make a pest of himself, but he couldn't understand her sudden coldness.

"A little."

Tyler nodded trying to think of what else he could say. Tracy couldn't have made it plainer that she didn't want to see him. "What's going on, Tracy?"

"Look, Tyler, I'm glad you stopped by. I've been thinking. I'm going to be pretty busy for the next several months, and I won't have very much free time."

"Busy with what?" Tyler didn't mean to sound so impatient, but he knew what books Tracy had been assigned. Christ, he had given her most of them. And unless she had gotten a new assignment she hadn't told him about, there wasn't anything else that demanding going on with her work.

"I'm thinking about writing a novel," she said. "And I really don't want to talk about it." The irritation in her voice was quite noticeable.

"I see. Afraid I might interfere with your creativity?"

"Something like that."

Tyler was mad now. He had done everything but jump through hoops for her, and now she didn't want him bothering her. "Well, I'll see you around." He heard her apartment door close as he heavy-footed it down the hallway that led to the outside. What was it that Jason had said? It was probably just one of those romances that flamed up when you were traveling in a foreign country. Once you got back to the real world and your normal life, there was nothing to it. It was burned out. This bit of wisdom from a brother who hadn't even dated in high school, much less been involved in a serious relationship with anyone. Tyler hadn't believed it, though. He honestly thought he and Tracy had something special going on. They enjoyed so many things—the same foods, a love for travel, the arts, and their work, not to mention their sex life. But now, thinking about it, maybe he had just been a chump. He couldn't remember Tracy ever doing anything for him, not that he had asked. He hadn't been brought up that way. It had been enough just to see how much she appreciated the things he did for her. Now he wondered if that was all an act on her part just to get good manuscripts.

He climbed into his car and slammed the door shut. Well, if that was the way she wanted it, he could find someone else to take her place. Finding attractive, available women had never been his problem. He tried thinking of someone he could call, but in the end, the effort it required just didn't seem worth it. He needed to start concentrating on work again. Before he loused that up as well. Jason had made it clear that everyone was starting to notice how slack he had been. It was time for him to focus on his own career.

As he was driving back to the office he thought about the sheets of paper Tracy had been holding and what he had been able to see on one on them. It was an outline with notes about lightning. How strange, he thought.

Once back at his office, Tyler worked late into the night. He knew he hadn't been performing up to his father's expectations for the past several months, and it couldn't have been more apparent than at the meeting that day. The manuscript he tried to push through for publication was ineffectual and repetitive of so many others that had already been published. It was something Kane Publishing would lose money on. Well, no more. That was the last time he would try something like that. He knew what was good work, and he knew what was suitable for Kane Publishing. In the past, before getting involved with Tracy, he had consistently come up with the best sellers. He still could. And he would begin with *Then There Was Light*. He needed to get back into his role as associate editor and heir apparent to the Kane Publishing empire. Trying to figure out what it was that Tracy wanted from him could come later—if then.

"You have a minute?" Caldwell walked into Tyler's office and closed the door.

Tyler had been expecting to get a lecture. He deserved it. In fact, he deserved a lot worse, considering how he had been behaving. "Sure, but I think I can save you some time."

Caldwell sat down on a small sofa facing the desk where his son was working. "How's that?"

"I know I have been stinking up the place these past few months. But I'm determined to get back on track. Just give me this next month to come up with something; I think I will surprise you."

"Is there any particular reason why you think you can suddenly start pulling your weight again?"

"Let's just say I have had my eyes opened."

Caldwell nodded. He was sure it had something to do with the girl Tyler was seeing, but since Tyler had chosen not to tell him about her, he didn't want to bring it up—not unless he had to. Tyler would know that Jason had told him about her and then blame Jason for interfering. "All right. Let's see what comes out of the next editorial staff meeting."

"By the way, I really like Aislinn. I think she will bring a lot into the company."

"That seems to be the unanimous feeling," Caldwell said as he headed back to his office.

Chapter Nine

Writing is to descend like a miner to the depths of the mine with a lamp on your forehead, a light whose dubious brightness falsifies everything, whose wick is in permanent danger of explosion, whose blinking illumination in the coal dust exhausts and corrodes your eyes.

Blaise Cendrars Sauser

"Aislinn, this is Lottie. I'm sorry to be calling you so early, but can you tell me what the laws are regarding slander and liable?"

Aislinn raised up on one elbow and tried to adjust her eyes on the clock next to her bed. It was 4:30 in the morning. Saturday morning. Who in the world was Lottie? Gradually her mind cleared.

"Miss Howard?"

"Please just call me Lottie. Miss Howard is so formal, don't you think?"

Aislinn looked at the soft white ball of fur still sleeping on the pillow next to her and turned on a lamp next to the phone. "It depends a lot on whether you mean saying something false about someone or writing something false about someone. Slander usually refers to an untruth that is deliberately said. Liable usually refers to an untruth that is deliberately written."

"What if the people being written about are dead, and what is being written is really bad, but true?"

"Then there is no liability, just so long as what is being written is true."

"Thank you, my dear. How is that little Hemingway?"

Aislinn didn't have the heart to tell her that he was still asleep and that she would be too if she hadn't called. "He is just fine."

"Well, thank you for your help. I'll be talking to you later. Bye, now."

"Good bye, Lottie."

Aislinn replaced the phone and sat up in bed. Hemingway looked at her and wagged his tail, just barely. "What on earth was that all about," she asked out loud.

Now fully awake, she decided to get up. By getting an extra early start, she would be able to make some headway on that pile of manuscripts in her office. She walked Hemingway outside in the back yard, showered and dressed, ate a bowl of cereal, and fixed a cup of coffee to sip while she worked. She also wrote a note to Caldwell thanking him for showing her such a pleasant time during her brief visit to New York. By the time she did all of that, the sun was just starting to peek over the horizon.

Thankfully, most of the manuscripts that had come in were picture books. They weren't necessarily the easiest to edit and evaluate, but they normally didn't take as long to finish as manuscripts written for older children, like middle grade or young adult novels. By mid morning, Aislinn was ready to take a break. It would be a good time to go to the hospital to see Robert. Before shutting down her computer, she went on-line to check her e-mail. Almost immediately, the instant message appeared. *You had better be careful! The Predator.* That was all it said. That was enough. It was obviously threatening in tone, just like the last phone message she had received. The threatening nature of the e-mails and the phone messages were escalating, and Aislinn was definitely concerned.

Aislinn saved the e-mail and shut down. She couldn't even imagine how anyone could be tapped into her computer that way. She needed to tell someone about it and get advice on how to deal with it, but she didn't know anyone she could talk to. *Come again for the* Ifá *and the*

Merindilogún, the botanica shop keeper had told her when he gave her the blue and white beads. *Soon you will feel the need.* Maybe now was the time.

* * *

Tracy had been working nonstop on her manuscript, *The Enlightened*, only taking time to eat a handful of Ritz crackers and drink a diet cola. She was irritated at Tyler for dropping by like that, and it was only after he left that she realized she still had her typed notes in her hand. Hopefully he wasn't able to read them, though.

Thinking about it now, she probably shouldn't have acted so hateful toward Tyler. He was nice enough, and all he had ever wanted was to help her. She might still need him to help her. After all, he had read *Then There Was Light.* So if anyone were to notice the similarities between that manuscript and her novel, other than Snow Henderson, it would be Tyler. It was just that he was clingy sometimes, and that worried her. She had too many dreams she wanted to accomplish before giving in to becoming some sort of emotional prop. She wasn't going to do it for her own family, and she wasn't going to do it for Tyler Caldwell either. He really needed to grow up. She sat back down in front of her computer. If he came around again, she just wouldn't answer the door, at least for the next week or so.

In fact, she had already decided to take the next week off. If the writing kept going well, she would be able to finish the first draft by then. That was using a lot of the material from *Then There Was Light*, but she felt sure enough of herself and the changes she was making that no one would be able to recognize it. After that, it would just be a matter of polishing it. She could do that in the evenings when she came home from the office. Certainly, by the end of the month, she should have it ready to submit.

She looked through the manuscript once more, comparing it to her notes. Surprisingly, Snow Henderson had integrated a lot of data on lightning and electrical injuries with her own personal experiences. According to what she had written, eighty percent of lightning-strike victims survived, but twenty-five percent of the survivors suffered major aftereffects. Many of these aftereffects were characterized by medical professionals as fakery or imagined. Snow had documented all of her experiences, however, and many of them could only be classified as paranormal sequelae—"the gifts" as she called them.

Immediately following each of the lightning hits, Snow had experienced different degrees of altered consciousness, confusion, disorientation, and amnesia. Headaches developed within the first six hours along with a certain amount of distractibility. Then, after several months, other aftereffects involving neuro and emotional behavior, sensory perception and physical disorders developed. This was in keeping with the statistics she produced indicating the highest percentages of injury resulting in lightning strikes involved memory deficit, paresthesia, depression, and stiff joints.

But that was where the similarities between Snow's lightning-strike experiences and others stopped. Each of the six times she had experienced a lightning strike, she had seen an aura, purple in color, that left her feeling calm and at peace. All of her senses became more acute and involved in what was going on around her. Her energy level soared. Things she had never been able to do prior to the strikes she now had the ability to do. Most remarkably, she seemed to develop an uncanny ability to intuit things. It were as though she had crossed into another dimension, and in doing so, she could read people's minds. The theme that kept running through Snow's story was that she was a lightning-strike survivor trying desperately to move towards either resolution or acceptance not of the fact that she was still alive, but that she was now in possession of "the gifts."

Tracy had named her protagonist Gideon, after the hero of faithing from the Book of Judges in the Bible. The name Gideon was Hebrew and it meant great warrior. There seemed to be some sort of special irony in choosing that particular name.

One of the statistics she had gleaned from Snow's manuscript was that eighty-five percent of lightning victims were children and young men ages 10-35. Her character, Gideon, was 35 years old, and, like Snow, he had survived several lightning strikes. He also had intuitive flashes resulting from those strikes. In her story, however, he would use his newly-developed intuition for his own gain. That was what people wanted to read about anyway. Greed, sex, violence, and love—those were the elements that made up a successful novel, in Tracy's opinion. *The Enlightened* would have them all. And when she got it published, she would be able to get pretty much whatever she wanted in the world of publishing. Smiling, Tracy popped open another can of diet cola and began typing away on the computer.

* * *

Robert had been discharged by the time Aislinn arrived at the hospital. Not only had he been discharged, he was already making his rounds. Aislinn tracked him down in the children's ward.

"I see you are looking better." Aislinn walked into the large, sunny room with wall-to-wall beds, most of which were occupied by children of various ages.

Robert was wearing a silly-looking hat and making funny faces to a small, freckle-faced boy in one of the beds. He looked up and grinned. "You know what they say. You can't keep a good man down."

She walked over and kissed him lightly on the cheek which immediately caused an eruption of giggles among the several young patients. Two bandages covered each side of his neck, but they were small. "How do you feel?"

"Not too shabby. Not too shabby at all. Of course, Dr. Turner is being mean to me." There was another burst of giggles. "He says I have to take it easy for the next week to ten days. By then I should be good as new—better, in fact."

"I'm glad." Aislinn glanced around at the children who for one reason or another were assigned to the ward. A broken leg in a cast here, a bandaged head there. A couple of others barely awake. "Is Dr. Marchánt being nice to all of you?" she asked.

There was a loud chorus of "yes."

"That's good, because if he isn't, he doesn't get dessert." The children laughed openly this time, even the two Aislinn thought had been sleeping.

Robert walked with Aislinn out into the hall. "We ought to take this act on the road. You're really good."

"Thanks, but I think I'll pass. I don't look as good in a hat as you do." Then in a more serious tone, "Do you need anything? How about at your apartment? Do you want me to pick up some groceries for you or anything like that?"

"Groceries? What are groceries?"

Aislinn frowned. Robert had always been terrible about eating regularly, even when they were married. He ate healthy foods whenever he did eat, but actually getting around to eating wasn't his top priority. There were always too many other more important things to take care of. More than once Aislinn had prepared a special candlelight dinner only to wind up eating by herself and saving Robert's portion for left-overs.

"No, I'm fine. Really. I'll probably work short days for a while. I don't want Josh operating on me again any time soon."

"Well, I'll be off on some errands then. Call me later and maybe I'll fix you a pot of homemade chicken soup." She knew Robert loved soup, especially chicken soup.

"That suits me." He walked her to the elevator and waited until the doors closed. Then, with his note pad in his hand, he headed down the hall to check on some other patients.

The shopkeeper was standing by the door when Aislinn got there. "I was expecting you," he said when she entered the botanica. For some reason it didn't surprise Aislinn when he said it. He noticed that she was wearing the blue and white beads and smiled. "This is good," he said. That didn't surprise her either.

The man's name was Pichardo, and he was a Santerian priest, Aislinn was soon to learn. "You have come to be seen with *Ifá* and *Merindilogún*," he stated. They will delve into your past, present and future; your questions will be answered." He looked into her eyes and sensed her nervousness. "Do not be anxious. You will learn how to make your life harmonious with the will of *Olodumare*, the *orishas* and the universe. It is *Ifá* and the *orishas* who will speak and advise as to what is the best path for you to follow." Aislinn listened to Pichardo as he led her through the maze of brightly-colored objects and the mixture of smells to the back of the shop and behind a closed curtain.

The small room itself was a storage area. A square grass mat had been placed in the center of the floor in preparation, and it was on this mat that Pichardo motioned for Aislinn to sit opposite him.

"First of all, this is not 'fortune-telling.'" His Hispanic accent was heavy, and the unusual names he spoke of were made even more difficult for Aislinn to understand by their unfamiliarity. "The *Ifá* and the *Elegba* shells will tell you how to bring your life into harmony." Pichardo then began praying, first to *Olodumare*, then to the *orishas* and to the *Eggun* asking their permission to do the work and asking them to speak about the situation affecting the life of the person coming to be seen—Aislinn. Pichardo opened a small wooden box that contained several cowrie shells. He cast them onto the mat in front of Aislinn. "These tell us the essential *Odu* or sign that is with you," he explained. "The *Odu* speaks of your life, the road you are on, how you came to be on that road, and where the path leads."

Aislinn watched fascinated. She had never even so much as had her palm read at the county fair. Now she was communicating with *orishas* and other spirits through a Santerian priest. Pichardo placed in one of Aislinn's hands a white powder substance. "This is eggshell," he said. In her other hand he placed a red stone. He called it a lodestone. He asked Aislinn to separate the objects and shake them. He repeated this, using objects of glass and metal. Satisfied, he removed all of the objects. "Now we have your personal *ashé* or spiritual energy. This will tell us whether something positive, *Iré,* or negative, *Osogbo,* is accompanying you and where it comes from."

An hour later Pichardo said that *Elegba* was satisfied. Everything had been said. The consultation was concluded. Aislinn offered to pay him, but he refused. "Another time, another way," he said.

Driving back home, Aislinn thought about everything Pichardo had told her. A negative force had entered her life, but it was weak. It fed on jealousy, greed, and impure motives. Soon it would leave, and she would have nothing else to fear. Aislinn interpreted that to mean those horrible e-mail messages and phone calls she had been getting. For some odd reason, the number sixteen kept coming up in Pichardo's conversation. He explained its significance in this world and the unseen world, but she wasn't sure she really understood his meaning. It had something to do with the basic building blocks of Destiny—her Destiny. "Remember it," he told her. "In time it will have a special meaning in your life." Pichardo had also told her something else. "There are twin faces, separate places, and a love for which you must choose." What could that mean, she muttered? When she had asked him, all he said was that she would know the truth when she was ready.

Once back home, with Hemingway taken care of and a big pot of chicken soup simmering on the stove, Aislinn settled back down to work. As she struggled to edit a particularly badly written nonfiction chapter book on extinct species of the Florida Everglades, her mind kept wandering back to New York and to the man she had met there. Caldwell had been so nice to her. She wondered if he was that way with everyone.

Finally, a little before six o'clock, Aislinn shut down her computer. She would have to go over the extinct species manuscript once more, but at least she had made progress on it. Robert still hadn't called, and she wondered if perhaps he had forgotten about her invitation for home-made soup. Just then the phone rang. It was probably him, she thought, and smiling, she answered.

"You sound happy. Do you always sound that way when you answer the phone?" It was Caldwell.

* * *

For the first time in over ten years, Caldwell had slept in late on Saturday. For whatever reason, his internal clock simply had not gone off. Frederick, not knowing what to do, had kept his breakfast warm in the oven and simply let him sleep. Finally, about ten o'clock, Caldwell came out of his bedroom looking refreshed, energized, and, if Frederick knew anything about him at all, happy.

"With all this rain we have been getting, I didn't think I would go to the house this weekend, but it has turned off so pretty I've changed my mind," he announced.

Frederick poured some fresh coffee into a cup and placed it in front of Caldwell at the kitchen table. "Yes, sir."

"Don't pack much. Just enough for the one night. While we are there, I thought I would open up one of the guest bedrooms—the one overlooking the gardens."

"Yes, sir." In all the time Frederick had worked for Caldwell Kane, other than the bedrooms used by him, his two sons, and, of course, Frederick himself, all of the other bedrooms had remained closed up. It was interesting that Caldwell now suddenly wanted one opened. Frederick wondered if it had any connection to his happy demeanor he was exhibiting. Of course he had heard stories of when his wife was still alive about the wonderful parties that were held there at the country home. All of the rooms had been used at that time for various occasions and an assortment of guests. Then, when she died, either because he didn't want to bother with entertaining or because it was too painful not to have her with him, most of the house was closed off. This new revelation was indeed exciting.

As soon as the breakfast dishes were washed and put away, Frederick began packing. A lot of things he always kept "on the ready" anyway just in case Caldwell decided to go somewhere at the last minute. So packing took little time even for longer trips. An hour later they were traveling east toward the shore. Frederick had called the housekeeper from the apartment to prepare her. Other than that, nothing else needed to be done.

Frederick sat in the front with Dan. Caldwell read in the backseat as he normally did with manuscript pages scattered around him. After a while, Dan glanced over at Frederick. "What's going on with the boss?"

Frederick cut his eyes toward the back to make sure they weren't being overheard. "I'm not sure. He wants to open up one of the guest rooms. Has he met someone?"

Dan grinned big and toothy and squared his cap on his head. "I would probably say that is a good guess." Then he told Frederick about the young editor who had flown in from West Palm Beach in order to attend the staff meeting.

"That probably explains it then," said Frederick glancing out the window at the beautiful oak and maple trees growing along the highway. "It's about time, too, if I might say so."

Dan continued to grin. He had thought Ms. Marchánt had a nice manner about her—sort of soft and feminine. She was a hell of a looker, too, although he would never say anything like that to Caldwell Kane. It had concerned him slightly that she wanted to see where Sidney-Talbert Publishing House was located, but that wasn't any of his business. And unless he found out that there was something about it that his boss should know, he would keep it to himself.

Once they got to the mansion, Caldwell immediately went through each room. He wanted to make sure he was opening the best room with the best view. Mrs. Hutchinson, the housekeeper, scurried around right behind him like a well-fed setting hen, more than willing to give him her opinion on whatever she saw him looking at: the over-stuffed chair covered in a chintz with a pink and yellow cabbage rose print, the rich brocade valances and draperies, the four-poster bed and lace canopy, the 19th century Kermanshah carpet, the marble-topped antique dry sink. She voiced her advice freely. In the end, he picked out the first room they had looked at—quiet, pastel colors, beautiful antiques, and it overlooked the gardens. Mrs. Hutchinson assured him it would be aired properly and new linens would be used on the bed whenever it was needed.

With that taken care of, Caldwell went into the library in order to go over some budget figures for the previous quarter. He also wanted to find a copy of his grandmother's book of poetry, *A Dusting of Petals*, to give to Aislinn as a present when she visited. He couldn't get over how good he felt, how vibrant. Ever since his wife died, his entire focus had been his work. All of his time and energy went to Kane Publishing House. Now all of a sudden he felt like doing other things. Things like going to the theater, taking long walks, visiting the latest Edna Hibel exhibition at the Metropolitan Museum of Art, going on a picnic in Central Park. Things he thought that Aislinn would enjoy doing. The grandfather clock in the hall struck six times. On an impulse, he picked up the phone and dialed a "1" and the area code "516" followed by Aislinn's number. He didn't even realize he had it memorized. She answered on the second ring.

After his initial enthusiastic hello, Caldwell suddenly found himself at a loss for words. He was acting totally out of character by even call-ing her. In fact, he felt like an awkward school boy—she had that kind of effect on him.

"I am so happy you called," Aislinn told him, immediately making him feel less idiotic. "I have been thinking about all of that wonderful Greek food we had. It was such a pretty restaurant."

The truth was, Caldwell hadn't noticed anything about the restau-rant until Aislinn had pointed things out to him—the fountain, the dif-ferent blooming plants, the music, the wallpaper, even the designs on the table linens and dishes. She noticed everything. "It was pretty good, wasn't it?" he said. Then changing the subject, "I mainly was calling to make sure you made it home all right."

"That's so nice of you. Yes, everything was fine when I got home. No leaking water heaters or warm refrigerators." She heard him laugh. They had shared horror stories while eating their Greek dinner of things breaking down in their homes whenever they traveled.

"And Hemingway? How did he make it with your neighbor?"

"He made it fine, too. I think Mrs. Howard—Lottie—really has a soft spot for Hemingway, and he for her. They've become pretty good buddies."

"Listen, Aislinn, I am at the shore just for the one night, and it occurred to me, that is, if you would like to, that maybe when you come back for the next meeting that maybe you would stay an extra night or two and I could show you around the Hamptons. There is plenty of room here." He stopped talking, afraid he had perhaps said too much and that he sounded like a complete fool. He really hadn't intended to invite her to stay at the house yet, but it just sort of popped out. And he had never been very good about waiting for things, especially when he had already made up his mind. He put the phone up closer to his ear to see if he could hear anything.

"I would enjoy that very much. If you are sure it wouldn't be putting anyone out?"

"Not at all." He made an effort to tone down his enthusiasm. "Half of these rooms don't get used any more. It will be nice to have someone staying here in one of them."

From her office window, Aislinn saw a car drive into her driveway. It was Robert. Hemingway started yelping his little piercing screams to let Robert know that he had heard him.

"Oh dear, someone is at the door, Caldwell."

"Oh, that's all right. I have to get back to work now. I'll be talking to you again soon."

After Caldwell hung up Aislinn skipped down the stairs to the front door. "I thought you had forgotten," she said when Robert came in.

"Now how could anyone forget about being invited for homemade chicken soup?"

Aislinn laughed. Knowing Robert, he had probably gotten busy with something at the hospital and only just now remembered about the soup. She ushered him into the kitchen where he plopped down on one of the stools with Hemingway in his arms.

After hanging up the phone, Caldwell sat for several minutes staring at it. Smiling. He knew he had to get in control of himself. There was a lot to do. And, after all, Aislinn was working for him now. Still. He hadn't felt this happy in years, and he knew without a doubt that it was all because of Aislinn.

He picked up the folder that had the word "budget" printed in bold black letters on the front and started flipping through the reports. Thirty minutes later he was still flipping through the reports, wondering who it was that had gone to visit Aislinn.

Part Two

Chapter Ten

The need to express oneself in writing springs from a mal-adjustment to life, or from an inner conflict which the adolescent (or the grown man) cannot resolve in action. Those to whom action comes as easily as breathing rarely feel the need to break loose from the real, to rise above, and describe it . . . I do not mean that it is enough to be maladjusted to become a great writer, but writing is, for some, a method of resolving a conflict, provided they have the necessary talent.

Andre Maurois

"It has to be in here somewhere. It's written on a plain sheet of paper. Did you look under the carpet?"

Lottie pulled up one corner of the carpet in order for Eliane to get down on her hands and knees and get a better look. The two women had been searching the bedroom for over an hour, looking for a poem that Lottie had written when she was a young girl. It was the missing piece to *My Father's Keeper*. Once Lottie had that, she would be able to complete her book.

It had been three weeks since Lottie had started her rewrite. Working day and night, never had she felt so driven to complete anything as much as she did *My Father's Keeper*. Of course, the photographs had been the catalyst. They brought back not only the memories of the things that occurred, but the emotions she felt at the time.

So many times as a child she had felt neglected and unappreciated. Her mother's pregnancy had been considered "late." Both of her parents were already in their forties by the time she was born. She wasn't a pretty baby, marked with ugly red splotches and an even uglier disposition that didn't improve as she got older. Big and awkward for her

The House of Kane

age with unruly red hair made even worse by the south Florida humidity, Lottie was painfully shy. With so many people—important people—constantly flowing in and out of the house, she was expected to be just another ornamental object and not a very pretty one at that; excluded from the entertainment, always in the background, quiet and usually unobserved. Many times she wanted to jump up and down and scream for attention. But she knew that wouldn't give her the kind of attention she so desperately craved. Better for her to remain hidden; then if ever she walked away and closed the door, she would be noticed.

When she became older she found comfort in watching the lives of people who were far happier than she was, for it gave her something to aspire to. But it was even more comforting to watch lives that were far worse, because then, and only then, did she feel advantaged. It was later that whatever positive feelings she had tried to latch onto began turning dark and forbidding. It was C.T. who pointed out to her that most people exist in a sort of numbing mediocrity of real life held in check by a system of compromise. She could find true happiness, but only by not allowing others to control her. It was her choice.

Strangely enough, Lottie felt no malice toward her mother and father. They had done the best they could with what they knew at that time. It was the way they had been brought up, and their parents before them. So her purpose in writing the book wasn't to set any record straight. There was no one left to care anyway. Nor was it to teach any kind of moral lesson. Lottie had accepted her father's abusive behavior and the influence of that behavior on her fate long ago. If anything, the emotion she felt most strongly was fear—fear of forgetting the one thing in her life that was more precious than life itself. Fear of not being able to reach back and uncover the reason why she was alive today. She had come dangerously close. Now, in writing it all down, she was able to once again remember a love that encouraged her to overcome the brutal insanity of her childhood and make her complete as a person. It didn't even matter if her story got published, just so long as she had it recorded.

Henry Flagler had already founded the vast empire of Standard Oil with partners John D. Rockefeller and Samuel Andrews by the time he first visited Florida. Recognizing the state's potential for growth, he immediately set about building several grand hotels, starting first in St. Augustine with the Hotel Ponce de Leon, that would mark the beginning of the Gilded Age. To interlink the hotels and accommodate travelers to his new resorts which later included Palm Beach, Miami and eventually Key West, he also purchased the Jacksonville, St. Augustine & Halifax Railroad which became the Florida East Coast Railway company. It was after the construction of two Palm Beach hotels, the Royal Poinciana Hotel overlooking Lake Worth and The Breakers Hotel on the ocean, that serious discussion began taking place to complete that final link of railroad to Key West. That was when Clifford Howard became involved.

Originally, Palm Beach was to be the terminus of the Flagler railroad, but several wealthy businessmen wanted Flagler to continue the railroad from Miami to Key West. To help convince him of the need, Flagler was offered land from private landowners, the Florida East Coast Canal and Transportation Company, and the Boston and Florida Atlantic Coast Land Company in exchange for laying rail tracks.

It was Howard who came up with this plan, and it was Howard who implemented it. Young, aggressive, and ambitious, Clifford Howard was a graduate of Trinity College, a small Methodist college in North Carolina that had moved from Randolf County to Durham and later to be renamed Duke University. His family was heavily involved in North Carolina politics, his father the campaign manager for the State

Republican Party, and for a while he thought he, too, would follow the same career course.

The spring following his graduation he traveled to Palm Beach on holiday, and it was there that he was introduced for the first time to the old money of Palm Beach society and a young woman named Cecille Dexter. They were married within the year and other than to attend his father's funeral, Clifford never returned to North Carolina, not even with their infant daughter, Lottie, when she was born several years later.

With the help of Cecille's father, a district court judge appointed by the State, Clifford opened his own law practice and soon established a name for himself within the Palm Beach community. His friendly, open Southern nature that had been instilled in him since childhood wore well with the residents living on what was considered the most prestigious residential island in the world. He established a bond and trust with the people who were already successful in business. And because of his seemingly unending energy, it was Clifford who was called upon to head up various events and brokerage large and sometimes questionable business dealings. He worked tirelessly and never disappointed those who had given him their trust. He didn't disappoint them in helping persuade Flagler to agree to extend the railway from Miami to Key West, either. It took seven years to complete the construction of the overseas railway, requiring many engineering innovations as well as vast amounts of labor and monetary resources. At any time during the construction, over four thousand men were employed. Five hurricanes threatened to halt the project before its completion. Despite everything, this final link of the Florida East Coast Railway was finally completed in 1912, the year before Henry Flagler's death.

With Clifford's involvement in the completion of the railway first to Miami, then to Key West, his own future was secured. He now had a beautiful home, a loving wife, and a daughter who soon would be entering her teenage years. What Howard didn't know was the state of desperation his young daughter was caught in: thoughts of suicide, extreme depression, self mutilation. Only her friend, C.T., knew. And only C.T. was able to help.

Lottie had included everything in her story. Everything except for the poem she had written that night just before C.T. found her in the intracoastal—the eve of her sixteenth birthday. A few minutes more would have been too late. Her parents had gone out for the evening, and by the time they returned, Lottie was already in bed asleep, her soiled, soggy clothes taken away to be discarded by C.T. They never knew that their daughter had tried to take her own life.

"I think I found something!" Eliane removed a folded, yellowed piece of paper stuck inside the valance hanging in front of the bedroom window and climbed back down a step stool. She handed it to Lottie without unfolding it. "Is this what you are looking for?"

Lottie didn't have to open it. Tears filled her eyes. She nodded and quickly left the room leaving Eliane to straighten everything. Back in her office, sitting in her big chair, Lottie read the page from her past.

The Same Cannot Always Be So

The same cannot always be so,
for time will not allow it.

Like the softly touched note of treble, muted,
lost in a gentle breeze;
Or the innermost leaf of bloom unfolded,
its fragrant beauty unseen,

So the same cannot always be so.

Once I laughed at fickle change,
so complete was our love without.
But death came along and slipped you away,
and replaced my laughter with doubt.

And like the soft cadence no longer heard,
or the withered flower forgotten,

To me time does not bring relief.

It was a simple poem, written by a sensitive child on the verge of becoming a desperate woman. There was no doubt that Lottie would have ended it that night had it not been for her friend. C.T. had given her courage. In his quiet way, he had taught her that it was all right to be herself, even when those around her criticized her every move. And he taught her love, so pure that even after the passing of so many years, she still felt it.

* * *

Robert removed his reading glasses and rubbed his eyes. He was working on this month's progress report to present at the Board of Directors meeting. It was more of a courtesy than anything else. The Board members never questioned his financial statements or his plans for the future of West Palm Beach Regional. Robert had been sleeping more since his surgery. It wasn't that he felt tired. Quite the opposite. Yet, there were times when he would suddenly be overcome with fatigue. A couple of times he had even fallen asleep at his desk while he was working. He hadn't mentioned it to anyone, not even Josh, telling himself that it was all part of the recovery. Besides, he was monitoring his own blood pressure and it always checked out all right. And, it had only been three weeks since the surgery, so he was bound to still be feeling some of the side effects.

The new Alzheimer's unit was entering its final construction phase, ahead of the scheduled completion date and within budget. Other administrative problems seemed to have leveled off as well. West Palm Beach Regional was finally becoming the well-tuned business it was meant to be. The only negative thing that had come up at all in recent weeks was the discovery of some missing drugs from the lab dispensing room. Either due to some careless record-keeping or out-and-out theft, several bottles of pain medications—primarily Oxycontin—had disappeared from a locked cabinet.

One of the other doctors first discovered the drugs missing and reported it to Robert. Not wanting to take any chances, Robert immediately notified the special drug enforcement unit of the Palm Beach County Sheriff's Department who, in turn, put an undercover agent working in the hospital. Only Robert knew about Agent Healy.

Robert glanced at his watch. It was already past three o'clock. He was running late for his rounds. He put his report aside, grabbed his notepad, and walked down the hall to the nurses' station. Nurse Peters smiled and slid a stack of patients' files toward him. Even though she was off duty, she had stayed around on the pretext that she needed to work on the computer, knowing Robert always checked over his patients' files before going on his rounds. It was about the only time she could get him to notice her, and she wasn't sure he even noticed her then.

"Can I get you anything else? Coffee? A nice massage?" she asked in her deepest, most seductive voice.

Robert ignored her comment and her voice and began scanning over each file and making notes to himself. Whether it was from how he was standing over the counter, or from that god-awful smelly perfume Nurse Peters was wearing, he suddenly felt light-headed and nauseous. He grabbed the counter and slumped forward.

"Doctor, are you all right?"

When he didn't answer, Margaret paged Dr. Turner. Thirty minutes later Robert was back in a hospital bed hooked up to various monitors and irritated at the world.

He wasn't the only one who was irritated. "Why in the hell didn't you tell me about the fatigue?" Josh was furious, and justifiably so.

"I just didn't want to admit there was a problem, I guess."

Josh shook his head. "As far as I can tell, it isn't your carotid arteries. The stents are where they are supposed to be. There isn't any blockage—no clots. And there isn't any hemorrhaging. The lab should have the results of your blood work within the hour. I'll let you know what I find out. In the meantime, my friend, you are staying put. Got that?"

Robert didn't answer. He knew there was a problem. He knew that night Aislinn fixed soup for him. The reason he was late was because he had fallen asleep, something that never would have happened before his surgery. He had behaved foolishly. He had done exactly what he always told his patients not to do, and that was to notify him immediately if they noticed anything out of the ordinary. Now he might have to pay a price for it. After Josh left he had just barely closed his eyes when he heard a light tap on the door. It was Agent Healy.

"I don't know if it's a good sign or a bad sign when the doctors in this place become the patients."

Robert motioned for him to come in. "Were you able to find out anything yet?"

Healy pulled up a chair and took possession of it. He was a large man, somewhat unkempt, and judging from all of the pieces of paper he pulled first out of one pocket, then another, a terribly disorganized one. Eventually he tracked down what he was searching for. He handed Robert several photographs. "These were taken by the surveillance camera I installed last week."

The photographs were black and white and grainy and had been taken in time sequence, but, even so, there was no doubt who the person in the photos was. It was Margaret Peters. The photos clearly showed her opening the locked cabinet, removing several bottles, and then putting the bottles in her pocketbook. The photos had been developed with the date and time they were taken. "We have a video of her, too," Healy said. Then he handed Robert his notes. "These are the times when she was on duty and when she went off duty. Each time she went to the cabinet, she was already off duty."

Robert nodded. "O.K. Good work. Will she be arrested?"

"Apparently she has gone for the day, but she'll get picked up and taken in for questioning. Hopefully she'll confess once she sees the evidence we have. Then it will be up to the District Attorney's office as to whether charges will be filed. I'm pretty sure they will be. She was probably selling the drugs, and that's a felony."

Robert didn't know whether to feel sorry for Nurse Peters or angry as hell. He had heard of other hospitals having trouble with drug theft. Usually the person caught stealing the drugs was a young intern or someone new on the maintenance staff. Nurse Peters had been working at the hospital a long time, even before he was named chief surgeon. Now her life was ruined and all because of greed. Well, hopefully it was over and he didn't have to worry about that problem any longer. His eyelids felt heavy. Unable to fight it, he fell into a sound sleep.

* * *

Margaret Peters left the hospital after making sure Robert was settled comfortably in a private room. She would go home, shower, and change clothes. Then she would go back and sit with Robert just in case he needed anything.

It was all because of that ex-wife of his—Aislinn—that he was sick. If she wasn't still around causing trouble, he would get on with his life instead of brooding over her so much. That's what was making him sick. Margaret slammed on the car brakes, barely avoiding a pickup truck that had pulled out in front of her. Angrily she rolled down the window and yelled: "You fuck'n moron. You trying to get us both killed?"

The driver of the pickup responded with a vulgar universal hand signal which infuriated Margaret even more. She stomped on the accelerator and screeched through the intersection. She was tired of playing games with Aislinn. If she was to have any chance at all with Robert, Aislinn had to be out of the picture—totally.

She turned left off Flagler Drive and headed west. When she got to the El Cid historical district she turned left again onto a narrow, tree-lined street planted heavily with orange and yellow crotons that was situated only a block from the intracoastal waterway. She slowed down as she approached the two-story, Spanish-style home behind the stucco wall and large, black wrought-iron gates.

Dark clouds were building out over the ocean. The wind was also picking up. Several large drops of rain splashed on her windshield. She hesitated by the driveway entrance looking for any signs of Aislinn or that mangy dog of hers. She saw nothing. Usually, at night, she would see a light in one of the upstairs rooms. But being as it was still daylight, she couldn't even see that much. Just then the front door opened and Aislinn came rushing out of the house wearing cut-off jeans and a pink tank top and carrying the dog. Margaret drove on past the house and stopped at the stop sign at the end of the street. She watched Aislinn through her side mirror wiggling her skinny ass down the side-walk and then turn into her neighbor's yard. After a few minutes, Margaret turned around and drove slowly back. Apparently, she was visiting her neighbor.

Margaret parked a short ways down the street and got out of her car. The rain was getting heavier now, but she didn't really give a big damn. She found the long pole behind the hedge where she had left it and stuck it through the opening of the gate until it reached the release switch. Pressing that, the gate swung open.

Within minutes she was inside the yard. She hurried up the back porch steps and tried the door. It opened. Once inside the kitchen she quickly searched through several drawers until she found a sheet of pa-per she could write on and a pen. *LEAVE THIS PLACE!*, she wrote. *YOU HAVE BEEN WARNED FOR THE LAST TIME! The Predator.* On the way out she saw a porcelain tea pot tucked daintily on a corner display shelf. It looked old. She picked it up and threw it on the floor, shattering it completely.

Driving home, Margaret smiled and hummed a little tune. A woman living alone like that in a big, creaky house. She was bound to be scared shitless. Especially when she saw that The Predator had ac-tually been in her house. She drove west on Forest Hill Boulevard, crossed over I-95, and exited south. A few miles later she turned onto her own street of small, single-storied houses. At one time, it had been a nice, clean neighborhood of mostly white stucco houses and neatly kept yards. Now, the houses were painted blue or chartreuse, and mostly Cubans and Nicaraguans lived there. Everyone else who could afford to moved out years ago. Trucks, vans, and old cars were parked on both sides of the street; some were parked in the yards. It didn't matter. Most of the yards didn't have any grass anyway. She parked her own car in the driveway and got out. As soon as she did, two sheriff's patrol cars pulled up behind her, blocking any possible exit.

"Mrs. Peters? Margaret Peters?" one of the deputies asked as he walked toward her.

"Yes. What is this all about?"

"You are under arrest. You'll have to come with us."

Each deputy took her by the arm and expertly handcuffed her hands behind her back. Then they loaded her into the back seat of one of the patrol cars. Several neighbors peered out their windows; a few came outside and stood in their small yards to get a better look. Only Margaret said anything, and she could be heard screaming curse words at the officers as they backed out of her driveway and drove down the street.

* * *

Peculiar. That was the only word to describe it. Peculiar. Aislinn had been working through the latest batch of manuscripts that she had received from Lorraine McLaughlin at Kane Publishing House when Lottie called. She had sounded upset at first, then downright giddy. She asked if Aislinn could come over for a glass of iced tea. She wanted to talk to her—immediately, if possible.

Aislinn didn't even bother to shut down her computer. She simply put on a pair of tennis shoes, grabbed Hemingway, and rushed out the door. It was so unusual for Lottie to actually invite her over for anything, much less a glass of tea. It was even more unusual for her to sound the way she had. Of course, ever since she had asked Aislinn to call her Lottie, Aislinn had noticed a lot of differences about her.

Aislinn took a deep breath and rang the front doorbell. She just hoped that everything was all right. Too many times she had heard Robert recount stories of patients behaving in unusual ways because of strokes or other illnesses. Especially older patients. Lottie wasn't young any more. Things happened.

Lottie answered the door slightly breathless and looking about the way Aislinn felt. Aislinn hadn't even bothered to put any makeup on earlier that morning, thinking she was going to be working inside all day, and she didn't really want to waste the time fixing herself up if she didn't need to. Lottie's hair was uncombed, her normally perfect fingerwaves twisted every which way, and a couple of the buttons on her dress were fastened in the wrong holes.

"Are you all right?" asked Aislinn as soon as Lottie answered the door.

"Thank you for coming over," she said standing back so Aislinn and Hemingway could go in. "I know I must have sounded strange, but I really wanted to talk to you."

Aislinn followed Lottie into her sitting room where a tray had already been set up with two glasses of iced tea. Next to the tray was what appeared to be a manuscript.

"Several months ago I sent you a manuscript to edit. The title was *My Father's Keeper.*"

"I remember reading a manuscript with that title, but it was written by someone I believe was named Latham Hunt. Was that you?"

Lottie nodded. "L.H. Lottie Howard. I used my initials. It was the first time I had ever seriously thought about trying to get anything I had written published, and, well, I just felt a little strange about it, especially you being my neighbor and all. That was the reason for the subterfuge."

"I understand." Aislinn did understand. A lot of people were embarrassed or insecure about letting strangers read their work. Writing was such a deeply personal thing. Using another name provided some distance and a level of comfort which they otherwise didn't have.

"Anyway, after thinking about your suggestions, I have finally come up with something that I feel might be worth reading."

Aislinn glanced at the manuscript. "I see you kept the title—it's a good title."

"I don't expect you to read it here and now, but I did feel I needed to explain to you why I wrote the things in it that I did." She smoothed the folds of her dress, ignoring the mismatched buttons. "Things were so different when I was growing up. Not at all like they are now with young women free to do pretty much as they please. They have so many more choices. When I was growing up, there were very few choices, and everything was written in stone—at least it was that way in the Howard household."

Aislinn sipped her tea and sat back on the sofa with Hemingway on her lap. This was obviously something important that Lottie wanted to talk about. The work she had to do at home could wait.

"You see, it was improper for people of different classes to mingle. It was especially improper for people of different races to mingle. It just wasn't done." For the next hour and a half, Lottie talked about what it was like growing up as the daughter of Clifford Howard.

"And you never found out what happened to C.T.?" asked Aislinn when Lottie finished talking.

"No. The night before my sixteenth birthday—the night I almost took my life—my parents were in their bedroom getting ready to go out for the evening. I thought they were going out to celebrate a big land development deal my father had just completed. That's what I had been told. One of my father's friends was on the State Board of Highways and Transportation, and he was always getting advance information on where roads were being planned or what land was going to be sold. Of course, now it would be considered unethical and, in some cases, illegal to pass that type of information out for personal gain, but back then, there was a tight group of wealthy businessmen, my father being one of them, who looked out after each other. I was going to my room for some reason when I heard my name mentioned, and even though I knew better, I listened outside their closed door. I remember hearing my father telling my mother what an embarrassment I was. He didn't even want to take me out with them. What I hadn't realized at the time was that all of us had been invited to dinner by one of his business associates. It also happened to be a birthday dinner for his sixteen-year-old daughter. Rather than take me and suffer through the inevitable comparisons that would be made, my parents had told me it was just another business dinner.

"Of course, I had always felt my parents' disapproval. But on that night, hearing my father say those words out loud was more than I could stand. After they left the house, I remember walking down to the intracoastal and not stopping until I was standing ankle-deep in the water. It was surprisingly warm; there was a slight breeze. It was during one of those seventeen-year cycles that the cicadas had emerged, and strangely enough I remember hesitating just long enough to listen to their sound mixed with the sounds of the tree frogs. As I waded deeper into the water, my dress billowed up around me. Gradually it became heavier until eventually pulling me under.

"I don't even know why C.T. came looking for me that evening. Somehow he found me, though. Here was this amazingly handsome, soft-spoken Black boy whose family had come from the bayous of Mississippi with hardly a pot to piss in, as they used to say, telling me how foolish I was to let what other people thought control how I felt about myself. The strange thing about it was that he had told me those things before. I guess I just wasn't ready to hear it until that night.

"He was very religious, you know, and was always reading his Bible. He had it with him that night, and he made me read a scripture from it. It worried me that I might get it wet, but he said he didn't mind. It wasn't the outside of it that mattered anyway.

"I was a new person after that. I remember telling myself that no one would ever hurt me again the way my parents had. The next day, when C.T. came over to the house with his daddy, he wanted to tell me something. He was so happy and excited. We walked down to the intracoastal. He told me he wanted to give me a birthday present before he told me his news." Lottie leaned forward and showed Aislinn a gold locket she was wearing.

"That is beautiful, Lottie."

"Lord only knows how long he must have saved up for it. I kissed him then and there—for the locket, for being my only friend, and for saving my life. That was when my mother found us. I never saw or heard from him again. You know the rest of the story."

Without realizing it, Aislinn had taken Lottie's hand and was holding it. What a terrible thing to go through life feeling unattractive and unloved—especially by your own parents. How ironic that it was Lottie her parents had turned to for help at the end of their lives.

"If it isn't good enough to get published, that is all right. I honestly think just the act of writing it all down has somehow set me free. I had buried so many things."

Aislinn carried the manuscript home with her giving Lottie her promise to be honest and up front with her criticism and evaluation. It was a remarkable story about the Gilded Age—a time in history that would never again be equaled, a story of the rich and powerful and their influence on the development of Palm Beach, and about an unloved child who was able to eventually see her own self-worth through the eyes of someone else.

On the way back to her house, Aislinn saw a car pull over to the curb and stop in front of her house. It was Josh Turner on his way home from the hospital. He waved and rolled down the window. "Have you talked to Robert yet?"

"No, what's happened?"

"I had to put him back in the hospital—as a patient. I'll be running more tests in the morning."

"Oh, Josh. What is it?"

"I honestly don't know yet. It might not be anything more than exhaustion. He really pushes himself hard, as I'm sure you already know." He reached out and scratched Hemingway on the head. "When you two were still living together, did you ever notice if Robert had any strange behavior patterns—anything out of the ordinary?"

"Not really. He always had so much energy. He could do loops around me. By nine o'clock I'd be ready to turn off the light and go to sleep and he would just be getting his second wind. He rarely went to sleep before one or two in the morning. I just thought he was one of those people who didn't require but three or four hours of sleep every night."

Josh nodded. "Doctors are notorious for not sleeping or just exist-ing on cat naps. We are trained that way in medical school. Well, I'll let you know if I find out anything. Like I said, he probably just needs to take a break from work for a couple of days." He glanced down at his watch. "Right now, I promised my wife I would take her out to dinner. I'm only an hour late."

Aislinn turned onto her walkway and put Hemingway down on the grass just in case he needed to do anything. She would finish reading over the manuscript she had been looking at before Lottie called—it wasn't that long—and then change clothes so she could go to the hospital to see Robert. Josh had said it might only be exhaustion. She hoped for his sake that it wasn't anything more serious.

Hemingway ran up the steps and waited for Aislinn to open the door. As soon as she did, he started to growl. Aislinn immediately picked him up. Something wasn't right inside the house for him to be disturbed like that. She made her way from the front of the house to the back, glancing into each room, until she got to the kitchen. There on the floor was her great grandmother's teapot, destroyed. Nothing else seemed to be out of place. Hemingway trembled in her arms as he continued to growl. Then she saw the note.

"That does it," she said out loud. "I don't care if that Santerian priest did say not to worry; I am worried." She picked up the phone and dialed the police.

* * *

"The boss wants to see you." Scott leaned inside Tracy's office and smiled. "He looks happy, too."

"Sheldon?"

Scott nodded.

Tracy put down what she was working on and stood up, smoothing her skirt, checking her blouse, fluffing her hair, and licking her lips. Scott stayed put, watching. "How do I look?" she asked.

"Great. Absolutely great."

Tracy ignored the growl he added and pushed past him out the door. It was about time someone wanted to see her. She had handed *The Enlightened* to Oscar Sheldon personally over two weeks ago. It was good work, and she knew it. Now it was just a matter of deciding how much she wanted for an advance and settling on how many copies to run in the first printing.

Sheldon's door was open and his secretary wasn't at her desk, so Tracy knocked and went in.

"Tracy, my dear. Come in and have a seat." Oscar Sheldon had been in the publishing business longer than Tracy had been alive. That was probably why he always treated her more like a child than his employee. He, along with his partner, Jonathan Talbert, built their business by buying out smaller publishers, thereby eliminating much of their competition. After successfully running the company for over twenty-five years, Talbert elected to take an early retirement, leaving Sheldon in control of one of the largest publishing houses in the country. The well-known fact that it wasn't the largest, however, that distinction being given to Kane Publishing House, continued to be a source of irritation for Sheldon and something which he tried to correct on a daily basis. The past year had been good at Sheldon-Talbert, the quarterly earnings slowly gaining on those at Kane Publishing. One more big seller could push them over the top.

Tracy picked out a straight-back leather chair, one in which she could give him full view of her legs when she crossed and uncrossed them.

"So, our little editor is also a writer." He sat back and smiled benevolently.

"I would like to think so, Mr. Sheldon." Tracy crossed her legs and tugged at her skirt demurely.

"When did you become so interested in lightning?"

Tracy had been preparing for this meeting ever since she first came up with the idea of rewriting *Then There Was Light*. She had rehearsed what she would say and how she would say it. She had asked herself every conceivable question that might get asked and come up with an answer for it.

"I guess you could say I was always fascinated by lightning, even as a child. Of course, my parents live in Florida, and, as I am sure you know, that is the lightning capital of the world."

He nodded and folded his hands in front of him. "Well, I like what you have done with this." He picked up the manuscript—her manuscript—that was on his desk. "I especially like that angle about "the gifts" your protagonist is left with after being struck by lightning. I have assigned Phil Herzog to edit it. It will be given top priority in order to get it into production as soon as possible. I want to include it in our spring releases, which doesn't give us much time. I'm giving it a $200,000 marketing budget. At the very least, we should plan on a twenty-city author tour, a national radio and print advertising campaign, and bookings on the *Today Show, Letterman, Oprah*, and maybe the book clubs—*Literary Guild, Book of the Month*. Does a fifty thousand dollar advance sound all right to you?"

Tracy smiled. "That will be fine."

"Good. Nancy has the contracts on her desk ready for you to sign."

Tracy glanced toward the door. His secretary had returned. "I was just wondering, how many. . ."

"Right now I intend to print 500,000 copies in the first run. That figure can be adjusted, of course, once I get the results back from marketing on the pre-publicity and reviews we do. Anything else?"

Tracy uncrossed her legs and stood up. It was even better than she had hoped. Now she just had to be patient. If the book proved to be any success at all, she would be able to get anything she wanted from Sheldon. "Thank you, Oscar," she said still smiling.

Chapter Eleven

A writer writes not because he is educated but because he is driven by the need to communicate. Behind the need to communicate is the need to share. Behind the need to share is the need to be understood. The writer wants to be understood much more than he wants to be respected or praised or even loved. And that, perhaps, is what makes him different from others.

Leo Rosten

The clinic was operated out of an old brownstone on the west end of the run-down neighborhood. The medical staff was small, but dedicated; the operating budget, practically non-existent. Still, it served a useful purpose, and there wasn't a day that went by that the small waiting room wasn't filled with patients who couldn't afford to go anywhere else for treatment. None of the people who went to the clinic had medical insurance. It was here that the Professor went on those infrequent occasions when his mind cleared, the normal functions of daily existence were once again important, and he made an attempt at living some sort of normal, productive life.

He sat in a corner holding one of his bags on his lap, the one that contained most of his military mementos. He liked to talk to the doctor about that part of his life, and the young doctor always seemed interested. Small children of various ages played on the floor nearby while men and women sitting and standing all around him chattered in foreign languages—mostly Italian and Spanish the best he could tell. He had been waiting for over two hours but he didn't mind. He had plenty of time.

"Hello, Professor. I didn't see you sitting there. Come on in." The doctor, dressed casually in a black knit sports shirt and khaki trousers, smiled and shook the Professor's hand. Then he put his arm around the Professor's shoulders and walked with him into one of the private examination rooms. After getting the Professor's weight, the doctor motioned to a chair for the Professor to sit in while he got out the monitor to take his blood pressure. "So, how have you been? I haven't seen you around lately." The doctor pumped the black rubber ball and watched the indicator. "Looks good," he said after a moment. "How are the headaches?"

"Right now, good," the Professor answered. "I had hell to pay when that last storm rolled through here, though."

"Hold out your arm. I want to take a little blood."

The professor did as the doctor asked.

After the doctor filled two vials, he pressed a wad of cotton that had been dipped in alcohol on the spot where the needle had entered the arm. "Hold that for me, will you?" Then he got out a Band-Aid and covered it. "If anything turns up in your lab work, I'll let you know the next time you come by." He made some notes in the Professor's file and then sat down on a stool facing him.

"That was a mean storm, all right. My wife and I had planned to get away for a short break, but had to cancel at the last minute." He sighed. "Maybe next month, before it starts to get cold." He smiled at the Professor. "Any other problems you want to talk about?"

"It's the strangest thing. Ever since that storm I have been clear-headed. I even picked myself up a little part-time job a couple of weeks ago. Nothing much. Just washing dishes. But I like doing it. You know?"

The doctor nodded. "That's terrific, Professor." He had been looking after the Professor for several years now, trying to help him through his down times. It wasn't easy, though, when the Professor wouldn't take his medications. It was really too bad; he could be living a fairly normal life otherwise, unlike a lot of the other homeless people he treated. "Did anything in particular happen during the storm to bring about this change?"

"I don't know. It sounds crazy, but I think I was visited by an angel in a silver chariot."

Over the years the doctor had heard a lot of the Professor's stories, a lot of them memories from his past but mainly things brought on from hallucinations. The angel was a new one. "Did the angel say anything to you?"

"I don't think so. I just remember thinking that she was going to take care of my problem and that I wouldn't have to worry about it any more. So I haven't." The Professor laughed. "Shit, I can't even remember what the problem was now. I think it had something to do with light, though."

The doctor visited with the Professor for the next thirty minutes. He had developed a fondness for the Professor, in spite of his occasional bizarre behavior, and had found him to be an extremely sensitive and intelligent man, self-taught for the most part. Whenever the Professor came to the office, he usually brought a book to give the doctor, or something from his past that he wanted to share with him. On this particular day he had brought a sack full of military medals. Most of them he had received while serving with the US Army Special Forces. The Professor had been one of the first selected to be sent to Vietnam in the mid-1950's, during that time when the Army contributed only advisers to South Vietnamese government forces. He had been eighteen years old then, just out of boot camp, assigned to one of the high-ranking officers. It was obviously a source of great pride to the Professor. As he was leaving the doctor grabbed several boxes of medications, samples he had gotten from various pharmaceutical companies, and put them in the Professor's bag. "Try these if you get another headache. Maybe they will help."

The Professor thanked him and left. He always felt happy after visiting the doctor. He would go to work now. It was a good day. *For whoever lives by the truth comes into the light, so that it may be seen plainly that what he has done has been done through God* (John 3/21).

* * *

Ever since that evening when Aislinn discovered someone had broken into her house, she hadn't been able to sleep. She went to bed at her usual time, but just as she would doze off, something would startle her awake—an unfamiliar noise, a wrinkled sheet, just her mind playing tricks. At lease she was getting caught up with her work, but she definitely needed a break.

The police had figured out how the person entered the house. They found the stick hidden behind some bushes next to the gates. But they weren't able to give Aislinn much more information, other than to tell her to keep her house locked even if she was just going out for a few minutes.

Josh hadn't been able to turn up anything else where Robert was concerned. It was his judgment that Robert just needed to take some time off—away from the hospital. Convincing Robert to do it was another matter.

Aislinn picked up Hemingway and wandered over to the window. She felt tired. So far, Lorraine had sent four batches of manuscripts for Aislinn to read over before the next editorial staff meeting. Only a couple of the manuscripts really showed any promise, besides *Then There Was Light*, that is. A few of them had been well crafted, but they simply weren't strong enough. The others more than likely wouldn't even make it past the assistant editors.

One thing Aislinn hadn't known until she read over Lorraine's tracking information was that Caldwell's son, Tyler, read only nonfiction material. That meant that he would be the one to get *Then There Was Light* once it was passed on, and Aislinn had no doubt that it would be. It would be interesting to see how he presented it at the staff meeting.

Aislinn glanced at the pile of magazines she hadn't had time to get to. The latest issue of *Publisher's Weekly* was on the top. It was the issue that had the advance listing of spring forecasts for all of the publishing companies. Curious, Aislinn picked it up and thumbed through to the section where Kane Publishing House was listed. As usual, the listing was quite substantial and included fiction, nonfiction, children's and even some poetry. There were two titles under their new Spanish imprint as well. She read through several of the synopses for the new releases and then flipped over to the listing for Sheldon-Talbert. The first title she came to under the fiction category was something called *The Enlightened.* As Aislinn read through the descriptive synopsis, her heart started pounding. She read it through twice more just to make sure she hadn't misunderstood. Next to her desk she pulled out a manuscript from the pile she was taking with her to New York and compared parts of it with the synopsis. Entire passages were identical. There was no mistake. Of course, *The Enlightened* was fiction and the main character had been changed along with the setting, but without a doubt the story had been taken from *Then There Was Light.* Feeling light headed and slightly nauseous, Aislinn slumped down next to Hemingway on the small office sofa.

The editorial staff meeting was a week away. Rather than flying up the night before, she had told Caldwell she would fly up early on the morning of the meeting. That way, there wouldn't be the extra fuss or burden of the hotel since after the meeting they were planning to go directly to his home in the Hamptons. Caldwell had called Aislinn several times, primarily to ask her about her preferences for something or other. Did she eat pork? Did she like yellow? When was the last time she had been to the Guggenheim? He always tried to tie his purpose in calling to business, but Aislinn knew better, and in all honesty she felt flattered. It had been a long time since a man had shown her any attention other than the attention one gets professionally. She really wasn't quite sure what to do with it, and right now she was too tired and upset to even think about it. Caldwell was paying her good money to help him solve this problem. She needed to get as much information as she could before she saw him again. And at this point, she really didn't know which manuscript had been written first, although she strongly suspected that *Then There Was Light* was the original.

Aislinn picked up the phone and dialed her travel agent. Within a few minutes she had reserved two airline tickets, leaving Palm Beach International and arriving in Asheville, North Carolina. There was a beautiful new Biltmore Inn that had recently opened located on the Vanderbilt estate property, her agent had told her. She could stay there and rent a car to get around to where she needed to go.

She went downstairs and pulled out Hemingway's travel bag from the closet. Now all she had to do was convince Robert to take a couple of days off. She would enlist Josh's help if she had to. She picked up Hemingway, fluffed his top knot tied with a red bow, and put him in his bag. "You want to go see Robert? Of course you do." As she locked the door behind her she thought about the last time she took Hemingway to the hospital. "Maybe that mean, witchy nurse won't be there this time," she told Hemingway.

* * *

Tyler had been working day and night since getting the brush-off from Tracy, but he felt good. With the editorial staff meeting coming up in a few days, he knew he was more than prepared. A couple of new manuscripts had been submitted in just the past week that looked promising. His ace in the hole, of course, was *Then There Was Light*. Without a doubt, it would be a best seller.

"You want to go grab a bite to eat?" Jason stuck his head in the door of his brother's office.

"I think I'll take care of some errands instead. Maybe next time."

Jason nodded and continued down the hall. Things had been going pretty well lately. He sure hoped that shit-eating grin on Tyler's face didn't mean he was going to stir things up with that woman again.

Tyler hadn't even tried to call Tracy since that morning at her apartment, much less go see her. But now, with everything under control, maybe he would just drop by and see how she was doing. If she didn't want to see him, then he would leave. At least there wouldn't be any harm in just saying hello to a friend.

It was only a short distance from Kane Publishing House to Sheldon-Talbert. He parked in the lot in the rear of the building and entered through the back door. Rather than going directly to her office, he went to the reception area and gave the young woman behind the desk his name and reason for being there. The young woman with big blond hair wearing a tight-fitted green sweater smacked her gum and giggled as she dialed Tracy's office.

While waiting, Tyler looked around the reception area. Large posters of Sheldon-Talbert best sellers covered the walls. On one wall near the elevators was a poster listing the titles and brief synopses of the upcoming spring releases. First on the list was the novel, *The*

Enlightened, by Tracy Cord. He didn't even have to read the entire synopsis to recognize where it came from. "My god," he muttered under his breath.

He immediately pushed the elevator button taking him to the third floor where Tracy's office was located. By the time he got there, Tracy was coming out the door.

"Well, hello, stranger. This is a nice surprise. I have been thinking about you." She smiled her brilliant smile and kissed him lightly on his lips.

"We have to talk," said Tyler taking her by her arm and pushing her back into her office. "What in the world were you thinking?"

"What's wrong with you? I don't know what you are talking about."

The expression on her face told him that she did. "You plagiarized *Then There Was Light.* I read the synopsis, so don't deny it."

"Now, listen, Tyler. . ."

"No, you listen. You can't do this. You have to tell Sheldon you have changed your mind. Tell him you aren't ready to get it published yet. I don't give a shit what you tell him, you just get it off the list."

Tracy sat down in her desk chair and leaned back. "I won't do that."

"What do you mean, 'you won't do that?'"

"Listen, Tyler. Sheldon is giving me a $50,000 advance with a guarantee of 500,000 copies in the first run. Do you know what that means? This book will be huge. It will certainly be the biggest thing they have had around here lately. And that means I'll be able to get my own imprint, my own authors, whatever I want. Don't you see?"

Tyler was stunned. Of all the things to happen, being involved in helping the competition plagiarize someone else's work wasn't what he wanted. "I won't let you do it."

"You really don't have much choice, do you? Think about it. You were the one who gave me the manuscript to begin with. Along with several others, or have you forgotten? I don't think your daddy would understand, do you? Or big brother." Tracy got up and went over to perch on the arm of the chair where Tyler was slumped. "Only you and I even know about that other manuscript."

Tyler shook his head and got up to leave. "The author knows, Tracy. Have you forgotten her? The author who wrote *Then There Was Light?*"

* * *

As it turned out, Aislinn didn't have to enlist Josh's help or anyone else's to convince Robert to fly to Asheville with her for a couple of days. "That sounds like fun," he told Aislinn in his office. "I've been wanting to get away from here for a couple of days. This is as good a time as any."

Hemingway sniffed around the piles of papers and file boxes on Robert's desk before making himself completely at home by stretching out on the large ink blotter. Robert popped open a can of diet cola he found in the small refrigerator located under his credenza and poured half of it into a cup for Aislinn.

"We need to be at the airport by no later than 5:30 this afternoon. Why don't you just come over to the house and we can go together from there."

"Sounds good. I'll pack my hiking boots," he teased.

Aislinn picked up Hemingway and put him back into his travel bag. "Come on, my little hairy friend. I don't want Nurse Peters to find us in here and threaten us with the doggie cops for being unsanitary on Robert's desk."

"Oh, didn't I tell you? Nurse Peters is no longer with us."

Aislinn raised her eyebrows in surprise. "What happened? She seemed so—so—dedicated."

"She was caught stealing drugs. Apparently she had been doing it for some time and then selling them. It's a shame, really. She was a good nurse."

Aislinn shook her head in disbelief. She hadn't cared for the woman that much, but she didn't like to see anyone get into trouble. She kissed Robert's cheek. "I'll see you in a few hours, then. Don't be late," she reminded him.

With so little time, Aislinn went straight home to pack. When she got there, she saw a sheriff's patrol car parked in front of her house. It was Hank and Mario, the two deputies who had been on duty the night she reported someone breaking into her house. They got out of the car and followed Aislinn through the gates as she drove in. "Hello, deputies. Have you found out anything?"

"That's what we would like to talk to you about. Do you have a minute?"

"Of course. Come on in." Aislinn unlocked the back door and led the two men into the kitchen. They sat on two of the stools that were in front of the counter and adjusted various things hanging from their belts while Aislinn released Hemingway from his bag. Hank, the shorter of the two and the one who usually did all of the talking, waited until he had Aislinn's full attention. "Have you ever had any dealings with someone named Margaret Peters?"

Aislinn's heart jumped to her throat. Of all the things to have happen now. "Look, I can explain that. I had just gotten back from New York when I found out that my husband—or ex-husband—was in the hospital. Rather than leave Hemingway by himself, I took him with

157

me. I know dogs aren't supposed to be in the hospital, but Robert is chief surgeon there and . . ."

The looks on the officers' faces told her that what she was telling them made absolutely no sense. "Nurse Peters didn't report me for having Hemingway in the hospital?"

"No. Not that we know of. She has been arrested for stealing drugs from the hospital, and as part of the investigation, the computer she had access to at the hospital was confiscated. Apparently, she is the one who was sending you the e-mails and who broke into your house."

Aislinn pulled out a stool and plopped down. "Nurse Peters is The Predator? But I don't even know the woman. Why would she do something like that?"

"We were hoping you could tell us."

"How could she do it? How could she know when I was on the Internet?"

"It really isn't that hard. She made up a profile on you and added it to her buddy list, which works on the Instant Messenger. That way, whenever you went online, she would get a signal from her computer. By having the message already written, all she had to do was send it as soon as she knew you were on. She created a separate identify and screen name from the one she used at work. That way no one would know what she was up to. Apparently, when you reported it to your Internet server, they were able to identify who the screen name belonged to."

"Did she scare other people that way?"

"Not that we know of. Apparently she just didn't like you."

"Some other information was found on her computer, too—schedules and addresses," added Mario.

Hank glanced at him and then back at Aislinn. "It would seem she spent quite a bit of time following you around."

Aislinn thought back to the few times she had been around Nurse Peters. She had the bedside manner of a rusty surgical clamp, but she always seemed to take good care of Robert—especially during his surgery. Maybe that was it. Maybe her interest in Robert was more than that of a nurse and she felt threatened by Aislinn. "I don't know what to say, except I am so glad that you found out."

The deputies got up and headed out the door. "Well, she won't be bothering you any more. From what we hear, she will have to serve time for the drug charges. The Internet server will probably have something to say about her using the computer illegally as well."

After showing the deputies out, Aislinn went back into the kitchen. She poured herself a glass of wine and carried it out to the sun porch. It was just all so strange. As far as she could remember, she had never done anything to Margaret Peters—certainly not intentionally. Pichardo, the Santerian priest, had told her that a negative force had entered her life, but it was weak. It fed on jealousy, greed, and impure motives. Soon it would leave, and she would have nothing else to fear. He had been right. Now, maybe she would be able to sleep at night. She still didn't know what the significance of the number sixteen was in her life, or what he had meant by "twin faces, separate places, and a love for which you must choose." He had told her when she was ready to learn the truth, she would understand. She would wait. For now she had other things to take care of, one of them involving a trip to the mountains of North Carolina in order to interview the person who supposedly wrote *Then There Was Light*.

* * *

Caldwell was acting like a kid, and he knew it. So did everyone else who was around him. Whistling in the hall, singing in his office, playing practical jokes on his employees; he was smitten, there was no doubt about it. Now everything he did had to have the "Aislinn factor," as Lorraine McLaughlin called it, figured into the equation. At Kane Publishing House, everyone had been warned to either clean up their offices or find other employment. No more clutter. On the home front, he had instructed his housekeeper at the Hamptons to clean the old estate home from top to bottom—not that it needed it. And in New York, in the past three weeks he had sent Frederick out of the apartment with so many of his clothes to the dry cleaners, the proprietor of the establishment was seriously considering an early retirement.

With only a few days remaining before he saw her again, his moods were as unpredictable as the summer temperatures in the city. He verged on being outright silly one minute, only to fall into a borderline psychotic depression the next. The much-anticipated arrival of Aislinn was not only going to be a relief to Caldwell, it was going to be a relief to everyone who knew him. Her effect on his behavior once she actually arrived was anyone's guess. But one thing was certain, it had to be one hell of a lot better than the way he was behaving now.

The one person who was thoroughly enjoying the little drama as it played out was Lorraine McLaughlin. She had known Caldwell when he was still in knee britches. She had known his wife and had suffered along with the family through the ordeal of losing her to cancer. Now, out of the den of emotional chaos, she could be heard saying repeatedly, "It's about time."

She and Aislinn had talked on the phone several times, mostly about business, but on personal matters as well. Aislinn was so easy to talk to. She was a good listener. And she was intelligent. As far as Lorraine was concerned, if Aislinn and Caldwell were to get together, it would be the best thing that could ever happened—even if it did mean putting up with some of Caldwell's foolishness. It was about time.

As Lorraine prepared to mail out another stack of rejection letters, her private telephone line rang. She had given out that number to only a few people—mostly family and close friends—to save them from having to go through the main switchboard. She had also given it to Aislinn.

"Hello, Lorraine. This is Aislinn."

"Well, hello, pretty lady. Did you get that last batch of manuscripts I sent to you?"

"I sure did. Thanks. In fact, I have finished going through all of them but a couple. Lorraine, this might sound a little peculiar, but I was wondering if you could help me with something."

"Of course. You know I will be happy to. What's up?" Lorraine immediately recognized the tension in Aislinn's voice. She was such an innocent. She would never be good at playing poker. She broadcasted her feelings too much.

"I was just glancing over the latest issue of *Publisher's Weekly* and the listing of spring releases. There is a novel titled *The Enlightened* listed under Sheldon-Talbert, and it is authored by someone named Tracy Cord. Do you think you could check around—maybe call someone at Sheldon-Talbert—and find out who this Tracy Cord is?"

Lorraine knew immediately what was going on. Aislinn had stumbled onto something that was part of the problem Caldwell had hired her for in the first place. Even though Aislinn had never discussed it with her, her own instincts were still pretty sharp, even if she was seventy-two years old. "That won't be difficult at all. I know one of the women who works in marketing there. I'll call her."

"I appreciate this so much, Lorraine. I am flying to Asheville later this afternoon, but I'll be back in a couple of days. I'll call you then."

Lorraine hung up the phone and pulled out her directory. She soon found the listing for her friend. Maybe she could meet her for lunch.

Aislinn had said she was flying to Asheville. The only Asheville she knew of was in the mountains of North Carolina. Wasn't that near where that lady lived who wrote *Then There Was Light?* Lorraine picked up the phone and quickly dialed the number for Sheldon-Talbert.

Chapter Twelve

Like stones, words are laborious and unforgiving, and the fitting of them together, like the fitting of stones, demands great patience and strength of purpose and particular skill.

Edmund Morrison

Snow Henderson picked another handful of snap beans, tossed them into the plastic bucket tied with a rope around her waist, and stood up straight. She was getting another one of those feelings again. Where her vision got cloudy and there was a high-pitched humming sound in her ears. When the humming stopped, her vision cleared, and that's when it happened. Some people called it being clairvoyant, being able to see into the future like that. Snow just called it "the gift." Something she had been given when the lightning struck her.

She hadn't received the gift in a while now, not since James Luther fell off his tractor and almost bled to death when the dang thing ran over him. But lately, she had been getting it—the cloudiness and the humming. Each day it was a little stronger; the feeling lasted a little longer. Each day the image was getting clearer.

There weren't many beans left in the garden now. Most had either already been picked or had dried up. She'd probably be able to get enough to can a few more jars and maybe find a couple more decent squash and a mess of late okra. That along with all the tomatoes and corn she had already fixed would be enough to carry her through the winter.

As she bent over to begin her picking, a bright light exploded in her face, just as the lightning had done, causing her to fall to the ground and squeeze her eyes shut tightly. The beans she had just picked spilled from her bucket. She saw reds and yellows and greens and blues; circles and squares and triangles. Then the colors and forms combined into swirls of different colors and different shapes. The humming was so loud she thought her skull would crack open. And when she opened her eyes, she saw a pretty young woman with bright blue eyes and brown hair that curled softly around her face coming toward her. She was smiling and carrying a small, white-haired dog. Snow watched the woman approach her. She wanted to talk about her book she had written. She wanted to know about it.

As quickly as it had come, the image disappeared along with the bright light and the humming sound, replaced with just the hint of a breeze and the gentle rustling of newly-turned leaves. Snow was left with a feeling of peace and quiet. And just as sure as she was lying in the middle of her vegetable garden, she knew a woman was coming to see her about her book. She also knew that meeting her would forever change her life.

* * *

"I'm not sure I totally understand what this Caldwell Kane—Is that his name?"

"Yes."

"What Caldwell Kane has hired you to do. I mean, are you supposed to edit the manuscripts that have been sent to him? Or are you being paid to be some sort of private detective?"

Aislinn had put off telling Robert her reason for suddenly wanting to pick up and fly to Asheville, North Carolina, until the two of them were aboard the plane and in the air with Hemingway safely stowed and secure in his travel bag at her feet. The fact that Robert was slightly upset because he had jumped to the wrong conclusion in assuming that it was going to be some sort of mini vacation wasn't her fault. The fact that she was making the trip on behalf of a man named Caldwell Kane didn't seem to be sitting too well with him either. Which was why she hadn't mentioned it until now. Instinctively, she knew that Robert would feel somewhat jealous. In spite of their unusual relationship of living separately and respecting each other's individuality, Robert did tend to be territorial at times.

Sensing the tension between Robert and Aislinn, Hemingway whimpered softly. Aislinn reached into one of the many flaps of her shoulder bag and found a dog treat to give to him. "There's a good boy," she said sticking it inside his bag. "It's all right.

"Caldwell doesn't even know about this yet," Aislinn explained. "I am making this trip on my own. If there is some doubt regarding the authorship of *Then There Was Light,* then I need to get it settled before I can recommend it to Kane Publishing House to be published. I have to know who actually wrote the manuscript." She felt it best not to go into any more detail, especially about the fact that Sheldon-Talbert seemed to have gotten hold of quite a few of the Kane submissions.

"Well, it just seems to me that you are going a little beyond—in fact, a lot beyond—the call of duty here." He glanced over at her. "Are you sure this is just a professional concern?"

Just then the steward came around with the drink cart. Aislinn immediately requested two white wines. "We can still enjoy ourselves," she said ignoring his question. "And, according to the national weather report, the Blue Ridge Mountains are already beginning to show some color in the higher altitudes." She held her glass out and touched it to Robert's smiling. "Cheers."

It worked. Robert got over his touchiness and by the time they landed he was visibly back to his usual, good-natured self. So much so, that when they went to pick up the car the travel agent had reserved, he exchanged it for a four-by-four, Jeep Cherokee "in order to get a better view of everything," he said. If it made Robert happy, it suited Aislinn, just so long as she didn't have to drive the thing. She had never mastered shifting gears, and trying to learn on the hair-pin turns of the two-lane road on the Blue Ridge did not seem to her to be a very smart thing to do.

It was just getting dark by the time they turned onto the long drive leading to the Inn at the Biltmore. Within minutes they could see the Inn, a sprawling, irregular-shaped white stone monolith flanked by mountains. Rising on a hillside overlooking the mountain-rimmed area, it reflected the last of the sun's rays. Robert let out a long, low whistle. The Inn and the surrounding Appalachian mountains were ab-solutely breathtaking. "This sure beats emptying bedpans."

"Robert!" Aislinn laughed in spite of herself. "When have you ever emptied a bedpan?"

"Oh, you would be surprised. The stories I could tell you . . ."

As soon as Robert pulled up to the entrance, staff was on hand to help with the luggage and escort Robert and Aislinn into the lobby. One helpful young man said, "If you would like, they are still serving tea on the veranda."

Robert looked at Aislinn and silently mouthed, "tea on the ve-randa." Within minutes, Robert and Aislinn were settled comfortably on a wicker settee with deep, soft cushions covered in chintz. Aislinn sipped a cup of hot tea while Robert had opted for something a little stronger. The waiter had called it a Blue Ridge Mist, and it involved gin and Irish whiskey, among other things. A butler's tray with as-sorted sandwiches and pastries had been left on a table next to them in order that they could help themselves. Hemingway was wedged be-tween them happily chewing on his stringy. Stretching out in front of them for as far as they could see were the great Smokey Mountains.

Aislinn silently watched the darkness of dusk fill in the gray half-tones of the remaining daylight as it moved from the valley below upward toward the sky. She couldn't help but wonder what the next day would bring. The post office in Laurel Gorge would be the first place she would go to see if she could get some information on where she might locate Snow Henderson. The only address she had for Snow was Rural Route 3 in Laurel Gorge. She had contacted the main post office in Asheville before leaving West Palm Beach, and had gotten the name of the carrier for Laurel Gorge, a Mr. Bullock. But that could wait. Tomorrow would take care of itself. For now, she just wanted to enjoy the feeling of peacefulness and total serenity. Robert took her hand and held it, as though he also had the same thoughts.

Robert was a big man, over six feet tall and at least two hundred pounds. Whenever he did sleep in a bed, he required a great deal of room not only because of his size, but because he kicked and thrashed around a great deal in his sleep. While they had been married, they had an agreement that whoever fell asleep first got to stay in the bed, while the other could sleep in the guest room. It was the only way either of them could get any rest—Robert, his three or four hours of sleep, and Aislinn's eight hours. This arrangement didn't preclude the many pleasant hours spent together in each other's arms before falling to sleep, however. The actual physical act of love-making was good, but more than that was what they gave to complete one another—the respect, the sharing, and the love that extended beyond the bed. No matter where they were or what was going on in their lives, that love would always remain.

Aislinn awoke the next morning with one arm hanging off the sofa where she had slept. Eager to get an early start, she quickly showered and dressed, not particularly concerned about the amount of noise she was making. After a great deal of prodding, cajoling, and a bribe of a steak dinner later that evening in the restaurant on the grounds at the Biltmore Estate, she finally managed to get Robert unearthed from the mound of silk sheets, pillows, and down-filled comforters he was burrowed under.

"It must be the mountain air," he mumbled as he staggered toward the bathroom. While he was showering, Aislinn ordered room service, thinking it would save time. As soon as Robert was dressed, their breakfast arrived and by eating it on the terrace off their room, it felt like they were extending the wonderful moments they had shared the night before. At least that is what Aislinn told Robert.

Thirty minutes later, with Hemingway in Aislinn's lap and Robert behind the wheel, they drove across the Blue Ridge Parkway until they were able to take the first exit toward the small mountain town of Laurel Gorge. Between the many curves in the road, Robert wanting to stop and get out to admire the view at every "vista," and Hemingway's upset stomach, it took a little longer to get to Laurel Gorge than Aislinn anticipated. And when they did, they almost missed it. There were a few stores and a one-pump gas station, but that was about all. Aislinn spotted the American flag hanging from a pole in front of one of the stores.

"Let's stop there," she said pointing to the flag. "Hopefully, that is a post office."

He pulled into the diagonal parking space and set the brake. "You go ahead. I'll walk Hemingway first and then come on in."

A bell tinkled lightly when Aislinn opened the door. Near the rear of the store a thin, wiry man stood up from behind the counter and looked expectantly at Aislinn. He held a newspaper in his hands, and a cup of steaming coffee in one of the biggest mugs Aislinn had ever seen rested near his elbow. A plastic tag with the name George Bullock dangled from his shirt pocket.

"I was hoping you could help me," she said smiling. "I am trying to locate someone named Snow Henderson. Do you by any chance know her?"

The man's eyes narrowed into thin slits and out of his mouth materialized a much-chewed toothpick that he had apparently been storing there. "You that woman with the white dog who wants to talk to her about her book?"

Just then Robert came in carrying Hemingway. "Hello," he greeted the man.

"Yup. I reckon you are."

The man repeated the directions three times, each time making it sound like he was sending them in a completely different direction. Finally, Robert said he thought he knew where to go.

"You folks watch out fer them dogs out there, ya hear?"

"Dogs?" Aislinn asked.

"Yup. Snow's got a pack of 'em. Most of 'em are friendly, 'cept fer the black 'un. You watch out fer the black 'un. He'll gobble up that little white thing you got there like one of them doggie treats."

"Thank you. We will."

Once back in the jeep, Robert started laughing. "Are you sure you want to go through with this? I mean, you don't even know who this Snow Henderson is, do you? Have you even talked to her?"

"Well, no, I haven't. But that's all right. She's expecting me."

"How could she be expecting you?" Robert laughed again, obviously enjoying himself. "These people around here barely have mail service, let alone any modern conveniences like the telephone or fax or computers."

"All I know is, that man back there asked me if I was the woman with the white dog who wanted to talk to her about her book. Snow must have told him I was coming."

"You're kidding, right?"

"No, I'm not. You see, she is clairvoyant. Ever since she was struck by lightning, she has had the ability to see things in the future."

"I guess if I was hit by lightning and lived to talk about it, I would be psychic, too."

"Well, she was struck six times, and each time she was left with some extraordinary power or sense. That's what she wrote her book about—if she actually did write it."

Robert took Aislinn's hand and squeezed it. "Look. I'll do whatever you want. If you want to find this Snow Henderson, we'll find Snow Henderson. That black dog, be damned." He started laughing again as he ground the gear into reverse, but so did Aislinn. She couldn't help herself whenever she was around Robert.

Five miles up the road, Robert shifted down and turned onto a narrow, two-lane gravel road that cut into the granite rock of the mountain. There were no signs to indicate they were even on the right road; just a large boulder on the side of the road where they turned that pretty much fit the description given to them by the man at the post office.

The thick undergrowth swiped the sides of the Jeep as it banked around the narrow curves, down the looping turns and quickly back up again so abrupt that Hemingway started to whine. Aislinn held him tightly and murmured into his soft fur near his ear. "It's all right, baby dog. We'll soon be there." At least she hoped so.

The village of Laurel Gorge could no longer be seen, having given way to an occasional trailer parked at an odd angle. Near the road, just off the shoulder, were country mailboxes—leaning in and out or hardly standing at all, all victims of a wayward or careless snowplow. Occasionally small, wood-framed houses could be seen scattered through the thick woods—some lived in, some apparently abandoned—unpainted, for the most part, and also leaning. Soon, they too disappeared.

After another swooping plunge in the road, Robert downshifted once again, turned sharply to the left and stopped. Loose gravel and dust settled around them. They were at the end of the road. Just ahead of them was a house, most of which was wood frame, but it looked like a room made from concrete blocks had been attached to one side. In the front yard were the dismantled remains of car engines and a rusted-out truck, its hood still open. A nearby ditch was filled with old tires. Piles of firewood, to have called them stacks would have indicated some semblance of uniformity, seemed to spring up from patches of dirt. One pile had made it to the front porch. Robert and Aislinn sat staring without saying anything. Hemingway wriggled to get free from Aislinn's hold, glad to at last be somewhere.

"You don't have to go through with this, you know. I can back out of here right now and we can be on our way." Robert glanced toward the front of the house where most of the porch was sagging either from the weight of the wood piled there, weather rot, or some other form of destruction.

"No, I've come this far. I don't want to give up just yet," said Aislinn with her face still buried in Hemingway's fur. "Do you see any . . ."

"Dogs?" Just then a dozen or so dogs, all of them large and all of them barking, came running toward the Jeep. The dog that appeared to be the leader of the pack—a black dog—growled and lunged repeatedly at the Jeep on the driver's side, covering it with saliva and what seemed to be the remains of something hastily eaten. Then they stopped. As quickly as that, the dogs stopped barking, stopped lunging, and the whole pack disappeared somewhere behind the house.

A woman came out of the front door and stood looking toward the Jeep, her hand shielding her eyes from the sun's glare. She was wearing faded jeans and what looked like a man's flannel shirt. She was tall and slender, and her gray-streaked hair was pulled back from her face in a tight braid that fell over one shoulder.

Aislinn took a deep breath. "Well, here goes." With Hemingway still in her arms, she climbed out of the Jeep. Concerned for Aislinn's safety, Robert quickly joined her, standing as close to her and Hemingway as possible without impeding her movement toward the house.

The inside of the house wasn't as bad as what Aislinn had expected after seeing the yard. It was old, of course, and everything had a worn look about it, but it was tidy and clean.

"We don't get many visitors up here. That's why the front yard is Treat's," Snow explained, looking out the front window. A man they hadn't noticed when they drove in was hunched over the front end of the rusted truck. "But the back yard is mine." She led her visitors outside to the back of the house. Flowers were growing everywhere. There was even a small fountain spilling water into a pond filled with water lilies. "It's gettin' late in the season now, so a lot of things is quit bloomin'. You should see it in the spring, though. The mountains is just full of redbud and dogwood." She reached down and pinched a dead flower head from one of the marigolds. After crushing it in her hand, she scattered it on the ground. "They just reseed themselves," she said wiping her hand on her leg.

"That big sunny spot over there is the vegetable garden," she said pointing. "We can grow just about anything we need. And that dead pine next to it is where I was struck by lightning the last time. They found Black Dog right next to me, all laid out like and glassy eyed. But he recovered. It just made him a little ornery is all. It singed all my hair, and for the longest time I kept smellin' somethin' like burnt chicken feathers. Turns out it burnt the hairs in my nose, too, but once they grew back I could smell things better than I ever could." She looked at Robert then. "You don't need to be worrying about them dogs. They won't bother you now."

He smiled unconvinced. "That's nice."

Back inside Snow fixed Aislinn and Robert some sassafras tea. "We get quite a bit of it growing around here," she said, referring to the sassafras plant. "I believe you want to know about my book," she said suddenly looking directly at Aislinn.

"Yes. I would like for you to tell me about your experiences that led you to write it in the first place."

And so Snow told her story from beginning to end, expressing herself just as she had in the manuscript in the language of someone who had been born and reared in the mountains of North Carolina. Her memory of each episode was uncanny. "But that's one of them gifts, you see. Being able to remember things in so much detail. Energy is another one. That's how I was able to do all that gardening out back."

"You mean you did that all by yourself?" asked Robert.

"Sure did. Every last lick of it." She grinned proudly. "Pretty, ain't it?"

She told Aislinn that even though she only finished the eighth grade, she knew enough about writing to be able to get everything down in cursive. Then she had paid some woman in Asheville to actually type it for her. "Two hundred dollars it cost me to get it typed. Course, I kept my hand-written copy. I'm sorta proud of it, ya know. You can hardly see the erase marks."

"Well, I think it is a wonderful story, Snow. I think it stands a good chance at getting published."

Snow smiled. "Heck, fire, do you think I might make enough money to get that two hundred dollars back?"

"Oh, my," said Aislinn. "You will get your two hundred dollars back and much, much more."

As Aislinn and Robert were leaving, Aislinn promised she would be back in touch with Snow through Mr. Bullock, the man at the Laurel Gorge post office, just as soon as she knew anything definite about *Then There Was Light* getting published. "If everything works out, would you and Treat like to make a trip to New York?"

Snow thought for a moment. "I ain't ever been to New York," she said. "Treat ain't either." She glanced at the mound of tires and the old, greasy engine parts. "I don't know," she said.

"That's all right. We can talk about it more later."

The pack of dogs chased the Jeep back to the first turn off in the road and then disappeared into the woods. "I feel like I have just taken a step back into time to a place I have only read about," said Robert wrestling with the steering wheel as the Jeep bumped its way back toward a paved road.

"I know. So do I. It's remarkable, isn't it, that someone like Snow could have written something so extraordinary."

"You think she wrote it?"

"Without a doubt."

* * *

Caldwell couldn't remember ever being so well organized and well prepared for anything in his entire life as he was for Aislinn's visit. With the editorial staff meeting being only a few days away now, he had pretty much already determined which of the manuscripts he thought were quality material. Tyler had been working practically non-stop ever since their little chat. Caldwell just hoped he had something worthwhile he could present at the meeting, not like that Vietnam story he tried to push through the last time. Finding and identifying good material was what Tyler had always done best. He did a good job with keeping up with the markets, and he seemed to know what would sell. Whereas Jason's interests were more attuned toward the financial end of the business. He seemed to thrive on creating budgets, flow charts, and monthly and year-end reports. His reward came from seeing the large, black, multiple-digit figures on the bottom line. Tyler and Jason would one day make a good team; that is, if Tyler kept his nose clean. Only time would tell.

Caldwell walked down the hall to Tyler's office. The door was closed so he knocked and poked his head in. "How's it going?"

Tyler was sitting at his desk and surrounded with the usual books and stacks of paper—in-coming manuscripts still to be read, manuscripts already rejected, query letters, and miscellaneous correspondence. Next to the phone was a large bottle of antacid pills. He looked up from the page he was reading and stared blankly at his father. The dark circles under his eyes indicated he hadn't been getting much sleep.

"Oh, hi. Everything is fine. Just fine."

Caldwell nodded. He knew his son probably better than anyone alive. And whenever he got that blank distant stare on his face, it usually meant things weren't going too well. "Anything you need help with?"

Tyler smiled. "No, not a thing."

Caldwell nodded. "I see you're taking those pills again. Is it your stomach?"

Tyler glanced at the pills. "Oh no," he said shoving the bottle into his desk drawer. "I was looking for something and forgot to put them back."

"Well, if you do need anything . . ."

Tyler smiled broadly. "Sure thing. Thanks."

Caldwell continued down the hall nearly getting knocked down by Lorraine McLaughlin.

"Oh, excuse me. I guess I wasn't looking where I was going."

"You haven't been drinking, have you, Mrs. McLaughlin," Caldwell teased.

"No, not yet, but I'm seriously thinking about it," she answered, obviously upset about something.

Caldwell watched her go back to her office. Was it just him, or was everyone going a little nuts? He went through the lobby and out the front door. Aislinn had admired the flowers planted there when she visited the last time. He wanted to be sure there was something pretty for her to admire when she came again. The two planter boxes were brimming with a mixture of colorful flowers—petunias and marigolds, he thought, but he didn't know for sure, and some red spikey things. The important thing was, they were pretty. Satisfied, he went back inside and returned to his office. He wanted to call Aislinn, but she had told him she was going to be away for a couple of days. Instead, he picked up another manuscript to read. He really didn't feel like it, but it helped pass the time.

* * *

Tyler continued to stare at the papers on his desk, not even knowing what he was reading. If ever he had messed up big time, this was it. How could he have been so blind. When he first started giving manuscripts to Tracy, he honestly thought it wouldn't matter. It couldn't hurt anyone. After all, Kane Publishing Company was publishing all it could handle. He just wanted to help Tracy get ahead in her career since it obviously was so important to her. When she actually succeeded in getting several of them published and they made it to the *Times* list of best sellers, he had felt proud that he had been a part of it.

But this thing with *Then There Was Light* was something else entirely. She wasn't going to back down. Sheldon-Talbert had given her a contract, and she was going to enjoy it for all it was worth. If he said anything, she would probably take legal action against him; that is, Sheldon-Talbert would on Tracy's behalf, and they had a bank of lawyers that could do it. If she had to, she would swear that she had written *The Enlightened* first, and if there was any similarity between it and another manuscript, it was either a coincidence or the other person had plagiarized her work. In the entire history of Kane Publishing House, there had never been a legal dispute involving the courts. The thought of it now made Tyler's stomach churn. He dumped three tablets from the bottle he had shoved in his desk drawer moments earlier and put all three in his mouth. The last thing he wanted was another bout with diarrhea.

Once again, he began sorting through the pile of manuscripts he had been reading to see if there was anything he could present at the editorial staff meeting in place of *Then There Was Light*. So far, the only thing he had come up with was a young-adult novel that dealt with the subject of Alzheimer's disease. It was good, but it was a far cry from *Then There Was Light*. The only other thing he had was a nonfiction work on the history of the United States Air Force flying team, the Blue Angels.

Tyler stood up and walked over to his window. Maybe Tracy could get away with it. Maybe the person who wrote *Then There Was Light* would never know. He would know, though. And just thinking about it made him physically ill.

Chapter Thirteen

A man writes to throw off the poison which he has accumulated because of his false way of life. He is trying to recapture his innocence, yet all he succeeds in doing (by writing) is to inoculate the world with a virus of his disillusionment. No man would set a word down on paper if he had the courage to live out what he believed in.

Henry Miller

Thanks to the helpful travel agent, Aislinn had taken with her at least a dozen or so maps and a brochure that talked about every historical landmark and point of interest on the Blue Ridge Parkway this side of the Tennessee border. After their visit with Snow, Aislinn and Robert spent the rest of the day exploring the little-traveled Cherohala Skyway that carried them along the ridge tops of the Appalachian Mountains and through several small villages each with its own craft shop. Eventually, in the early hours of dusk, they returned to the Biltmore Estate to have the steak dinner Aislinn had promised Robert earlier that morning.

The next day, they again got an early start, making their way back to Asheville to turn the Jeep in and catch their flight back to West Palm Beach. It was late afternoon by the time Robert dropped Aislinn off at her home. He carried her luggage into the house as well as a hand-stitched quilt, a box of mountain apples, and a paper bag with several jars of crabapple preserves. The quilt and apples she had purchased in one of the mountain craft stores. The home-made preserves were from Snow.

"Are you hungry? Would you like an omelet?" asked Aislinn putting Hemingway down and following him into the house.

"No. Thanks anyway. I'd better get going. I want to stop by the hospital and check on things."

Aislinn nodded and pulled Hemingway's stringy out of his travel bag. "Here's your stringy," she said handing it to the small dog. He immediately trotted off with it in his mouth to check on the rest of the house.

"I really had a nice time," said Robert. "Thanks for asking me to go along."

"I couldn't have found Snow without you." Aislinn laughed. "It was fun, wasn't it?"

"Heck fire, woman, I even got to meet Black Dog," Robert answered in an extremely poor impersonation of a mountain dialect. Then in a more serious tone, "When are you flying to New York?"

"Day after tomorrow. That gives me just enough time to get myself organized for the meeting."

"I hope everything goes well for you."

"Thanks."

Aislinn sensed a hesitation in Robert. He was holding back from saying something. She wasn't sure, but she suspected it had to do with Caldwell. "I'll let you know when I get back."

Robert backed out of the driveway and drove up Flagler toward the hospital. For some reason he was feeling slightly deflated, and he suspected it had to do with the man Aislinn was flying to New York to see. She obviously cared for him in ways other than professional, whether she admitted it to him or not, not that it was any of his business. She deserved to have a full and happy life with someone she loved. It's just that he had never even considered that it might be with someone other than him. He had meant it when he told Aislinn he had enjoyed himself. It had been so long since he had taken any time away from his patients and the hospital. He had been a little surprised at himself that he didn't even want to call while he was gone to find out how things were going. Maybe that was an indication that he needed to make a change. He had been pushing hard long enough.

Seeing Aislinn enjoying her work so much made him realize how much he was missing in his own work. He could remember when it had been fun. Every operation had been a challenge he looked forward to. Now, it seemed that everything was a problem—the surgeries he performed, the hospital he was trying to build, that business with Nurse Peters. The local papers were having a regular field day with that one, especially now that it had been discovered that she not only stole drugs, she misused hospital equipment. And then there was his own health. None of it brought him any pleasure. He felt tired all of the time. Instead of looking forward to each day, he dreaded it. Whatever goal he accomplished for the hospital, whatever surgery he performed, it was just something to cross off his endless list. It was one thing less he had to worry about, only to be replaced by something else. He didn't feel the passion he had once felt for what he did—at least not like Aislinn. The sad thing was, he didn't know what else he could do. Medicine had been his whole life. There was nothing else.

Robert turned into the hospital entrance and drove around back to his reserved parking space. Once inside he was greeted by other doctors, staff members and volunteers as he made his way to his office on the second floor. "Welcome back, doctor." "Have a good trip?" "Nice to see you back." Robert nodded and gave a brief reply to each of them.

The mail that had come in during his absence was stacked neatly on his desk. As he glanced through it, one envelope in particular caught his attention. It was from Absey Laboratories, one of the pharmaceutical research companies that the hospital worked with. The last he had heard, they were in the process of expanding their technology into stem cell research, something which Robert was particularly interested in because of its potential in advancing cures for diseases affecting the brain.

He located his letter opener and slit open the envelope. Inside was a single, type-written letter from Dr. Leonard Moulton, CEO of Absey Laboratories, inviting Robert to visit him at their administrative offices in Richmond, Virginia, to discuss the possibility of Robert participating in the new stem-cell research program. Robert sat down and read the letter again. He had never actually been involved in research, but it was something he had always been interested in doing. Maybe this was the change he needed.

Carefully he folded the letter and put it back in the envelope. He picked up his notepad and headed out the door toward the nurses' station to look at his patients' charts. Naturally, he would have to give this a great deal of consideration, but deep down he already knew what his decision would be.

* * *

Clarence Tyrell Wood was feeling better than he had felt in a long time. Ever since the storm—ever since seeing the angel—his mind had cleared. The voices had become quiet. He was still sleeping behind the trash bins at Sheldon-Talbert Publishing House, but that was out of necessity until he earned enough money to be able to afford a small room close to where he worked.

Tony Esposito and Jenny Cha, the husband and wife who owned and operated the small deli where he washed dishes, had offered to let him use the storage room in back of the restaurant for free, but Clarence couldn't accept that. He would wait. Eventually he would have enough money saved to be able to rent something. For now, he would stay where he was.

Tony and Jenny had helped other homeless men—mostly Vietnam vets who were having a hard time of it. Tony himself had served with the US Marines, and he had met Jenny while stationed near Cambodia. He had brought her back with him as a young master sergeant to the United States, and as soon as he got his honorary discharge, the two of them bought what amounted to a rat-infested hole-in-the-wall on one of the side streets a few blocks off Manhattan. It took a lot of hard work, but eventually they cleaned it up, made it into a small diner, and named it the Backstreet Deli. Now, after twenty years, it was still providing a good income for them.

Most of their customers came from the nearby neighborhoods. Occasionally people stopped by from the other side of town. They had a reputation for having fresh breads, good salads, sour pickles, and lean meats. As far as Tony was concerned, that was all that mattered.

Jenny had brought into the union an understanding of Eastern practices and philosophy. Her knowledge of acupuncture and herbs was extensive, and when Clarence first started working at the deli, she encouraged him to drink a hot tea she prepared for him on a daily basis. That along with a couple of acupuncture treatments soon made the headaches along with the delusions he experienced disappear. The occasional alterations in earth's magnetic force field no longer brought discomfort or concern. His thoughts became coherent and rational. All of the things that had once produced anxiety and debilitating pain, were now memories carefully sorted, analyzed, defined, and categorized. He remembered things from his childhood and what it was like growing up in south Florida, and he could distinguish those things from his time spent in the military as a young man. He understood his past and the present, and for the first time in many years, he looked forward to the future.

Most days, Clarence washed dishes. He also kept the floors and counters clean. Occasionally, when the deli was really busy, he helped wait on people. Tony and Jenny trusted him, and he always did a good job. Back at the trash bins behind Sheldon-Talbert, he still kept his cart with all his bags of books and other possessions, but he was no longer fearful of leaving them behind whenever he went to work. He awoke each morning feeling rested and alive and eager to go to work. The parallel lines and the number seven were no longer of paramount importance in his life. He continued to use the restroom inside the big publishing house to wash up each morning and then again each evening. No one ever complained or said anything to him. And Tony had given him some work clothes to wear which were a lot nicer than what he had.

So things were finally working out for Clarence. Everything in his life seemed to be settling into place. The only thing that didn't fit into any of the categories or definitions, no matter how much he tried to analyze it, was a certain brown envelope that contained the page with the words, *Then There Was Light* by Snow Henderson, typed on it. But that was why the angel had appeared to him. Eventually, he would understand and he would be able to put it away with all of his other things.

* * *

Aislinn was still thinking about Robert when she finished unpacking her things and went back downstairs to check her phone messages. He seemed to really enjoy going to Asheville with her. She couldn't remember ever seeing him so relaxed—certainly not since she had known him. She just wasn't sure how much good it did, though. Once they returned home, he had obviously become uptight again. Lately, he didn't seem to be able to handle all of the stress that went along with his job the way he once did. She only hoped that he would be able to make the necessary adjustments in his life before it was too late. His body was already warning him. It was up to him now.

Lorraine had called from New York, apparently the same evening that Aislinn and Robert had left for Asheville. She wanted to talk to Aislinn as soon as possible—it didn't matter what time she got in. Aislinn carried the phone into the den and sat back on the sofa, pulling her legs up under her. Hemingway curled up next to her, chomping on stringy. Lorraine must have been close to the phone because she answered immediately.

"Hi, Lorraine. We just got back about an hour ago. Is everything all right? You sounded a little worried."

The fact that Aislinn had said, *We just got back,* didn't go unnoticed by Lorraine. She suspected it was her ex-husband she was referring to, but she would deal with that little situation later. Right now there was something else on her mind.

"Aislinn, I talked to my friend at Sheldon-Talbert, the woman in marketing I mentioned to you?"

"Yes. Was she able to tell you anything?"

"Apparently, this Tracy Cord is a real piece of work. She has been with Sheldon-Talbert about four years now. She started out as a reader and has advanced up the ladder to associate editor mainly through finding choice material to publish. It's because of her that Sheldon-Talbert has had so many best sellers published in the last couple of years. Now, it seems, she has also written a novel called *The Enlightened.*"

"It sounds like she is extremely ambitious as well as talented," offered Aislinn.

"I don't know about that. My friend didn't have all the facts, but she had heard that Ms. Cord was fired from her last job as a journalist because she misrepresented something she had written. Apparently she made up several stories and passed them off as true. She almost received a Pulitzer for them, but she got caught. Of course, she was using a different name then."

Aislinn rubbed her forehead. She didn't like what she was hearing. If the woman had a history of being professionally dishonest, it stood to reason that she could have stolen Snow's work as well.

"There's something else you need to know." Lorraine was obviously having trouble saying it.

"Listen, Lorraine, don't tell me anything you don't want to. If you feel you are betraying your friend's trust, I can accept that."

"No. It's not that."

Aislinn heard her sigh into the phone. "Apparently Tyler Kane has been dating Tracy for some time now. My friend told me that a lot of the other editors at Sheldon-Talbert suspect that he might have helped her find some of those manuscripts that got published—maybe even gave her some that had been submitted to Kane Publishing. It could just be professional jealousy on their part, but the odds of her getting her hands on so many manuscripts, especially when they didn't go through the normal channels of submission, seem a little high."

Now Aislinn understood Lorraine's hesitation. Of all the people she would least want to hurt, it was Caldwell Kane. The very idea that his own son was mishandling materials sent to Kane Publishing House was difficult to understand or deal with.

"Lorraine, there might be a real simple explanation here. I'm not going to jump to any conclusions, so don't you, either. Meanwhile, we'll just keep this information between the two of us for now. I'll know more after the meeting. Do you agree?"

"I don't plan to tell another living soul. I'm just glad I could talk to you about it. You can't imagine how this has upset me. All of them are like my own family—Caldwell, Jason, and Tyler. If anything happens to one of them, it hurts me deeply."

"I understand. I honestly do, Lorraine. We'll get this sorted out, and then everything will be all right—even better than before." At least that is what Aislinn was hoping. She knew without a doubt that Snow had written *Then There Was Light*, and that *The Enlightened* was a poor imitation of it, camouflaged as a work of fiction.

Changing the subject, Aislinn asked, "How is Caldwell?"

"All I can tell you is, if you don't hurry and get up here, he'll have to be committed. I've never seen a man so eager to see a woman as he is to see you," she answered candidly.

Aislinn smiled. "I'm looking forward to seeing him as well."

After hanging up her immediate concern was for Tyler. He had been so friendly and pleasant to her when she met him. She had recognized an innocence about him that usually becomes lost or diminished with life's more difficult experiences. She remembered the first evening in New York when Caldwell had taken her to the Greek restaurant for dinner. For some reason when Caldwell was talking about Tyler, she had remembered her grandmother's words, *People give strange things in the name of love, when in fact all they have to do is give of themselves.* Now she knew why.

Chapter Fourteen

Fundamentally, all writing is about the same thing; it's about dying, about the brief flicker of time we have here, and the frustration that it creates.

Mordecai Richler

Caldwell had been calling Aislinn every day—sometimes two or three times—just to talk about anything and everything that came to mind. The strange thing about it was that very little of their conversations actually had anything to do with the manuscripts being sent to Kane Publishing House. Somehow that entire subject had gotten shoved back behind more personal discussions. He was convinced he was going through some sort of second childhood. If not that, then he had completely lost his mind.

Ever since his wife's death, there had been no other woman in Caldwell's life. Kane Publishing Company was what mattered; that was what took his all of his attention and energy. And then something curious happened. It was almost as though he knew just from hearing about her and reading her books that it was inevitable he would fall in love with Aislinn. After meeting her for the first time in the airport, he was convinced of it. Now, deciding what to do with it was the problem. He was several years older than Aislinn, he still wasn't clear on what kind of relationship existed between her and her ex-husband, and even though she always sounded pleased and happy to hear from him, he didn't know what she thought about him. He wasn't even sure he wanted to know. Worrying about it was driving him nuts. And, yet, he was happier right now than he had been in years.

Her flight was due in at 7:45 a.m. If it was on time, they wouldn't have any trouble getting back to the office by nine o'clock, which was when the editorial staff meeting was scheduled to start. If they were delayed for any reason, Mrs. McLaughlin had been instructed to hold up the meeting until Aislinn and Caldwell got there.

Actually, it really wasn't necessary for him to even go to the airport to meet her, but there was simply no way he was not going. He had thought of very little else in the four weeks she had last visited. Now that he was actually going to see her again, he didn't want to waste a single moment of the time they could spend together.

Dan wasn't in the most cheerful of moods when he picked up Caldwell at his apartment due to the extreme early hour. Seeing Frederick at the door with a sour expression and rolling his eyes as Caldwell left didn't help matters any either, but he brightened considerably once they got to the airport and he was able to find a cup of strong black coffee. If anything, he was glad the day had finally arrived when his boss would get to see Aislinn Marchánt again. Everyone who spent any time around Caldwell Kane was feeling slightly off-center, not knowing what to expect with his mood swings. Frederick had been in a blue funk for a couple of weeks over all of the extra duties he had been given in order to get Caldwell organized and in shape for his visitor. Even Mrs. Hutchinson, the housekeeper at the Hamptons, had been put to the test with her extra burdens and responsibilities that exceeded well beyond the norm in preparation of Aislinn's first visit there.

Caldwell Kane wasn't the type of man to fool around. He knew his own mind, and he didn't shy away from making decisions. The way Dan had it figured out, this visit would be the determining one: it would determine whether Caldwell really was in love with Aislinn, or if he was just experiencing a testosterone surge. For Caldwell's sake, Dan hoped that Aislinn was everything Caldwell believed she was. Life was simply too short to go through it without someone to love. Dan also hoped for Caldwell's sake that Aislinn had the same feelings for him.

Dan carried his steaming cup past several arrival gates toward the exit where he had parked the limo. If her flight was on time, it would be another thirty minutes before she arrived. There were only a few people waiting that time of morning. Off to one side, sitting alone and staring blankly into space was Caldwell Kane. "Jeesus," muttered Dan as he walked through the open electronic doors to go wait in the limo.

* * *

Aislinn didn't know which was making her more nervous—seeing Caldwell again in person, or having to deal with the problem this Tracy Cord had created. Talking to him on the phone each day was one thing. There was a comfort level built in by the physical distance separating them which made it easier to talk about matters that normally would not have been discussed until much later in the relationship. Without even trying, Aislinn found herself caring whether Frederick's back pain was eased with the new medication, or if Dan won at his last weekly poker game, or if Mrs. Hutchinson had found a suitable replacement for the young woman who normally did all of the laundry at the Hamptons home but who had taken maternity leave. Unaware of when it happened, Aislinn had involved herself into Caldwell's concerns and into his life, just as he had done in her own, and she loved every minute of it.

Aislinn pulled off the dress she had on and threw it on top of the pile of other clothes she had already tried. Nothing seemed to look good on her, including the soft brown pants suit that had looked perfectly fine to wear when she tried it on the night before. "This is ridiculous," she said to Hemingway who was curled in a tight ball on her pillow trying to sleep. "What difference does it make what I wear?" But it did make a difference. In spite of what she told herself, she wanted to look pretty for Caldwell, and yet professional. The fact that it was four o'clock in the morning when she was trying to make that decision didn't help.

Without a doubt, Caldwell had awakened something within her. She loved Robert and she always would, but ever since meeting Caldwell Kane, she had started feeling things that before she had only experienced in her imagination and written about in her novels. It was silly. In fact, nothing about her feelings for Caldwell made any sense. And yet, everything about them made sense. The one thing that Aislinn had missed the most in her relationship with Robert was knowing that she could always depend on him to be there for her. He never was. It was always the hospital or his patients that came first. Whether it was true or not, the message she got from that over the three years they were married was that she didn't matter enough to be in a place of priority. The moment of truth—that defining moment—finally came when Aislinn's father died and Robert was too busy taking care of other people to even go to the funeral with her. It was then that Aislinn decided she would rather live as a woman alone than to repeatedly be disappointed.

Looking back on everything now, it was probably all for the best. She and Robert remained close. Of course, Aislinn developed a couple of new worry lines in her face and a few new gray hairs, but, she eventually walked away with a deeper understanding of who she was and what she wanted in life—or at least what she didn't want. She had been drawn to Caldwell naturally out of their mutual love of books as well as other things, but also because he so tangibly represented the very thing Aislinn needed and wanted the most: he was there for her. Analyzing her feelings for Caldwell did absolutely no good. She had definitely been struck by that mythological arrow from the bow of Cupid, and like it or not, there was nothing she could do about it.

Aislinn pulled a two-piece, pale yellow knit suit out of the closet and put it on. "This will have to do," she told Hemingway. An hour later, ticket in hand, she boarded her plane. Hemingway had been happily relocated with Lottie, and Aislinn's baggage was checked since she had packed for a longer stay this time. She kept with her the bag containing her laptop and notebook which she wrote in, and another shoulder bag that held several manuscripts which she would recommend to the editorial staff if no one else did. Included with these was Lottie's book, *My Father's Keeper*. She didn't tell Lottie she was going to take it with her. She didn't want to unnecessarily get her hopes up. But it was one of the manuscripts she wanted to discuss with Tyler, since it was nonfiction, and she felt fairly confident he would like it enough to want to pursue it. *Then There Was Light*, on the other hand, was another matter.

* * *

Ever since finishing the rewrite of *My Father's Keeper*, Lottie's energy had been soaring. Writing the story the way she did, not to place blame but to tell of her life during a period in time that could never be repeated, gave her a sense of renewal, a sense of purpose and, strangely enough, hope. Now with the manuscript in Aislinn's hands, Lottie wanted to move on to something else constructive and creative; namely, she wanted to refurbish the old house.

Things had been the same for too long. It was her house, after all, and she could decorate it as she pleased. Other than making an office out of one of the downstairs parlors off the central hall, everything had remained just the way it was when her parents were still living there. It was time for a change.

She hired a contractor she knew and an architect who specialized in renovating old homes. She familiarized herself with terms like "historical integrity," and learned the differences between such processes as stylized leaf and floral work, and sponging, stenciling, and marbleizing.

The home had originally been furnished in the high Victorian style where each room was crammed full of furniture, heavy fabrics were used in abundance, and every available surface was overflowing with knickknacks. Such displays were a means of showing off the Howard's cultural interests, prosperity and status. With the passing of time, Mrs. Howard, Lottie's mother, became interested in the popular Aesthetic Movement, where furniture was inspired by Elizabethan, Classical Greek and traditional Georgian forms, and fabrics were generally lighter and more subtly colored. It was Lottie's desire to stay within the character of the home's "Old Florida" architecture, but adopt a cleaner and more up-to-date look in the interior. It was also time to bring the plumbing and electrical wiring up to code, which meant several of the walls had to be broken into and then replastered.

Since Hemingway was her boarder, she was careful to keep him out of harm's way with so much going on. Quite often, the two of them could be found in the backyard sitting under a particularly large ficus tree and watching all of the activity from a safe distance. Occasionally, Lottie would have her trunk next to her so she could once again go through the photographs at her leisure. Other times she would have her sewing basket as she undertook some sort of sewing project usually involving tatting and crocheting.

She never strayed from the house too far or for too long in case a question arose requiring her attention or a decision needed to be made.

With the implementation of each plan, new problems arose and additional decisions were required. Most people would have been distraught over all of the noise and confusion of seeing their home torn apart, but Lottie was enjoying every minute of it. Just as writing her book, *My Father's Keeper,* had been therapeutic for Lottie, she found that by creating a home that suited her own tastes she was once again releasing something from deep within her soul—something that was an expression of herself.

Chapter Fifteen

*To write is to make oneself the echo of what cannot cease speaking—
and since it cannot, in order to become its echo I have, in a way, to
silence it. I bring to this incessant speech the decisiveness,
the authority of my own silence.*

Maurice Blanchot

Aislinn's flight was on time. Dan took the two bags she had with
her and locked them in the limo. Then he went to the baggage claim
area to pick up her other suitcase. While this was going on Caldwell
and Aislinn were grinning at each other like a couple of kids seeing
Disney World for the first time.

"How have you been?" Caldwell asked Aislinn for the third time.

"Fine. Really fine."

"Well, you look . . ." Caldwell's eyes covered Aislinn once more in
one, full, comprehensive glance, "beautiful."

Aislinn was glad she had decided on the yellow knit.

"Sir, I believe you have a meeting to go to." Dan had been waiting
by the limo assuming Caldwell and Aislinn would come on out to
where it was parked. When they hadn't come out after fifteen minutes,
he went back into the large waiting area to find them still standing
where he had left them and still grinning.

"Oh, right. Let's get on our way then." Caldwell guided Aislinn
past several arrival gates to the exit. An hour and a half later they drove
up to Kane Publishing House. Dan let them out at the front entrance
and quickly retrieved the two small bags Aislinn needed. The rest of
her luggage he would keep for her. She and Caldwell were so busy
discussing the flower boxes by the entrance that she would have gone

off and left the two bags on the sidewalk if Dan hadn't said something to remind her.

Lorraine McLaughlin was watching for them from her office window, and as soon as she saw the limo pull up, she went outside to greet Aislinn. Even though the two women had met for the first time only a month earlier, they had become good friends during that time. Because of her age, and because of her close relationship to the Kane family, Lorraine had never befriended any of the other female staff members working at Kane. Most of the other women were quite a bit younger with husbands and children, and she really didn't have that much in common with them. Aislinn was different. She was easy to talk to, she was concerned about Kane Publishing House, but more than that, she cared for the Kane family—at least Caldwell. Lorraine felt she had a true comrade on her side—someone she could confide in and trust. With any luck at all, Aislinn would also become part of the Kane family, and nothing would please Lorraine more.

"There's that pretty girl," she greeted Aislinn. "I was beginning to think Caldwell had decided to take you on to the Hamptons and not even bother coming into work today."

"Now, Mrs. McLaughlin, you know me better than that."

"We'll talk later," Lorraine whispered as she led Aislinn into the conference room.

Everyone was already sitting at the table waiting to start the meeting. As before coffee and pastries had been set out, and flowers decorated the large walnut conference table. Tyler was the first person to welcome Aislinn back and to ask about her flight while Caldwell fixed her and himself a cup of coffee. Several of the people in attendance observed that he served her coffee black with a little sugar which made for speculation that he was apparently already aware of how she preferred it.

When Tyler finished talking, Jason, more reserved, shook her hand. "It's nice to see you again, Aislinn."

"Thank you, Jason. It's nice to be here." Aislinn smiled up at Caldwell as he set the coffee in front of her. Then she pulled out the manuscripts along with her notes from the bag she had brought with her that she had earmarked earlier as good candidates for possible publication. Caldwell had asked her to feel free to discuss any manuscript she liked if it wasn't brought up by one of the other editors. For the next three hours, each of the associate editors discussed the pros and cons of the manuscripts they were interested in seeing get published. So far, there were no surprises. All but two of the manuscripts she had marked for possible publication were being brought up by each of the editors and discussed. Those two were similar to something Kane had already published in recent years and, therefore, couldn't be used. The meeting went pretty much as Aislinn had predicted, but Tyler hadn't talked about his selections yet.

It was 12:30 when sandwiches were brought in, and after a brief break the meeting resumed. Tyler was the first to start following the break, and he immediately launched into a discussion on the manuscript that discussed the history of the Blue Angels, the United States Air Force flying team. Everyone agreed with his assessment of it. It would make a good nonfiction supplement to the middle-grade educational curricula, and could be sold in both the trade and library markets. Next on his list for discussion was a young adult novel, *The Thoughts of One*, which was a heart-rendering story of a young girl who had lost her grandmother to Alzheimer's disease. This, too, was accepted by the other editors to be a good choice for the young adult market. The only downside to each of them, of course, was that the markets in which they would be placed were limited. Neither manuscript would bring in the revenues that an adult best seller would.

Aislinn made more notes and slipped each manuscript into the accepted pile after it was discussed. The only remaining manuscript in the stack she had brought with her to discuss at the meeting was *Then There Was Light.* She looked at Tyler expectantly.

"Well, that's all I have at this time," he announced.

Aislinn was devastated. She glanced over at Lorraine who was staring down at her own notebook. This meant that Tyler was somehow involved with the mishandling of manuscripts sent to Kane Publishing House—certainly Snow Henderson's manuscript. She felt Caldwell's hand. "Are you all right?" he asked apparently sensing something was wrong.

"Yes," she answered unsteadily. She took a drink of water and then breathed in deeply. How in heaven's name could she tell Caldwell that his own son was working against the company. She had been hired to help discover the truth, regardless of what that truth was. Keeping it inside and not exposing it would only make things worse in the long run. She pulled out her copy of *Then There Was Light.* "Tyler, perhaps you didn't get a copy of this?" She wanted to give him every benefit of the doubt. However, the expression on his face when he saw the title told her he had seen it. She pushed on. "I personally found this to be one of the best nonfiction testimonials, if you will, I have ever read. It's exciting, it's honest, and it has a certain element of the unexplained that most readers like. I truly think it can be a best seller."

Tyler scooted down in his chair as Aislinn talked about the subject and theme of the story and the unusual way it was presented by the author.

"Have you read it, Tyler?" asked Caldwell when she had finished.

"Yes, I have."

"What is your opinion of it?"

Tyler didn't hesitate. "I think Aislinn is right on the money."

Aislinn glanced again at Lorraine and this time found her looking at her. At least he didn't lie to his father, her look seemed to say.

"Well, then, Mrs. McLaughlin, if you will see to it that the others get a copy of this?" He glanced around the table, "I would like your comments on my desk by no later than Monday."

The other editors sensed something had just happened, but they didn't understand quite what it was. Now, out of curiosity, they couldn't wait to read *Then There Was Light*.

When the meeting was finally over, Caldwell took Aislinn back to his office to wait while he returned some phone calls before leaving for the weekend. Aislinn felt sick. She knew she wouldn't be able to go to the Hamptons with Caldwell until she told him what was going on. He might not even want her to go with him after that.

"This won't take long," he said smiling at her and picking up the phone. "Then we'll be on our way. Make yourself comfortable."

Aislinn tried to smile, but couldn't. She couldn't even sit down. She should never have gotten involved in the first place. Now, it was too late.

There was a tap on the door and Tyler poked his head in. "Am I interrupting anything?" he asked coming in and closing the door behind him.

Caldwell motioned for him to come in. Apparently the person he was calling wasn't in. "Well, that was easy. He can just call me back the first of the week." He looked at Aislinn then back at Tyler. "Have I missed something here?"

"I need to tell you something, Dad, before it gets any worse than it already is."

"Why don't I go find Lorraine," said Aislinn. "Maybe she needs some help with something." Aislinn walked toward the door.

"Please don't leave, Aislinn." Tyler put his hand out. "I want you to hear this, too."

Aislinn sat down then. For the next thirty minutes Tyler talked. He made no excuses; he only presented the facts in a clear, straightforward manner. A couple of times Caldwell interrupted him with an exclamation—out of shock and anger more than anything else, but Aislinn doubted if he even realized it. When Tyler had finished telling everything, he said he was sorry. Aislinn felt her heart break for him. The silence in the room was ear-shattering.

"I'm not going to tell you that what you did was totally stupid," said Caldwell. "I think you already know that." He ran his hand through his hair. "What we need to do now is figure out how to proceed from this point on."

"Caldwell, I don't want to be in the way. Maybe it would be better if I go back home and visit the Hamptons with you another time." Aislinn could sense the pain Tyler was feeling. He, of all people, needed to spend some time with Caldwell—to be reassured if nothing else.

"I wouldn't even think of it. If you don't mind, though, I want to see if I can get hold of Oscar Sheldon. There's always the chance that we can settle this like gentlemen and not get the lawyers involved, even if I do think Sheldon is a jackass. Do you mind waiting for just a few minutes?"

"Of course not. This takes priority over everything else right now as far as I am concerned." Aislinn went over and sat next to Tyler who had collapsed on the sofa. "I am so sorry about this, Tyler."

"Don't be. It needed to all come out. I don't think I could have lived with myself otherwise."

The two sat quietly while Caldwell placed the call. He finally got hold of Sheldon, but when he explained the situation, Sheldon refused to discuss it further. "At the very least, you need to question the woman who claims to have written *The Enlightened,*" said Caldwell. He was obviously getting upset. "Fine. If that's the way you want to play it. You will be hearing from our attorneys." He slammed the phone down. "I told you he was a jackass." He stood up and walked over to where Aislinn and his son were sitting. "The main problem I see that we have here is actually proving that this Tracy Cord, or whatever her name is, plagiarized Snow Henderson's work. We have to have something concrete."

"Man, I really screwed up this time." Tyler shook his head.

"Well, if it will make you feel any better, Snow Henderson is quite a woman. She is exactly the way she sounds in her book. She is direct, honest, and hardworking. It will mean so much to her if her story does get published."

"You've met her?" asked Caldwell.

Aislinn told him how she had come across the advance summary of *The Enlightened* in the spring forecasts of *Publisher's Weekly*. "It was just too similar to *Then There Was Light* to be a coincidence. I wanted to know which one was the original."

"So you went to North Carolina and found Snow Henderson?" he asked Aislinn, smiling. "So you went to North Carolina and found Snow Henderson," he repeated, this time making it sound like a statement.

"I know, it sounds crazy," said Aislinn. She looked at Tyler. "You might as well know everything. I suspected someone—one of the associate editors—was taking submissions sent to Kane Publishing and giving them to Sheldon-Talbert. Since most of the best sellers they had recently published were nonfiction, and since that is your area of expertise, I couldn't help but think that you were somehow involved, Tyler. These things happen. We get caught up in something that seems innocent enough, but, too late, we realize it is something else entirely." She looked at Caldwell. "That is where I have been the past couple of days. Snow showed me her hand-written original while I was there. She also told me about each of the lightning episodes in her story. I am convinced that she wrote it."

"Well, there is nothing else we can do for now. Let's get out of here and enjoy our weekend."

Tyler got up to leave.

"I'll want to talk to you later," Caldwell told him.

After he left Aislinn said, "Don't be too hard on him, Caldwell. He is the second child, the second son, at that."

"I don't understand."

"There has always been someone ahead of him. It is hard to be in that position especially when that someone is as smart and motivated as Jason. I am sure there have been many times when Tyler wanted to overtake Jason as the older sibling, competitively speaking. Instead, he has learned to rely on his charm. The second born often become skilled at developing social skills, because it is important to them that they are liked. I'm sure his motive in trying to help Tracy wasn't to harm Kane Publishing Company but because he wanted her to like him."

Caldwell stood looking at Aislinn. Then, without saying anything he drew her close and wrapped his arms around her. "Thank you, Aislinn," he whispered.

On the way out Caldwell instructed Lorraine to get hold of Donald Leer, the company's lawyer. "Ask him to drive out to the shore on Saturday and I'll feed him lunch," Caldwell. "I'll call him tonight and let him know what is going on. Tell Tyler and Jason I'd like for them to be there, too." Lorraine didn't know what had taken place. She had seen the dejected look on Tyler's face when he left his father's office.

She didn't know where Jason was. And now, looking at Caldwell and Aislinn leaving together for the weekend at the Hamptons, she couldn't totally read Aislinn, but Caldwell had never looked happier. "Oh, by the way, what are you doing Saturday for lunch, Mrs. McLaughlin?" Caldwell asked.

"Nothing. Do you need something?"

"I'll send Dan for you. You need to get away from the office more often."

Aislinn smiled at her as she and Caldwell disappeared into the limo. They hadn't gone a block when Aislinn suddenly sat up straight. "I've just thought of something."

"What? Did you leave something back at the office? Because if you did, Mrs. McLaughlin can . . ."

"No, that's not it." She took Caldwell's hand. "Would you mind if we went by Sheldon-Talbert Publishing House?"

Caldwell hesitated for a moment and then leaned forward. "Take us by Sheldon-Talbert Publishing House, Dan."

Dan turned right at the next corner and did a U-turn in the street which sent them back in the direction they had just come. "What is it about Sheldon-Talbert Publishing House," he muttered under his breath. Within minutes they drove past the office building. "Do you want me to drive around back again, Aislinn?"

"Yes, if you don't mind."

Caldwell raised his eyebrows. "I asked Dan to show me where Sheldon-Talbert was located the last time I was here," explained Aislinn.

The large silver limo turned off the main boulevard onto the driveway leading behind the publishing house to the parking lot in the rear. Aislinn craned her neck to look out of the windows.

"What is it?" asked Caldwell.

Then she saw him. His clothes were nicer, and he had gotten a haircut and shave since the last time she saw him, but he was there. Next to the trash bins. "Stop here, Dan." As soon as he stopped, she opened the door and got out.

"Wait, Aislinn." Without hesitating, Caldwell jumped out with her.

Dan, not wanting any trouble for his employer and his employer's friend, felt it best that he be as close to both of them as possible. He, too, got out and stood out of the way, but near enough should he be needed.

"What are you looking for?" Caldwell asked as he glanced around the area. Then he saw him.

Chapter Sixteen

The worth of a book is to be measured by what you can carry away from it.

James Bryce

Oscar Sheldon had been in the publishing business for almost as long as Caldwell Kane. He had built up a reputation for being ruthless, competitive, and hard-driving when it came to running his business. But most of all he was known for his temper, and right now it was taking on dimensions of mammoth proportions.

"Find Tracy Cord—NOW!" he yelled to Nancy, his secretary, who immediately went flying down the hall. When she didn't find Tracy in her office, she sent out what was equivalent to an all-points bulletin used by the law enforcement agencies in an attempt to locate her. She had never seen Sheldon so angry, and she sure didn't want any of that anger to touch her. By the time several minutes had passed and she still hadn't found Tracy, tears started to well up in her eyes. She was going to lose her job over this—she just knew it.

Back in Sheldon's office, thick cigar smoke circled the desk where he sat. Black ashes spilled down the front of his tie, but either he didn't notice or he didn't care. He had pulled out a copy of *The Enlightened*, practically ripping each page as he finished glancing over it. It was bad enough that this could happen in his firm, but to have that cocky bastard Caldwell Kane of all people call him on it was just about more than he could stand. Still, he shouldn't have spoken to him the way he did.

Sheldon had suspected that the manuscript might not be Tracy's work. After all, he had been around the block a few times. He had a pretty good instinct about these things. But he had chosen not to question her about it. He was too eager to get another best seller. Now, with Kane on his ass, if he pursued the publication of it, he stood to lose not only his reputation but his entire company. Even if he didn't publish it, Kane was pious enough to probably want to take him to court anyway just on the principle of the thing. Well, he wasn't going to let that happen. He would have to put a stop to all of it before it went any further, but the first thing he wanted to do was to see Tracy Cord and find out what in the hell she thought she was doing. He slammed the manuscript into the waste basket under his desk knocking it over and spilling its contents.

"Tracy Cord, get in here," he bellowed out the door, and Nancy, who was running from office to office looking for her, burst into tears.

* * *

It had been a good day. Tony had given Clarence a small raise even though he had only been working at the deli for slightly less than a month. And Jenny had also found some more clothes for Clarence— things Tony had outgrown and could no longer wear. "I like my own cooking too much," Tony had told Clarence while patting his stomach. "Jenny is threatening to put me on a diet."

Now, with the weekend coming up, Clarence was going to start looking around for someplace to live. Nothing fancy. Just someplace that he could call his own. There were several rooming houses that he walked by each day not too far from the deli. A room of his own would be nice. The plastic bags he carried all his stuff in were all right as far as keeping everything dry, but they were a nuisance to keep up with and they wouldn't last forever. And, besides, the weather would soon be changing. He sure didn't want to spend another cold winter outside if he could help it.

Clarence started rearranging his bags when he heard the engine. He knew without even looking that it was the same as before. The angel was returning. Perhaps now he would understand.

The long silver limo emerged from the alleyway and slowly circled the parking lot. It was so bright and shiny, it reminded Clarence of a chariot. He moved away from his hiding place behind the trash bins and stepped out into the open. The limo stopped, and a young woman got out. It was the same woman he had seen before. It was the angel.

Clarence was so intent on watching Aislinn that he didn't notice the other two men. When he saw them, he felt a little confused. He hadn't seen them before. The woman walked toward him.

"Hello. I am Aislinn Marchánt," she said softly. "What is your name?"

"Clarence Tyrell Wood."

"Do you mind if I talk to you for a moment?"

When the angel of the Lord appeared to Gideon, he said, "The Lord is with you, mighty warrior" (JDG 6), Clarence heard the voice say. "You came before," said Clarence.

"Yes, I did. And when I was here you spoke the words, 'Then There Was Light.' Do you remember that?"

Caldwell glanced over at Dan who had moved up slightly closer in order to hear the conversation.

"Yes. That is what was in that brown envelope," said Clarence. "Or I think it was." Clarence looked at Caldwell and Dan. "I sometimes get confused, but lately I have been a lot better," he explained. "I have a job now, too."

"Tell me about the envelope," encouraged Aislinn. "The brown envelope."

It took a little doing to follow what Clarence said. The part about a dog made no sense at all, but the rest of it, if looked at in a certain light, Aislinn understood. Apparently, Clarence believed in numerology, for he had mentioned the number seven several times. What had the Santerian priest said? That the number sixteen, which when broken down was also the number seven, had something to do with the basic building blocks of Destiny—her Destiny. "Remember it," the priest had told her. "In time it will have a special meaning in your life." Clarence seemed to be saying the same thing.

Caldwell looked down at Aislinn. "Is he saying that he saw the manuscript *Then There Was Light* in Tracy's apartment?"

"I think so," she said. "Of course, even if we present that as evidence, she could claim that it was her own manuscript that she wrote."

"*Then There Was Light*, by Snow Henderson," said Clarence.

"You saw the title page?" asked Caldwell.

"I saw what I saw," Clarence answered.

"That makes all the difference." Caldwell looked at Dan and smiled. Get something to write with. I want to know where we can get in touch with Clarence if and when we need to. "Clarence, I want to explain to you what you saw. That woman who had the brown envelope stole a manuscript from another woman, and now she is trying to claim that she wrote it herself. I don't think it will come to this, but if we have to go to court over it, would you be willing to testify about what you saw before a judge? Of course, I will pay you for your time and any expenses you incur." The last thing Caldwell wanted to do was take this to court, especially since it appeared that Clarence had broken into Tracy's apartment in order to see what was in the brown envelope. Otherwise, how else could he have seen the manuscript? He didn't want to make any unnecessary trouble for the guy if he could avoid it.

"I will do what I can," Clarence answered. *This is the verdict: Light has come into the world, but men loved darkness instead of light because their deeds were evil. Everyone who does evil hates the light, and will not come into the light for fear that his deeds will be exposed. But whoever lives by the truth comes into the light, so that it may be seen plainly that what he has done has been done through God* (John 3:19-22).

Caldwell handed Clarence his business card. "This is in case you need to get in touch with me for any reason."

"Thank you, Clarence, for talking to us." Aislinn offered her hand to the old man not knowing for sure if it would be accepted. It was.

"Did anyone ever tell you that you look like an angel?" Clarence asked.

"If not, she's going to be hearing it a lot from now on," said Caldwell.

Clarence watched until the limo disappeared from view. So now he had the answer to his problem about the brown envelope. He had known all along that there was something evil about it. But now that evil was going to be dealt with. *The unfolding of your words gives light; it gives understanding to the simple* (PSA 27:130).

It had been a good day.

* * *

"Are you spying on that poor old man again, Scott?" Darlene sashayed into his office, followed closely behind by Tracy Cord carrying a stack of manuscripts.

Scott was standing to one side of the window looking through a small area of the blinds he had separated with his fingers. Embarrassed to be caught, he tried to act like he was straightening the blind. "These damn things are cheap," he said yanking on the cord. "You'd think that Sheldon-Talbert could afford something better."

Darlene giggled. "Scott thinks the Professor is out to get him," she said to Tracy.

"I don't blame him. He gives me the creeps, too, always sneaking around." Tracy put the manuscripts down on Scott's desk. "Would you mind looking at these for me, Scott? I'm not going to be able to get to them."

"You go ahead and laugh if you want to, Darlene," Scott said ignoring Tracy's request, "but you're not going to believe what I just saw." He took a position behind his desk and sat down. "In fact, I am willing to bet that Sheldon would be interested in knowing what I saw, too."

Tracy walked over to the window and glanced out. "What did you see, Scott?"

Scott knew he had their interest. He would just lead them on for a while to pay Darlene back for teasing him. "Why should I tell you? You are already in good with the boss, Miss Author/Editor. Maybe I'll keep this bit of information for myself."

"Oh, come on, Scott. Tell us if you are going to. I've got things to do."

"Well, you know that big silver limousine that Caldwell Kane rides around in?"

Tracy snapped her head in the direction of Scott. "You mean Kane Publishing Company?"

"Yeah. That's right. It was just here. Parked right back there. And Caldwell Kane, his driver, and some woman got out and talked to the old man. They looked real chummy, too, writing stuff down, shaking hands." He looked at the two women smugly.

"Writing stuff down?" Tracy pulled the blinds open fully and took a good look. They weren't there now, but why had they talked to the Professor? She didn't like it one bit. She had caught the Professor several times following her around. She had even seen him hanging around where she lived. She wondered if it had anything to do with her book. Maybe Kane Publishing House was paying him to spy on her.

Without saying a word, she walked out of Scott's office. She wanted to talk to Sheldon—now. Darlene said something to her, but she didn't stop to respond. Tracy had been through a scandal once. She definitely didn't want to go through another one. Not if she could help it. If she got to Sheldon before anyone else did, she could make him believe that she was the one who had been plagiarized. As she marched down the hall toward Sheldon's office, she heard someone yelling her name. It was Sheldon. She immediately turned around, stopped by her office long enough to grab her purse, and walked right out of the building.

* * *

Robert felt a little foolish knocking on Miss Howard's front door. He had only seen the woman a couple of times, both times in her car getting ready to go someplace. But Aislinn hadn't told him when she would be back and he really wanted to talk to her.

There was a lot of hammering going on inside the house and the jaw-clenching, shrill noise of some kind of electrical tool. He doubted if anyone could hear him. He stepped off the front porch and walked around to the side of the house. There in the back under one of the biggest ficus trees he had ever seen was Miss Howard. She was sitting in a large, upholstered chair with a fold-out table positioned in front of her. Wallpaper books and fabric swatches and paint samples were everywhere. Hunkered down between Miss Howard's lap and the arm of the chair was Hemingway.

Hemingway saw Robert first and immediately jumped down from his cozy spot to run over and greet him. Miss Howard peered over her silver half-framed glasses to see what had gotten Hemingway's attention. "Well, hello, Robert. I didn't know you were here." She tried to sit forward in an effort to greet her guest.

"Please don't get up," said Robert bending down and picking up Hemingway. "It looks like you really have your hands full." He looked toward the house where a large metal trash bin had been placed for the purpose of keeping all of the waste and debris in one area. Chunks of dry wall and concrete were everywhere.

Lottie sank back into the comfort of her chair once more. "Well, it's about time to make some changes around here," she answered. "There are so many decisions that need to be made, though. It seems like every time I decide on something, there are three other things that need to be changed because of that one decision."

Robert smiled. "I know what you mean. Aislinn loves decorating, so in the past I have experienced the joy of what you are talking about."

"Speaking of Aislinn, are you looking for her, because if you are she's not here."

"I know. She told me she had to go to New York, but I was wondering if you knew when she is supposed to get back."

"I believe she said she would be at the Hamptons for the weekend but she would be returning home Monday morning. Her flight gets in around 9 o'clock."

Robert glanced back at the trash dumpster. Monday morning would be too late.

"I have a telephone number where she can be reached, if that will help."

"That would be so nice of you." Robert watched her heave her ample body forward and propel it out of the chair. "I'm sorry to be such a bother."

"Oh, it's no bother. I need to start thinking about dinner anyway." Lottie disappeared into the house and moments later returned with a sheet of paper. "I can't vouch if this is clean or not. You wouldn't believe the amount of dust taking out walls can produce." She handed him the paper.

"Thank you so much." Robert handed Hemingway to her. "Bye, little guy," he said scratching Hemingway's chin. "Thanks again, Miss Howard."

Lottie watched Robert back out of the driveway and drive off. It was obvious he had something important on his mind, otherwise it surely could have waited until Monday. She just hoped it wasn't something that would make Aislinn unhappy. A nice young woman like Aislinn didn't need to carry around a lot of burden. "Come on, Hemingway. Let's go see what Eliane has fixed us for dinner."

Chapter Seventeen

One age's oddities and curiosities are often another's masterpieces. It may be that it requires a long absorptive time for a unique style to be understood and then admired, or an original thought to be comprehended and then appreciated. The resistance to such phenomena is great. Most people prefer the easy and familiar . . . only the future reveres the original and daring style.

Doris Grumbach

Riding in the limousine to the Hamptons with Caldwell Kane was even more fun than Aislinn had imagined. Caldwell had thought of everything. When he told her he wasn't going to let that nasty business with Sheldon interrupt their weekend, he apparently meant it because from all appearances he was completely relaxed and happy.

Frederick had gone on ahead in order to help Mrs. Hutchinson get ready for their arrival. Before leaving, however, he had prepared a light snack of fresh fruit, miniature crab cakes and some sort of tiny cheese roll-ups for them to eat while traveling through the country. To go along with the food Caldwell had selected a Greek *retsina* wine similar to what they had their first evening together at the Apollo Restaurant.

With everything happening the way it did at the office, they had left later than Caldwell had wanted. "I really hope you can see it your first time while it's still daylight," he told Aislinn, referring to the old family home. "It was built by my grandfather and it has stayed in the family ever since."

Aislinn smiled and sipped her wine. "It must be nice to have that kind of tradition and heritage to enjoy with your sons. I never had that when I was growing up. My father's work required that we relocate every two or three years, so home was wherever I lived at that moment in time. I became very adept at packing my things and moving, and it wasn't difficult for me to meet new people since I had done it all my life. But I often envied my cousins who all seemed to stay in the same house they grew up in, even after they became adults."

"How provincial."

Aislinn laughed and put her hand on Caldwell's. "I know. I'm sure they envied me as much as I envied them. It's just that I had a tendency to romanticize things. I always stayed with my grandparents whenever my parents would take me to visit the family. They lived on a small farm in the Midwest, and I thought it was just about the most beautiful place I had ever seen. The green meadows, and the neat rows of corn and beans; the autumn foliage and the wonderful cooking smells in my grandmother's kitchen. And, of course, the chickens were really special. I was allowed to gather the eggs, you see."

Caldwell smiled. "Go on," he said.

"Everything had a natural, unforced pattern to it, and each time I would return for a visit, the pattern would still be there. Of course, I was never there long enough to see the other side of it—all of the hard work it took to run the farm, the years of too much rain on the crops and the years they struggled with droughts or disease. I only saw it as the one place in my life that would always remain the same, and it was beautiful."

"Are your grandparents still living?"

"No, they both died a few years ago. One of my cousins bought the farm from the estate, and the first thing he did was bulldoze down the farmhouse. He wanted more grazing land for his cattle. I haven't been back since."

"That's a shame."

"I know. It needed to be done, I guess. The house was old." Aislinn looked out the window just as the limousine made a right turn off the main road onto a narrow black-top lane.

"Good," said Caldwell glancing out the window. "We are almost there."

For the next several minutes, Caldwell explained to Aislinn what she was seeing from the car window. "This property that you are on now has been in the Kane family dating back well over a hundred years. Of course, it wasn't worth then what it is now. My grandfather mostly wanted a place where he could provide for a large family."

The limousine left the blacktop road and turned onto a private lane which meandered through towering oaks and pines. Caldwell lowered the window next to Aislinn. "If you listen, you can hear the ocean from here."

The closer they got to the ocean, the smaller the trees became, stunted by the salt air and sea breeze. Soon the landscape took on a more cultivated look. Flowering shrubs lined each side of the narrow road, an occasional garden bench nestled within shaded recesses. And then, suddenly, the road opened up onto a brick circular drive leading to the most magnificent estate Aislinn had ever seen. "Oh my goodness," she said.

"Do you like it?" Caldwell leaned forward anxiously trying to see the home from the same angle as Aislinn. When Aislinn didn't answer him, he began explaining more about the history of the home. "It really is a bit overwhelming when you see it for the first time," he said, almost apologetic. "It was patterned after an eighteenth century English castle. Jason and Tyler have been after me for years to renovate the place. I just don't seem to have the heart. It's been through two world wars, the Korean Conflict, Vietnam and The Depression. Changing it now just doesn't seem right somehow."

"Oh my goodness," Aislinn repeated as she stretched to see it from every window. In front of her was a three-story English Tudor with a beautiful gambrel shingled roof and dark-stained wooden beams. The mansion itself was surrounded by formal gardens and walkways.

Just when Caldwell was about to offer to take her back into the city, she looked over at him and smiled. "I think this is the most beautiful place I have ever seen."

"Do you really think so? I was so afraid you wouldn't like it—it's so big and all. Jason says it's too Gothic, and Tyler—well, he spends all of his time either at the pool or on the tennis courts when he is here."

By the time the limousine came to a stop at the front entrance, Mrs. Hutchinson along with several other members of the staff were waiting by the front porch steps to greet Caldwell and Aislinn. As soon as all the introductions had been made, everyone seemed to scramble in a different direction in order to tend to something that needed their immediate attention. Aislinn stood in the large entrance hall and watched her luggage disappear up the central stairs. Antique Persian rugs covered hardwood floors. Period moldings and beautiful paneling decorated the spacious rooms off to her left and right.

"There are nine fireplaces, all in working order I'm happy to say since it can get a little cold here, especially when the northerly wind comes off the ocean," said Caldwell. "All of the bedrooms are upstairs, each with a private bath and a private balcony that overlooks the ocean." He followed Aislinn's gaze, and whenever he saw her pause on something, he told her about what she was looking at. "I'm sure we can make you comfortable here," he said still concerned that it might not be the type of place Aislinn would enjoy.

"Oh, Caldwell, I am going to enjoy every single moment. I want to see everything. Will you have time to take me around and . . ."

"That is exactly what I plan on doing. I want you to see everything there is to see, and know everything there is to know—about me."

Aislinn looked away from a large portrait hanging near the first landing on the stairs and turned toward Caldwell. He had already made it pretty clear how he felt about her. At first she had avoided it, but now she no longer could. She needed to examine her own feelings and decide if she felt the same way. In the past month she and Caldwell had gotten to know each other as well as two people could. They had shared everything with each other; they had kept back no secrets. It happened so quickly, and, yet, Aislinn felt it was all somehow meant to be. "There are twin faces, separate places, and a love for which you must choose," the Santerian priest had told her the last time she visited the botanica. She hadn't known then what he meant. Now she did. She had been holding onto a love that was unfulfilling and unproductive probably because it was convenient. Her relationship with Robert suited her lifestyle at the moment. Maybe now it was time to move on to another kind of love; a love that could give her fulfillment and that sense of emotional well-being she had never experienced with Robert

"Caldwell, I . . ."

"Excuse me, sir." It was Mrs. Hutchinson. "Ms. Marchánt has a telephone call."

Caldwell nodded slightly. "Here, Aislinn," he said taking her by the hand. "You can use the phone in the library."

"How strange," said Aislinn. "The only person I gave this number to was Lottie Howard. I hope nothing has happened to Hemingway."

Caldwell led her down the hall to a large room that opened out onto a terrace. Walnut bookcases lined the walls. Groupings of rich, tan leather furniture graced the room, encircling a beautiful antique desk. After showing Aislinn where the phone was he quickly left the room in order to give her privacy. "Do you know who was calling?" he asked Mrs. Hutchinson, locating her in the kitchen.

"The gentleman said his name was Robert Marchánt," she answered.

* * *

"Aislinn, I'm really sorry to interrupt like this."

"Robert! Is anything wrong? You're not back in the hospital, are you? How did you get this number?"

"Miss Howard gave it to me. She told me you were coming back Monday morning, but I wanted to talk to you before then." He paused and cleared his throat. "The Hamptons. Is that where that publisher lives?"

"Caldwell. His name is Caldwell. And, yes, he has a home here. But that isn't why you needed to talk to me, is it?"

"No. And what you do and where you go is none of my business. The reason I wanted to talk to you is that I have been offered a position with a large medical research company, Absey Laboratories—maybe you've heard of them?"

Aislinn said she hadn't, but, then, she would have had no reason to.

"They are the leading company in stem cell research. Dr. Bernard Moulton has asked me to head up their program that deals with diseases involving the brain. It will be coordinated as a joint effort with the University of Virginia Medical School in Richmond."

"When would he want you to start? What about West Palm Beach Regional Hospital?" Aislinn sat down at the desk and tried to close her mind to everything except what Robert was telling her.

"Dr. Moulton wants me to start immediately. That means I have no more than a week to find my replacement and make the recommendation to the Board of Directors. I'm going to recommend Josh, by the way. In the meantime, I'll need to fly to Richmond and get things started on that end." Silence filled the line. "I know it's sudden; these things always are. But I think it's time for me to make a change."

"Perhaps it is." Aislinn tried to sound happy, and probably it really was a good move on Robert's part. It's just that she wasn't prepared for it to happen so soon. "Will I see you before you leave?"

"I don't know. If not, I'll let you know where I am once I get settled in Richmond." After a moment, Robert said, "You could always come with me, you know."

Aislinn glanced out of the window. A flock of seagulls was flying low on the gray horizon. "I know. But I honestly don't think that is what either of us wants."

"Take care of yourself. And, Aislinn?"

"Yes."

"I hope the publisher is able to give you what you need."

After she hung up, Aislinn sat staring at the phone. He hadn't asked about her meeting, not that he wasn't interested. It's just that it would never occur to him. For him, there would always be more important things to think about. In a few minutes there was a light tap on the door and Caldwell stood in the doorway. "Aislinn? Do you need anything?"

Aislinn took a deep breath and smiled. "Not a thing. Everything is fine."

Caldwell started to enter the room, but then hesitated.

"That was Robert," Aislinn said.

"Oh?"

"He has been asked by Absey Laboratories to head up a research project involving stem cells. The University of Virginia Medical School is also involved, so Robert will be going to Richmond."

"Oh. Well, that sounds interesting. Doesn't it?"

Aislinn felt Caldwell studying her face. "Yes," she answered. Then she got up and walked over to where Caldwell was hovering somewhat self-consciously. Standing on her tiptoes, she reached up and kissed him tenderly on the mouth.

* * *

Caldwell, it seemed, had every minute planned. He wanted to make sure that Aislinn not only enjoyed herself while spending the weekend at his home in the Hamptons, but that she got to know him totally and completely. He already knew how he felt about her, but he wanted to give her all she needed including the time to decide for herself how she felt about him. He was a patient man; he would wait. But in the meantime, Aislinn's happiness was his responsibility, and he intended to see to it.

They started out early the next morning exploring the island in Caldwell's Land Rover. "There are a lot of famous and interesting characters living around here, not to mention some beautiful homes," explained Caldwell. By lunch time, they had driven from one end of the island to the other, stopping several times to take in a particularly breath-taking view or walk on the beach. When they got back to the estate, Aislinn had just enough time to change for lunch. As she walked down the hall toward the dining room, she heard several voices. Apparently the others were already there.

Donald Leer, the publishing firm's attorney, was laughing with Caldwell when she entered the room. Jason and Tyler were talking with Lorraine. "There she is," said Caldwell rushing over to Aislinn and putting his arm around her. Donald was about the same age as Caldwell, and the two were obviously good friends. Short, a little on the heavy side, and extremely composed, he held Aislinn's hand warmly when she was introduced. "Well, this is quite a pleasure, Aislinn. I feel as though I already know you."

Aislinn felt her eyes widen. "I am afraid I am at a disadvantage," she murmured.

"Don't you worry, Aislinn," said Lorraine. "I can tell you everything about this man you need to know." Everyone laughed, and Aislinn couldn't help thinking that it seemed to be a much happier occasion than she had anticipated. Even Tyler seemed to be in a good humor.

Caldwell held out a chair for Aislinn and then sat next to her as the others also sat around the large dining room table. Lunch was an elegant occasion and something that Mrs. Hutchinson had gone to a great deal of trouble to prepare. When the wine had been served, Caldwell stood and raised his glass. "To love and friendship in the House of Kane."

"Here, here!" said Donald while everyone touched their glasses.

"After you called last night, I did some checking around." Donald speared his salad and glanced around the table. "Apparently this Tracy Cord person has disappeared. No one seems to know where she is. Sheldon wants to drop the matter. He understands now that this so-called novel she wrote was, in fact, someone else's work. Of course, it is up to you, Caldwell, if you want to pursue it."

Aislinn glanced at Tyler. Even though Tracy had betrayed his friendship, she knew the pain he must be feeling. After all, he had fallen in love with her.

"That's not my style, Donald. I think it is best if we just forget the matter and move onto more positive and productive things. Jason? Tyler? Do you agree?"

"Well, I for one certainly agree. Bad publicity is just that. It doesn't sell books," said Jason.

"I agree," said Tyler.

"Good. Then as far as I am concerned the matter is closed. Now, what I want to know, Lorraine, is how much wine did you drink in the limousine when Dan drove you over here this morning?"

"That is none of your business," she teased. Then to Aislinn, "I don't drink, and he knows it. He's just trying to find an excuse to fire me."

Aislinn laughed with the others. It was such a close bond between all of them, a bond that she knew Caldwell wanted her to be a part of.

That evening Caldwell took Aislinn into the city for dinner and to see a stage show. More and more she was seeing things about Caldwell that were normally hidden by his professional face, things she knew he was revealing only to her. She had never known that depth of trust and love before; she was almost frightened by it. Yet, it was the very thing she had wanted with Robert, but was never able to reach.

Later that night, back in her room, Aislinn was propped up in bed and writing in her notebook. She didn't feel her day was complete until she had worked at least some on her novel. She was getting close to the end now, but she didn't want to rush it. The ending, like the beginning, had to develop and unfold in its own time and at its own speed until the conclusion was finally satisfied. It was a many-faceted story about love and betrayal, and the complications brought about by two very different cultures. As it is in real life, so it was in Aislinn's novel. There was nothing that was black and white; there were only varying shades of gray. The love would remain, but her protagonist would move on with her life. She would choose the familiar path rather than a path that would repeatedly lead her to those things in life which she did not understand. *She could see the left wing of the house as well as the front façade.* Aislinn wrote, *She counted three chimneys, perhaps four, and there was what appeared to be a stone or oolite wall just beyond the house, probably indicating a garden or courtyard. She could see a thicket of trees, cypress trees. The image of a stone altar adorned with fresh flowers and fruits flashed through her mind. Santeria. Through the noise of the rain and windshield wipers, she could hear the pounding of the ocean surf coming from somewhere beyond the house. Standing on the front steps were two men. To one, her lover, she had promised everything; to the other, the priest, she had promised nothing. As she turned and drove away, she knew that the priest, dressed all in white except for the many strands of colorful yemaya beads, waited. He would always wait.*

"Aislinn?" There was a tap on her door.

Aislinn put down her notebook and got out of bed. She quickly slipped on her robe and went to the door. "Tyler?"

"I saw your light still on." He glanced inside her room. "I guess I couldn't sleep."

"Come in. I was just catching up on some writing, but I've about finished now." She led him to the sofa and chairs positioned in front of the large, multi-paned window overlooking the gardens and the two of them sat down.

"I didn't get a chance to thank you for all you have done." He put his head in his hands and looked back up. "I can't believe I was so stupid."

"It all worked out in the end. Don't be too hard on yourself. You know, Tyler, a lot worse things have been done in the name of love. This one was fixable. I'm sure each of us has learned something from it."

Tyler nodded.

"Will you try to locate Tracy?"

Tyler snorted. "I'm not that stupid. I might be a little slow sometimes, but I do learn." He smiled at Aislinn. "No, I was going the wrong way on a one-way street from the very beginning. Not like you and Dad."

Aislinn blinked her eyes in surprise.

"That's all right. You don't have to say anything. I just want you to know that whatever you and Dad decide, it is all right with Jason and me."

"The two of you have discussed it?"

"You might say it has been a hot topic of conversation ever since you came to that first editorial staff meeting. In all the years I have been working at Kane Publishing, not once has Dad ever had pastries at the editorial staff meeting, let alone flowers on the conference table; that is, until you came. Jason and I figured you must be someone pretty special." Tyler got up and walked to the door. "Goodnight, Aislinn."

Chapter Eighteen

In a sense the world dies every time a writer dies, because, if he is any good, he has been a wet nurse to humanity during his entire existence and has held earth close around him, like the little obstetrical toad that goes about with a cluster of eggs attached to his legs.

EB White

Aislinn stood unnoticed just off to one side dressed in a black satin gown covered with black lace. Her hair was swept up off her neck in a soft cluster of curls. Her only jewelry adornments were the diamond studs in her ears and the matching diamond bracelet, gifts from Caldwell.

The Waldorf Astoria ballroom sparkled from the floor to the chandeliers. White damask linens decorated with fresh flowers and flickering candles in crystal holders covered the small tables. At one end of the room a long table had been set up to display a multitude of books— this season's releases by Kane Publishing House. Her own book, *The Initiation,* had been placed front and center. Several other smaller tables had been strategically placed around the room as refreshment stations. In one corner a small chamber group softly played the music of Mozart, Bach, and Vivaldi.

Aislinn had been looking forward to this occasion, and now she wanted to enjoy it quietly for a moment on the fringe, so to speak, before taking part. Slowly the room began to fill with people. The glitter and rustle of gowns, the dark tailored suits, the sounds of happy conversations, and the bustle of servers weaving their way around the room presented a festive picture. Most of the people attending the annual party given by Kane Publishing House were new to the world of publishing. Some were fortunate to have been there many times. Over three hundred people had been invited, all were involved in some way with Kane Publishing House.

As Aislinn looked around the room she recognized Timothy Richards, the young man who had written the nonfiction work on Hadrian's Wall. His wife was with him, glowing with happiness. They were expecting their first child. Lottie Howard was the next person Aislinn recognized. Dressed in a beautiful bronze gown with a sequined bodice, her red hair usually fixed in finger waves had been restyled in a more sophisticated, contemporary look; she looked stunning. Her book, *My Father's Keeper*, had already been nominated for a Pulitzer. Standing next to one of the refreshment stations was Snow Henderson and her husband, Treat. *Then There Was Light* had sold over 500,000 copies in less than six weeks, and plans for a second printing were underway. A Spanish translation of it was also in the works. Half hidden behind a potted plant stood Clarence Tyrell Wood, the elderly Black man who had been so willing to sacrifice his personal freedom for what he believed was right and just. Lorraine had just given him a plate filled with several of the delicacies that had been prepared for the occasion. As Aislinn looked around, she couldn't help but reflect on how much each person had impacted her own life. So much had happened in such a short time.

"Hello, my darling. I'm here. Sorry I'm late." Caldwell walked up behind Aislinn and leaned down and kissed her. "One of the Spanish imprints was having trouble with their distribution center, but I think we got the problem resolved." He smiled at his bride and then glanced appreciatively around the room. "This has been quite a year, hasn't it?"

"I was just thinking the same thing. Everyone looks so happy. And you look so handsome." She reached up smiling and straightened his tie.

"Are you happy?" Caldwell put his arm around Aislinn and pulled her close to him.

"I never knew happiness could feel this way," she answered.

Just then there appeared to be a commotion of sorts next to one of the potted plants where Aislinn had last seen Clarence standing. Lottie was sobbing uncontrollably, and Clarence had his arms around her.

"What is that all about?" Caldwell said, taking Aislinn by the hand and walking over toward them.

When Lottie saw Aislinn, she smiled broadly and wiped her face with the handkerchief Clarence miraculously produced for her. "This is C.T.," she said to Aislinn.

Aislinn caught her breath and stared at Clarence. "C.T.?" she repeated. "Clarence is C.T.?"

"What's going on?" asked Caldwell.

"It's a long story," said Aislinn fighting back her own tears.

* * *

Much later, back in their bedroom at the estate, Aislinn and Caldwell held each other closely as Aislinn told the story of a young Black boy whose only crime was to save the daughter of the wealthy land developer from herself. "Clarence is C.T., the boy Lottie wrote about in her book." Aislinn sighed deeply and tenderly draped her arm across Caldwell's body. "She told me she is taking C.T. back home with her."

"To live?"

"That's right. Lottie has plenty of room, and she's still doing all of that remodeling. C.T. wants to help her with it. I think it will be wonderful for both of them." Aislinn felt the gentle rise and fall of Caldwell's chest. "I can't wait to see what all Lottie has done to her home."

"We'll go to West Palm next month, if you like. It will be cold as the dickens here, so we'll be ready for some of that south Florida sunshine and humidity." Knowing how much Aislinn loved her home, Caldwell had insisted when they got married that she keep it. They could both enjoy it whenever they wanted to get away from the frigid New York winters.

Aislinn reached up and kissed Caldwell. "I'd like that. The orange and grapefruit trees in the yard should be ready to pick by then. We can bring some back to share." She felt Caldwell sigh contentedly. "I'll even take you to meet that Santerian priest I told you about," she continued. "If you are good, he might give you some beads to wear."

"Oh, I'll be good," said Caldwell.

And Aislinn knew without a doubt he would be.

Coming Soon!

BARBARA CASEY
JUST LIKE FAMILY

All in one day, thirty-five-year-old Hallie Marsh is involved in a car accident, learns that the man she loves, works for, and is living with has found someone else, and that her mother is planning to leave her father for another man. With no job or a place to live, embittered, filled with anger, and wanting revenge, Hallie decides to take a year's sabbatical and write a novel that would reveal the unethical, if not illegal, real estate business practices of her former boss and lover. Her anger, however, is soon replaced by a fascination for four elderly and peculiar neighbors who have formed an alliance, bought an old run-down estate to fix up and live in just like family. It is these four people—a retired construction worker, a tobacco tenant farmer, a divorcee, and an immigrant from Vietnam—that Hallie writes about, and with this new focus Hallie overcomes her feelings of rage, she is able to cope with her mother's sudden death, and she finds true love.

For more information
visit: www.SpeakingVolumes.us

On Sale Now!

BARBARA CASEY
THE COACH'S WIFE

For more information
visit: www.SpeakingVolumes.us

On Sale Now!

STEPHEN STEELE
THE TROUBLE WITH MIRACLES SERIES

For more information
visit: www.SpeakingVolumes.us

www.ingramcontent.com/pod-product-compliance
Lightning Source LLC
Chambersburg PA
CBHW050515260626
47157CB00004B/1329